# DRUMENDUS

## MISSION TO THE DRUM PLANET

Andrew Ashwin

# DRUMENDUS

## MISSION TO THE DRUM PLANET

The Book Guild Ltd

First published in Great Britain in 2022 by
The Book Guild Ltd
Unit E2 Airfield Business Park,
Harrison Road, Market Harborough,
Leicestershire. LE16 7UL
Tel: 0116 2792299
www.bookguild.co.uk
Email: info@bookguild.co.uk
Twitter: @bookguild

Typeset in 12pt Minion Pro

Printed and bound in Great Britain by 4edge Limited

ISBN 978 1915352 231

British Library Cataloguing in Publication Data.
A catalogue record for this book is available from the British Library.

*For Rosie and Ellie,*
*who inspired the creation of Drumendus*

# CHAPTER 1
# THE PURPLE HALO

Ella Crinkle gazed up at the planet Drumendus. It hung above Earth like a giant purple marble in the night sky, tantalisingly close, yet so mysterious.

'Mercury, Venus, Earth, Drumendus, Mars,' Ella recited in rhythm, imagining herself zooming across the solar system at the speed of light, 'Jupiter, Saturn, Uranus, Neptune!' A deep longing welled up inside her, as it so often did. 'One day, I'll be an astronaut,' she whispered. 'One day, I'll visit *you*, Drumendus.' She paused, then added, 'If Aunt Belinda can do it, so can I.'

Ella was desperate to follow in the footsteps of her world-famous aunt, Belinda Crinkle, the first person in history to walk on another planet, twenty-five years ago. Not to mention her uncle, Otto Crinkle, the *second* person in history to walk on another planet. Space travel was in Ella's blood, and she constantly dreamed of breathing the Drumendus air, exploring the purple landscape and, above all, *hearing* the legendary sounds of Earth's sibling planet.

'The first thing that hits you is the extraordinary drumming noise from deep below the ground,' Aunt Belinda had said on TV after returning to Earth all those years ago. 'Well, that and the fact you can wander around in normal clothes, without a care in the world – no need for a fancy spacesuit, and no bouncing across the surface, metres at a time. Trust gravity to spoil the fun! But the *sounds* are like nothing you can imagine: the wind, the water, even the birdsong are just so intense… so beautiful… and really rather terrifying.'

Aunt Belinda herself coined the nickname *Drumendus* on the first day of the mission. The planet was duly renamed, which cemented her iconic status across the world. '*Drumendus* is much more memorable than *Purple-1812*,' she had remarked at the time.

Despite the global triumph of the Drumendus Landing, a huge cloud hung over the mission for a single, tragic reason: only one Crinkle astronaut returned home alive.

Uncle Otto fell ill and died on the voyage back home. That's all the public knew, but Ella was sure there was more to it than that. Every time she asked Aunt Belinda about it, she was shut down instantly –

and it wasn't like her aunt to miss an opportunity to tell a Drumendus story.

Why all the secrecy? What really happened to her uncle up there, in the vastness of space?

A flurry of purple lightning bolts flashed across Drumendus, startling Ella back to the reality of the chilly summer's evening in Belton-on-Snare. A familiar dread came over her as she remembered what tomorrow had in store.

𝄞

St Hildegard's School Hall was crammed full of pupils and teachers waiting to go home for the summer. The end-of-year assembly had been as chaotic and rowdy as ever, and it was now Ella's turn to play her trombone as a final musical offering. Her legs trembled as she looked out across the sea of faces and played the first notes of her piece. To her surprise, it wasn't the pupils who voiced their disapproval but the school pets, dotted around the hall in cages, ready to be taken to their holiday homes. The hamsters and gerbils squeaked away each time Ella played a high note, and as the piece reached its final crescendo, form 8VE's famous chinchillas, Rall and Tando, stole the show with a perfectly timed series of screeches.

Ella lowered her trombone and bowed awkwardly to a smattering of applause and grumbling.

'Ah, the magic of music,' said the headteacher, Mrs Clapstick, ushering Ella to her seat. 'Thank you for that… interesting piece, "The Purple Halo", written by Ella herself. Gosh, so many… loud notes. I expect it's inspired by Drumendus, with that title?'

Ella nodded and shuffled in her chair. The murmuring swelled amongst the pupils.

'Settle down, thank you,' said Mrs Clapstick, but the unease in the hall continued, and heated discussions broke out between the older pupils and even some of the staff. 'I said, settle down!' She glared at a group of teachers in the corner, who visibly shrank into their chairs as silence descended. 'Yes, Drumendus is back in the news, with its extra-bright glow and… rather stormy weather. But there's no danger whatsoever, despite the hysteria flying around. I mean, *really*, many of these rumours are quite frankly absurd. Someone could report that a six-legged, seven-eyed squishy purple alien had been discovered in the Buckingham Palace gardens, and many people would think it was a Drumendus attack!' The pupils chuckled at the way she said *squishy*. 'Well, I'm not going to lose any sleep over a bit of bad weather up there, and neither should you. That barren planet has always been Earth's neighbour, and we are stuck with it. Not even the Drumendus fanatics are worried.' She turned to Ella unexpectedly and said, 'You're one of them, aren't you, dear – what do you call yourselves again?'

'Drumgazers,' Ella murmured, her face burning in embarrassment.

'That's it,' said Mrs Clapstick, her tone becoming more enthusiastic. 'Well, you *would* be a drumgazer, with your family history.' Ella knew what was coming. Mrs Clapstick never missed an opportunity to bring

4

up Ella's famous family past. The number of times the pupils had heard all about it… 'Most of you will know that Ella here is the niece of two world-famous astronauts,' she started.

Ella groaned and stared intently at the trombone balanced across her lap. Mrs Clapstick launched into the story of the Drumendus Landing, making the usual mistake of calling Aunt Belinda 'Bonnie'. She didn't bother to mention BASS – the British Agency of Space Study – or the team of astronauts and scientists that had made the mission possible in the first place.

Ella longed to be off the stage.

Mrs Clapstick banged the lectern in excitement, her face full of pride. 'What an honour to have a Crinkle sat here, in our midst.' She closed her eyes and took a few deep breaths, clearly exhausted from telling the story so theatrically.

It was precisely during this awkward pause that Ella's trombone chose to slide off her knee and clatter onto the wooden floorboards, much to the glee of the baying onlookers. Even the chinchillas seemed to laugh. Ella decided that this was officially the worst five minutes of her twelve-year-old life.

Mrs Clapstick waved her arms in the air in a feeble attempt to restore calm. 'A final word about leaving the school in a quiet and orderly—' she started, but the scraping of chair legs drowned her out as everyone stood up. She sighed and hobbled to the edge of the stage, stepping over Ella, who was scrabbling around on her hands and knees for her trombone. 'I give up,' she muttered. 'School dismissed.'

As Ella placed her trombone into its case, a scrunched-up piece of paper bounced off her head and landed on the scuffed floor beside her. She opened it and glanced down at the scrawled writing:

*Ella Crinkle, the famous LOSER!*

Her heart dropped. A pitiful attempt at her playing the trombone had been scribbled above the message. She looked over her shoulder to see a pupil known only as Drawl squeal with laughter, flanked by his two bullies-in-crime.

'That was pathetic, Crinkle,' Drawl said. 'I'd rather cook my own toes than listen to that awful racket!'

Mr Pulp, the music teacher, bustled over. 'And happy holidays to you too, Mr Drawl.' He was the only one in school who called him that. 'Now, if you're quite finished…?' Drawl scowled and shuffled off. His friends followed in obedient formation. Mr Pulp turned to Ella. 'It takes guts to play in assembly, Ella,' he said, 'and your trombone piece was certainly *not* awful.'

'Thanks… I think.'

'It might not have been everyone's cup of tea, but it had an *impact*. Music must have an impact, Ella, otherwise it belongs in a lift… if you know what I mean.'

'Not… really.'

'Good, good.' He beamed and toddled off.

Ella said her goodbyes to a couple of friends and

wandered out to Mum's car. She slung her trombone into the boot and jumped in the front, harrumphing as she wrestled to put her seatbelt on.

'I'm guessing "Hello" is out of the question?' Mum laughed. 'How was your performance?'

Ella slumped in her seat, blushing at the memory of it all. 'Okay, I suppose.'

'I bet it was more than *okay*.' Mum cleared her throat and changed her voice into that of an over-excited game-show host. 'Ella Crinkle – are you ready for your summer adventure with… *AUNT BELINDA*?'

Ella sat upright. 'Oops, I forgot about that. Are we going… *now*?'

'Of course – it's always at the start of the holidays,' said Mum, frowning. 'Remember?'

'But… I haven't packed.'

'I noticed.'

'I'm *not* wearing Aunt Belinda's clothes, no way!'

'Don't worry, it's all done. Your suitcase is in the boot.'

'Phew! Thanks.'

Mum drove away from the school gates. 'One more thing.'

Ella groaned. 'Not… the song?'

'Of course the song!'

Before Ella could protest further, Mum had launched in:

*'Aunt Belinda's holiday trip*
*Is the highlight of the year!'*

'Mum,' Ella cringed as they passed hordes of St Hildegard's pupils streaming along the pavement. 'Do we have to?'

'Yes! It's tradition.'

They turned onto the main road and sped away from school. Ella felt her spirits lift and her worries evaporate as she thought about her trip to Aunt Belinda's. Eventually, she broke into a wide grin and couldn't stop herself singing along with Mum:

*'Aunt Belinda's holiday trip*
*Is the highlight of the year!*
*She's number one, it's so much fun,*
*Let's all give her a cheer!*
*A giant...*
*Holiday... CHEEEEEER!*
*Yeah!'*

# CHAPTER 2
## RACKET LODGE

Ella's annual trip to Aunt Belinda's house was the high point of her summer, crammed full of fun, freedom, music and various cookery disasters. A cross between a homemade theme-park adventure and a disorganised summer camp, it was the one week of the year that Ella could be *herself* without worrying about anyone or anything else. Aunt Belinda had never really grown up, as she freely admitted, despite being the world's most famous astronaut. As a serial inventor and a hoarder of all things music-related, her house and garden were filled with weird and wonderful contraptions, most of which were built out of old instrument parts and few of which actually worked as intended. When she wasn't inventing things, she was planning her next project to pass the time in retirement. Last month alone, she swam around the Isle of Wight in her spacesuit, cycled a hundred miles playing a harmonica and even bounced across the county on a pogo stick whilst singing the Beatles' greatest hits, in alphabetical order, in French. The sprawling garden shed was where her ideas were born and her inventions brought to life.

Four hours after leaving Belton-on-Snare, Ella and Mum turned into Aunt Belinda's overgrown driveway in deepest Dorset and pulled up outside her tumbledown cottage, Racket Lodge. Ella jumped out of the car and ran to the open front door.

'Hello…? Aunt Belinda?'

'Helloooooooo!' a voice boomed out of the end of a drainpipe hanging down the wall. 'Welcome baaaaaaack! I'm just in the attic. This is my new-and-improved intercom system. Do you like it?'

Ella laughed. 'What, an old drain?'

Mum raised an eyebrow and smiled. 'Hi, Belinda,' she called into the pipe. 'Nothing's ever normal with you, is it?'

A wonky window carved into the roof flew open, and Ella watched as Aunt Belinda sprang into the sky above Racket Lodge, attached to a bizarre flying contraption.

'This is Josephine!' she called from her precarious mid-air position. 'Half catapult, half parachute.' She made a *ta-da!* gesture with her arms then grabbed the homemade musical instrument attached to her front. It was unlike anything Ella had ever seen, with dozens of tubes, pipes and funnels pointing upwards.

'I have to play a note to make the parachute work. The air blasts it open.'

'Stop explaining,' shouted Ella, 'and start playing, then!'

'Ah, yes, of course. Now, what was the note? Was it an F...? Or a C...?'

For a heart-stopping moment, Aunt Belinda plummeted towards the ground. She blew into her contraption until her face turned crimson, and to Ella's relief, a patchwork parachute opened up above her as the note echoed around the driveway like a ship's horn. Guiding the parachute down, she landed with a stumble and untangled herself.

'Looks like Josephine needs a bit of work,' she muttered, hugging Ella and Mum.

They unloaded the car, and Ella tried and failed to wriggle free from Mum's customary ten-second hug. 'Don't get upset,' Ella whispered to herself as a familiar feeling of sadness crept into her tummy. Why did this always happen? Mum went on her piano tour *every year*, and Ella had a brilliant time at Aunt Belinda's every year too.

'Have a good trip, Jude,' Aunt Belinda called to Mum, who reversed out of the scruffy drive. 'Where are you going again?'

'Northumberland,' sighed Mum, driving off into the early-evening sunshine, 'as always! Byeeeee!'

Aunt Belinda clapped her hands together and laughed, as if she were the happiest person alive. She put her arm around Ella. 'I'm delighted you're back. You keep me so young at heart.'

Ella smirked. 'I don't think you need *me* for that.'

'Now, let me remind you of the house rules.' Aunt Belinda scratched the mop of hair on her head. 'What are they again?'

'The garden shed is strictly out of bounds?'

'Ah, yes. And by the way, it's a lot more than a garden shed these days – it's a *top-secret* fortress containing wonders and marvels the likes of which the world has never seen!'

'Rrrright…' Ella nodded, trying not to laugh at her aunt's dramatics.

'And the punishment for snooping is…?'

'You sing "Baby Shark" at me for the rest of the day – with actions.'

'That's right. Next rule?'

'No stealing chocolate from the secret stash I don't know about?'

'Yes, that's another one. But you've forgotten the *main* rule.'

'Er… I'm not sure… Oh, *yeah*: fun must be had at all times?'

'Exactly!' Aunt Belinda chortled. She steered Ella into the cottage, then nipped back outside to pick up the tangled mess of parachute and brass tubes she had named Josephine. 'Ah, Freddie, do go in, dear,' Ella heard her say.

'Freddie?' Ella said to herself, turning around as her friend bounded in. 'Oh, hello,' she muttered, secretly thrilled.

'Hi.' Freddie beamed. For an instant, he looked as

though he were about to give her a hug. 'I saw your mum's car, so I thought I'd come over.'

Freddie Molto lived at the dairy farm a few minutes' walk up the road. He and Ella had become firm friends, sharing many summer adventures despite only seeing each other once a year. He was Ella's first and only pen pal.

'Freddie has called around a good few times today, haven't you, dear?' said Aunt Belinda, obviously unaware of the embarrassment she was causing. 'Very keen, indeed. Well, I think it's lovely. Let's eat, shall we?' She bustled off to the kitchen and returned with a plate stacked high with pizza slices and an enormous bowl of popcorn. 'Tuck in!'

Between eager mouthfuls and slurps of lemonade, Ella and Freddie shared stories of school and family life, without a care in the world. She felt so alive when they were together. Freddie was one of the few people who understood her; she didn't have to pretend to be cool or fashionable or somebody she wasn't.

As Ella scooped out the last kernels of popcorn from the bowl, her mind wandered, as it always did, back to Drumendus. 'I guess you've seen the storms up there?' she said. 'And the extra-bright halo?'

'Who hasn't?' said Freddie. 'It's all over the news too. My dad says it's the Draliens showing off their power.'

Aunt Belinda nearly spat out a mouthful of lemonade. 'What on Earth are Draliens?'

'Drumendus... aliens... *Draliens*.' Freddie sounded surprised that Aunt Belinda hadn't heard the name before. 'It's all over social media.'

'Ah, then that is precisely why I know nothing about Draliens.' Ella and Freddie shared a grin, and Aunt Belinda tutted. 'Draliens, indeed, I've never heard such nonsense.'

Ella sighed. 'Even if there aren't any... *Draliens*, the more active Drumendus gets, the more I want to go there. It's like... I'm drawn to it. But at the same time, I don't *really* fancy going, because it's far too dangerous, and I might never come back. Does that make any sense?' She noticed out of the corner of her eye that Freddie was nodding.

'Why, that makes perfect sense, Ella,' said Aunt Belinda. 'That's *exactly* how I felt when I was an astronaut. The lure of this mysterious planet on our doorstep was always there, ever since I was your age. I *had* to visit; in fact, I couldn't understand why anyone *wouldn't* want to! But I knew it would involve taking my life in my hands.'

Ella slumped back in her chair. 'Everyone thinks I'm weird for being a drumgazer.'

'Of course they do! They're quite happy on Earth, with their cosy lives, thanks very much. They don't want anything to do with Drumendus and its inconvenient behaviour. It might disturb their afternoon nap or... distract them as they sip their tea.'

'Would you ever go back?'

Aunt Belinda let out a long breath with puffed cheeks, as if she were about to say something she knew she shouldn't, then inhaled sharply and muttered, 'That's enough of that talk, I think. Time to clear up.'

She struggled to her feet from her favourite armchair, which had become so droopy over the years that most bottoms ended up resting on the carpet underneath.

'Miss Crinkle, I've missed your memorable banana smoothies,' Freddie said. 'Maybe we could help you blend the—'

'No, no, must be getting on,' she interrupted, scurrying out of the living room towards the back door.

Ella and Freddie glanced at each other. It wasn't like Aunt Belinda to act so strangely, but far more worryingly, it wasn't like her to refuse a banana smoothie. They wandered through to the kitchen with the leftovers, but there was nowhere to put the plates. Every surface was packed full of dismantled instruments, scraps of old machinery and half-built contraptions. Aunt Belinda was using the room as an overflow area for her garden shed – as if the vast shed, that she had extended numerous times over the years into a super-sized workshop, wasn't big enough! Countless dog-eared sheets of paper were stuck to the cupboard doors, each filled with indecipherable scribblings and frantic crossings-out. Ella was as inspired as she was baffled by the scene around her; she had never seen the kitchen in such a state.

'This is just *too* random,' she said, staring out of the window at her aunt, who had stomped down the garden to the shed, glancing around as she did so. 'She's up to something. Come on.'

Ella and Freddie tiptoed out of the back door and along an unkempt stone path.

'What are we doing?' whispered Freddie. 'The shed's forbidden territory.'

'I only want a quick look,' said Ella, creeping over to the nearest window.

The sound of opera singing wafted through an open skylight into the mild early-evening air.

Ella's jaw fell open as she peered through. 'Is… is that what I think it is?' she gasped.

Freddie squinted as he looked in, then turned to Ella. His eyes gleamed. 'What else can it be?'

# CHAPTER 3

# THE HAMMERKLAV

To Ella's astonishment, the inside of Aunt Belinda's sprawling garden shed had been transformed into a spotless high-tech launch station. A spacecraft the shape of an oversized grand piano stood majestically on a launchpad, with three formidable-looking rockets below it and boosters and fuel tanks attached to each side.

'I *knew* she was up to something!' Ella said, pressing her face against the glass.

'It looks so... *real*,' Freddie replied. 'So... *professional*. Not like—'

'Not like Aunt Belinda at all,' Ella joined in. 'She must be serious about this.'

A rope swinging from a branch above their heads

caught Freddie's attention. 'I want a better look…
through that window in the roof.'

'Er, I'm not sure that's the brightest ide—'

Freddie jumped with a grunt and grabbed the
rope. He tried to climb it but ended up pulling it
down instead. As his feet grazed the grass, the rope
flung itself upwards again, to his obvious horror.

'What's happening?' he yelled, clinging on. 'It's got
a mind of its own!'

Above his head, a colossal drum beater swung
down and slammed into a rusty old gong attached to
a branch.

*CLAAAAAAANG!*

The vibrations rattled Ella to the core, and Freddie
lost his grip and thudded to the grass.

The shed door burst open.

'WHO'S THERE?' thundered Aunt Belinda,
pounding towards Ella and Freddie holding a red
music stand. 'Mozart's mittens!' she said, staring at
the gong. 'That's the first time this contraption has
worked. I knew my days as a church bell ringer would
come in handy – that's what inspired this particular
trap.'

'Aren't you… angry we're out here?' stuttered Ella.

Aunt Belinda laughed. 'I can't be angry, dear. I
would've been just as curious at your age.'

'And… what about the "Baby Shark" punishment
for spying?'

'Hmm, yes, there is that… but, more importantly,
I'm guessing you… saw what's inside?'

Ella nodded.

'Well, as it's you two, I suppose I should show you the Hammerklav.'

'The *what*?' Ella and Freddie said at the same time.

'The Hammerklav; that's the name of my spaceship. It's the German word for piano... give or take a few letters.'

She led them inside the pristine launch station and up to the remarkable spaceship she had built. 'Twenty years of my life, at least,' she said proudly. 'And twenty more years as an astronaut before that!'

Inside the cramped cabin, there were unmistakable nods to Aunt Belinda's personality. The seat in the tiny living quarters was a reinforced piano stool with a flowery cushion, and the table was an upturned bass drum screwed to the floor. Even at the control panel, which looked just like those Ella had seen in pictures, some of the buttons and levers were fashioned out of guitar pegs and organ stops. A miniature statue of Mozart attached to the dashboard served as Aunt Belinda's 'lucky mascot'.

'I've coated the inside walls in an ultra-thick fireproof, heatproof, waterproof layer of paint, all of my own concoction,' Aunt Belinda said. 'There's violin polish in there, and trumpet valve oil... Oh, and vinegar, of course.'

'Vinegar?' said Freddie, scrunching up his nose at the thought. 'What does that do?'

'Oh, nothing – but the smell reminds me of chips.'

Ella explored the Hammerklav, deep in thought. At long last, she turned to Aunt Belinda. 'It's... incredible,' she said, gulping, barely able to continue.

Such love and attention had been poured into every detail of this extraordinary machine. 'Are you going to Drumendus?'

Aunt Belinda nodded slowly. 'That's the plan.'

'Soon?'

She nodded again. 'I've a few things to do up there.'

Freddie stomped over. 'There's no way this thing'll fly,' he declared with characteristic bluntness. 'Launching a spaceship from a back garden? No way!'

'Ah, that's where you're wrong,' Aunt Belinda said. 'Yes, some of my other projects have been… less than successful—'

'The self-playing violin that exploded. That's one.'

'Yes, thank you, Freddie.'

'And the—'

'There's no need to recount them *all*! Anyway, *this* project is different. It's the crowning moment of my life's work, and I've left no stone unturned. The Hammerklav is fuelled up and ready to go.'

'You must have had help?' Freddie persisted.

'Yes, lots! Hundreds of "what-if" conversations with my old scientist and astronaut friends, dozens of lunches where all sorts of wild ideas were thrown around after a few too many hot chocolates. Lots of folks have chipped in with their machines and inventions, quite happy to let a harmless retired astronaut borrow and test their designs in her "garden shed". I just take it a bit more seriously than they expect.' After a pause, she added, 'You think I'm the only one who dreams of building a spaceship? There are whole communities out there devoted to it, and some have done more than just dream, I can tell you!'

'But when will you go?' said Ella. 'What will you do when you get there? How will the *Hammer*… whatever it's called, get you back again?' She blurted out questions so rapidly that Aunt Belinda had no chance to respond. 'Is this all to do with your last mission… and what happened up there to…?' She trailed off.

A brief wary look crossed Aunt Belinda's face, as if Ella had guessed something she shouldn't have. 'I'll get back to Earth, don't you worry,' she said, ignoring most of Ella's questions. 'I've planned it all out. Meanwhile, you *must* promise to keep the Hammerklav a secret. Both of you. My mission isn't exactly… official. Understood?'

'Of course,' Ella said.

Aunt Belinda led them down the ladder to the launchpad below. 'One last surprise,' she said. 'I'm rather proud of this one. Then it's everybody out, okay?'

'I don't think I can take another surprise,' Ella muttered.

Aunt Belinda reached into her apron pocket and took out a chunky CD-player remote. Pointing it at the ceiling, she pressed the *Okay* button. Ella jumped as the roof screeched and shuddered into life. The sloping edges slid away from each other to reveal the clear Dorset sky.

There, directly above the Hammerklav, the planet Drumendus shone down.

'Beautiful, isn't it?' said Aunt Belinda. 'And people ask me if I'd like to go back. Really!' Silence descended, broken only by a strange buzzing noise overhead. She went to close the roof, but before the sides could slide together, the silhouette of a small object appeared in the sky, hovering above the launchpad. 'What is that?' she said.

'Uh-oh,' said Ella. 'It looks like a drone.'

'A drone?'

'Yep – with a camera. Someone's spying on you.'

'Oh dear, oh dear, that won't do,' Aunt Belinda said, her expression panicked. The drone swooped down for a closer look but collided with the roof. Its rotors sheared off, and it plummeted out of sight. They heard it clatter onto the stone pathway outside. 'That'll teach them.'

They rushed out and retrieved the damaged drone. A logo the shape of a musical note was printed on its side, with the initials *LL* in the centre of the design.

'What's *LL*?' Ella said.

Aunt Belinda sighed. '*Larry Lark*, of all people!' The name rang a bell in Ella's mind, but she couldn't think how. 'Nasty piece of work. Larry is desperate to be an astronaut, but he doesn't have what it takes – no backbone, you see. What he *does* have is money, and plenty of it. He's just built his own mission control centre on his private island. Madness! The day that man goes on a space mission will be the day I sing the national anthem at the World Cup Final!'

'I remember now,' said Ella. 'You've mentioned

him before. He's obsessed with Drumendus, isn't he? And he's obsessed with… you?'

'Yes. He can't stand the fact that a bumbling Crinkle like me was the first person on Drumendus. I do wish he'd leave me alone.'

Ella put her hand on her aunt's arm. 'He's just jealous. And for what it's worth, I'm proud of my aunt, even if she is a "bumbling Crinkle" – and that's coming from *another* bumbling Crinkle!'

'Thank you, Ella,' Aunt Belinda said, distracted. 'But *no-one* can know about my mission. Especially not *him*.'

'Too late,' Freddie said, inspecting the drone. 'Larry Lark will have live-streamed the footage, I reckon. And this isn't just any drone; this is the super-long-distance Dragon Drone 88! He's probably controlling it from miles away.'

'The sneaky devil – that's typical Larry. He'll do all he can to shut down my mission, and he would enjoy every minute.' She glanced over at Racket Lodge, then back at the launch station. 'Well, I'm not going to give him the chance.' Rushing into the cottage, she leapt up the stairs two at a time.

Ella followed her inside with Freddie. 'Wait… you're… launching the Hammerklav *now*?'

'I don't have a choice. Larry will know his drone crashed. He'll be on his way – with government reinforcements, I expect. Too *cowardly* to come on his own. Ella, dear, you can stay at Freddie's for a few days, okay?'

'Er, I'm not sure if—' started Freddie.

'I don't think so!' Ella interrupted. 'You're not going to Drumendus without us! *We're* coming with you. Aren't we, Freddie?'

'Er, I'm not sure if—'

'Don't be ridiculous, dear!' This time it was Aunt Belinda's turn to interrupt. 'You can't.'

Ella stood in her aunt's way and folded her arms. She felt a smile creep across her face. 'Aunt Belinda, it's me! You don't honestly think I'm going to pass up this chance?'

Wringing her hands together and screwing up her forehead, Aunt Belinda let out a sigh. 'I really *should* have accepted the offer of a banana smoothie earlier, shouldn't I? Then I wouldn't have left the house, and you two wouldn't have seen the Hammerklav, and...' Ella didn't move. 'I can't believe I'm saying this, but... there are prototype flight suits and helmets hanging up in the airing cupboard. Go and fetch them.'

'Right!' said Ella.

A few minutes later, the unlikely trio met on the landing wearing futuristic all-in-one spacesuits.

Aunt Belinda beamed. 'Let's go to Drumendus, shall we?'

# CHAPTER 4

# A CRUMPLED MAP

Freddie phoned home to let his family know he'd been invited on a 'last-minute trip away, for a night or three', and that Aunt Belinda was the designated responsible adult.

'Gosh, I've never been called that before,' Aunt Belinda said as she locked the Racket Lodge doors.

Freddie asked to speak to his older brother, then said urgently down the phone, 'If anyone official-looking drives down the lane, do *not* let them past. Do whatever you can, okay? Oh, no reason… Thanks – I owe you. See ya!'

Aunt Belinda led Ella and Freddie back to the launch station and up the ladder to the Hammerklav. 'I need at least half an hour to do the pre-launch tests. An hour, really, but needs must.'

For the first time, Ella noticed a second seat in the cockpit next to Aunt Belinda's. 'Er, what's that for?'

'Oh… I…' Aunt Belinda hesitated. 'I had the idea of a co-pilot but thought better of it in the end. Then I strapped Mozart the mascot in there but decided *he* looked better on the dashboard. So now it's yours and Freddie's! A bit snug, but it's better that way than rattling around. I'll secure you in when I'm done.' She nipped back down to the launchpad and busied herself with a multitude of checks.

Ella's gut began to twist up as reality hit her. Was she really about to launch into space and fly to Drumendus? Or was this another one of her vivid dreams? It was too much for her brain to take in, so she fixed her gaze on the Mozart mascot and thought about her favourite trombone music. Freddie, on the other hand, could hardly contain himself. He paced and fidgeted and couldn't stop humming, despite being 'very definitely *not* a singer', in his words.

After the longest half hour of Ella's life, Aunt Belinda finally edged into the Hammerklav cockpit. 'Helmets on. Let's strap you in.' Ella and Freddie squeezed into the seat and leaned back, their legs as high as their heads. Aunt Belinda attached them to the communications link and air supply. 'It won't be the most comfy ride, but it'll be worth it.' She looked out of the window and scanned the nearby lane. 'I can't believe Larry Lark hasn't arrived yet. Racket Lodge should be swarming with space officials by now.' She craned her neck to see further along the road. 'Wait a minute. Freddie! There are cows crossing the road!'

Freddie shook his fists victoriously. 'I *knew* my brother would think of something!'

Ella turned her head and caught a glimpse of the herd trundling over the lane, crossing aimlessly from one field to the other. A few cows munched away at the grass verge, in no mood to be moved along. A convoy of cars with tinted windows waited on the far side, and Freddie's dad waved his arms around to try and move the dozy Friesians along.

'Well, Larry and his minions had better keep their distance if they don't want to get sizzled.' She took her seat beside them and strapped herself in. 'This is it. Focus, Belinda, focus!'

Ella smiled as her aunt started singing a lengthy song she must have written to remind her of the pre-lift-off checks. Snippets such as 'access arm retracted', 'internal power activated' and 'escape system armed' came through the tinny speakers in her helmet, both fascinating and alarming her.

'Tanks to flight pressure,' Aunt Belinda declared. 'One minute to lift-off!'

Ella clenched her fists and used every ounce of energy she had to empty her mind of the growing fear and doubt. 'You're about to go to Drumendus!' she whispered to herself. 'This is what you've always wanted, Ella!' One of Mum's sayings popped into her head: '*Life's like music – you take it a beat at a time.*' There was nothing she could do now, so she may as well *try* and take this crazy experience 'a beat at a time'. She glanced over at Freddie. At least her best friend was coming with her. 'Are you ready?' she said, trying to sound positive.

'No. You?'

'No.'

'Excellent…'

'TEN, NINE, EIGHT,' Aunt Belinda belted out. 'Ignition sequence started.'

Ella's eyes seemed determined to close as the Hammerklav's rockets roared to life.

'SEVEN, SIX, FIVE…'

'Hey!' Freddie yelled. 'You won't get to do this again – keep your eyes open!'

Ella blinked a few times and nodded.

'FOUR, THREE, TWO, ONE…' Aunt Belinda tapped her statue of Mozart on the head. 'LIFT-OFF!'

The Hammerklav rose into the night sky, faster and faster until Ella felt as though she were turning inside out. She managed a quick look over at Freddie, whose body, like hers, was pinned to the seat from the g-force of lift-off. His stretched face sported a huge grin, and his eyes were so wide that they practically leapt out of his head.

Aunt Belinda carried on talking to herself in short bursts, little of which Ella understood. She then gave a thumbs-up and chuckled. 'All's going to plan, but it's a bumpy ride for a few more minutes. No worse than those funny rollercoaster things, though.' She paused. 'Well… perhaps a *little* worse.'

A few minutes later, the roaring and shuddering stopped as abruptly as it had started, and the weight bearing down on Ella's body lifted. Worry melted into wonder as she stared down at Earth. The shimmering lights of a thousand towns and cities made the dark expanse of the oceans yet more mysterious. Mountain ranges, lakes and forests stretched majestically across the land, punctuated by determined rivers weaving towards the sea.

Aunt Belinda patted Ella on the arm with her gloved hand. 'Congratulations, you two, you've just joined the astronaut club!'

&

As the hours ticked by, Earth became an ever-smaller ball of sea, land and cloud in the vast expanse of space. Ella moved to a quiet corner by a window and wrapped herself in a blanket that bore the comforting smell of Racket Lodge. Just as she was about to give in to the hypnotic beauty of the view outside and fall into a deep sleep, she noticed Freddie float over to her.

'Ella,' he said in a hushed voice. 'Your aunt is up to something.'

Ella sat up and rubbed her eyes. 'What do you mean?'

Freddie looked over his shoulder to check Aunt Belinda wasn't listening, then leaned in closer. 'Remember when she said, "I've things to do up there"?'

'Yeah,' said Ella, 'but that could mean anything. Do a few science experiments, take a few selfies, sing a few songs… I don't know!'

Freddie shook his head and held up a creased piece of paper that looked like a hand-drawn map of Drumendus. 'Look what I found.'

Ella tutted; she had seen dozens of maps like that, scattered all over Aunt Belinda's house. 'Part of her mission plans, obviously.'

Freddie lowered the map to a wall light. 'Look what's written on it: arrows and signs, all labelled *Otto*.'

'As in, my Uncle Otto?' said Ella, leaning in for a closer look.

'Of course! Who else does your aunt know called Otto? She's even labelled the map, *Where's Otto?*'

A bony hand swooped out of nowhere and snatched it away.

'How did you get this, young man?' Aunt Belinda said, glowering at them and stuffing the map into her pocket.

'I… I found it on the floor,' Freddie stuttered sheepishly. 'It must have… fallen from somewhere… during lift-off.'

'Really?'

'I was about to return it. Honest.'

'But you *had* to show Ella first, eh?' said Aunt Belinda, a faint smile crossing her lips as her expression softened. Freddie shrugged, and Aunt Belinda added, 'It's alright, Freddie. I was looking for it earlier, so you've actually done me a favour.'

'What does the map mean?' said Freddie, his confidence returning in an instant.

Ella coughed in embarrassment. 'You don't have to explain, Aunt Belinda,' she blurted out. 'This is *your* mission – we shouldn't even be here!'

'Yes, I think she *should* explain, actually,' Freddie

persisted. 'We're part of the *"astronaut club"* now, remember? Why are you really going to Drumendus, Miss Crinkle? You must be in so much trouble with everyone back on Earth, 'cos you're not… official.'

Aunt Belinda waved her hand dismissively. 'My *mission's* not official, but *I* certainly am, thank you – I'm the first person on Drumendus! And I'm *Commander* Crinkle, Freddie… but you can call me Belinda.' She sat herself down on the piano stool.

Freddie's impatience was clearly getting the better of him. 'Okay, but why have you got a map that labels Ella's *dead* uncle? Your *dead* brother?'

Aunt Belinda screwed up her face. 'Yes… I wanted to talk to you about that. But it's all rather top-secret. Otto's, er… not exactly… *dead.'*

Ella's body jerked in surprise. 'Either he *is* dead or he *isn't* dead,' she said eventually. The more confused she felt, the higher her voice became.

'What I mean is, I don't *think* he's dead,' said Aunt Belinda. 'If there's one person I know that could survive on Drumendus for a quarter of a century, it's your Uncle Otto.'

'But he died on the way back from your mission. It's common knowledge. Everyone learns about it in Year 2.'

Aunt Belinda's shoulders hunched forwards. 'That's what BASS – the British Agency of Space Study – *decided* had happened. In fact, Otto never left Drumendus.'

Ella's mouth hung open as she tried to comprehend what her aunt was saying.

'Why did BASS say Otto was dead?' said Freddie, his tone edgy.

'To stop them getting into trouble. Imagine the news reports and the public uproar if they'd found out we left somebody behind, to fend for himself!'

'But why didn't BASS try to rescue him?' Ella said.

'Oh, they did, but every mission failed. Whoops, that's also top-secret.'

'Why didn't *you* try?'

'Believe me, Ella, I would have, but I was fired as soon as I returned to Earth. You all think I retired a national hero, but BASS forced me to stop being an astronaut because I had come home without Otto. I was mission commander, and I had broken the sacred law of space travel: *never leave anyone behind.*'

Silence descended as Ella and Freddie tried to take it all in. Was everything Ella knew about her aunt and uncle a lie? If not, where did the truth end and the lies begin?

'And now,' said Aunt Belinda, trying to sound triumphant but clearly sensing Ella's unease, 'I'm putting it right. I'm going to rescue Otto and bring him home. It's taken over twenty years, but I've finally designed a spaceship that works. And here we all are.'

'So *that's* why there are two seats in the cockpit,' Freddie said. 'One for you and one for Otto.'

'Indeed… hmm, it'll be quite a squeeze on the way home. One of you will have to sit with me. Oh, well – cross that bridge, eh?'

Ella pulled her knees to her chest. 'I still don't

understand. Why did you leave Uncle Otto on Drumendus? Your own brother?'

Aunt Belinda sighed. 'It seems impossible, doesn't it? I struggle to make sense of it myself. Well, all I can do is tell you the story of our mission, all those years ago – the *real* story, I mean, not what you learned at school. I was going to do that before we landed, but you've rather beaten me to it.'

Freddie and Ella wrapped blankets around themselves.

'Are you sitting comfortably?' said Aunt Belinda, and nobody smiled. 'Sorry, bad time for a joke. And no, of course you aren't, this is the Hammerklav. Well, here goes...'

# CHAPTER 5
# OTTO'S CHOICE

A quarter of a century ago – who would have thought it? That summer was all of my dreams crammed into one huge piece of delicious astronaut chocolate cake. Everything I'd worked for my entire career was geared towards this mission, and now here I was, leading it, with my brother, Otto, to my left, and the best rocket scientist in the world, Celine Holiday, to my right. We were the first people attempting to land on Drumendus, and the world was watching.

The weeks beforehand were a bit of a blur. All I remember is being asked question after question, not about the things *I* wanted to talk about, like the experiments we would do and the species we hoped to study, but silly things like how many pairs of socks

I would pack and whether Otto was jealous that his sister was in charge. I wouldn't say Otto was *happy* that BASS made me the boss and not him, but we certainly weren't archenemies, as some folks reported. At least, I didn't *think* we were...

On launch day at BASS headquarters, Otto, Celine and I stood on the steps of our spaceship, the Leopold, alongside two other crew members who would stay in orbit in the command module while we three visited the surface. We wore our best fixed grins for the thousands of excitable journalists and enthusiasts who had come to witness take-off. Otto had barely spoken to me all week, he was so fed up at being in my shadow the whole time, but I was determined not to let it spoil the occasion. The last thing I recall before stepping into the Leopold is waving down at the splendid brass band from Yorkshire, who had serenaded us in with a most hearty rendition of 'The Planets.'

Lift-off was bang on time and the twenty-one-hour flight to Drumendus went perfectly to plan. It was a bit strange, really: all that celebrity hype, anticipation and frenzied activity on Earth, and here we were, calmly going about our business in space with not even the tiniest technical fault to report. I hoped that a little spider may have sneaked in and decided to join us on our mission – but no, the spiders stayed on Earth that day.

*This is too good to be true*, I remember thinking to myself. And, my goodness, it *was*.

We landed precisely where we wanted to, on a hill

on the edge of the Hidden Lands. There was no point touching down on the side of Drumendus facing Earth; that's just one vast ocean, as you know, with a few tiny islands dotted about. No, we decided that *real land* would be far more interesting. We didn't have much to go on when we started exploring – just a few vague maps, like the one you found about Otto. The Hidden Lands have always been a great mystery to us. Even today's high-tech space probes struggle to give us much of a clue – those wretched purple clouds hide everything from the photos they send back these days. What *was* utterly astonishing was how similar the planet was to Earth: we didn't need oxygen, we didn't need spacesuits – it was wonderful!

By day three on Drumendus, we had explored a fair chunk around the landing site. We'd got used to the purple tint that runs through everything and the breathtaking sounds all around us: the constant drumming from deep within the planet itself, which we called the 'heartbeat', the birdsong, the waterfalls, even the breeze – *so* vivid in our ears.

We found no signs of organised living – settlements, tracks, tools and such like. Celine and I slowly realised that we would have to let down the public back on Earth rather gently. All they wanted was for us to find harmless purple aliens with antennae and little round faces.

Otto, on the other hand, was certain that there *was* intelligent life on Drumendus, and he was desperate to find it. Drumendus had some sort of hold on him, enticing him ever further from the Leopold, tempting him to discover its secrets. He never said it, but it was clear he wanted to be the first person in history to find extraterrestrials. Then *he* would be the most famous person on Earth, not his younger sister.

The thunderstorms that day were beyond anything I could've imagined. The noise was so deafening that it shook our bones to the marrow, and the water bucketed down so hard that we couldn't see more than half a yard in front. We were forced to cut the day short and rush to the Leopold before it was blown off the hill and washed away. We squelched our way back as fast as we could, slipping and sliding through the treacly mud. Celine and I scrambled up the slope towards the Leopold.

'There's water in the cabin,' Celine said as she climbed the steps. 'In a couple of minutes, this thing won't fly.'

'Start the launch sequence,' I barked. 'Now!'

'But what about the pre-launch checks and lift-off protocol? BASS won't be happy if we—'

'Forget them!' I interrupted, determined to make sure we left Drumendus while we still could. 'We need to get off this planet and back to the command module!'

At the top of the hill, I looked over my shoulder to check that Otto was behind me.

He wasn't.

'Hurry, Otto,' I remember yelling down to him. 'There's no time!' I could barely see him through the torrent of rain, but he was clearly reluctant to move.

'Launch sequence engaged!' Celine shouted from the cockpit. 'I'd jump in if I were you, Commander.'

I climbed halfway up the ladder and looked down again. 'It's now or never, Otto. Please!' I begged. 'I have to seal the door for take-off!'

It was at that moment I knew he wouldn't come. He stared up at me, a strange stare that I *cannot* work out to this day. He was absolutely still, despite the rain lashing against his face and the wind doing its best to blow him over. The lure of Drumendus seemed too great for him to leave. It fixed him to the spot, *commanding* him to stay.

The Leopold stuttered to life. The water had breached the electrics and was causing havoc. Celine, who was strapped in and checking the dials in the cockpit, turned to me and said, 'Otto needs to get away from the hill or the rockets will toast him alive.'

I climbed into the cabin, grabbed the handle and pulled. Just before the clunk of the door sealed me inside, I screamed as loud as my voice would manage, 'OTTO, RUUUUUUUUN!'

I don't think he heard over the noise of the spacecraft and the storm.

The Leopold's rockets fired up, battling the water that had soaked them through. From the cockpit, I caught sight of Otto opening his arms in defiance, as if to say, '*My Drumendus adventure is just beginning.*' Then he smiled, shook his head and sprinted off towards the edge of the forest. He jumped into a ditch, surrounded by rocks and thick bushes.

That was the last I saw of him.

I banged my fists on my knees, lost for words. I was shocked, frustrated, terrified. Did that just happen? Did I just leave my brother alone on another planet? Or did he leave *himself* there? How could he do that? *Why* would he do that?

I tore myself away from the frenzy of questions in my mind and back to the reality of the Leopold, which, after yet more spluttering sounds from beneath our feet, shot upwards and climbed through the swirling purple clouds. Within seconds we were above the storm and bathed in bright sunlight, and I steeled myself for the bumpy ride out of Drumendus's atmosphere, trying not to focus on my brother miles below.

Once we were safely out of the purple planet's clutches and floating through space towards the orbiting command module, Celine turned to me and said, 'It's not your fault, Commander Crinkle.'

'But Otto, he...' I could hardly speak. 'I—'

'Otto made a choice, Belinda,' she said, her voice firm. 'He had time to get back to the Leopold. He chose not to. He *chose* to stay on Drumendus.'

She was right. Otto had made a choice, one that I could not for the life of me understand.

We radioed the incident to BASS. As soon as we landed on Earth, I was summoned to the chief's office and ordered to hand over my astronaut's badge. Despite protesting my innocence, he decided I was to blame for the whole thing. After all, I was Commander of the Leopold, and I was the one who ignored the rules and gave the go-ahead for the launch sequence to start. It was one of the worst days of my life.

The chief also decided that BASS would keep everything top-secret while they tried to find Otto and bring him home. When every mission failed, they chose to rewrite history, to stop them getting shut down in a whirlwind of public anger and disgrace. The story they concocted was that Otto fell gravely ill on the flight back to Earth, was whisked off to hospital, spent weeks there out of sight and sadly lost his life after a brave battle. Meanwhile, I would retire a national hero as the first person to set foot on Drumendus.

I was so confused at the time. How could they tell such lies? This was my brother! And how could they blame me for everything and cast me aside like that?

But none of that mattered to BASS. Their reputation was intact.

Storming out of their headquarters for the last time, I resolved to build my own spacecraft one day and find Otto myself. I wanted answers from my brother, and I wanted to bring him home.

I still do. And that's precisely why we're here.

# CHAPTER 6
# NATURE'S SYMPHONY

Aunt Belinda looked exhausted as she finished her story. 'Well, you two are the ninth and tenth people in the world to find out the truth about my first mission to Drumendus. Quite an exclusive club, I'd say.'

Ella leaned forwards, perplexed. 'So Uncle Otto *wanted* to stay on Drumendus?'

'I'll never be completely sure, Ella, but I know what I saw in those last few seconds before lift-off, and so does Celine.'

'But why? Why would he leave everything on Earth behind? And what would he do on Drumendus, all alone?'

'I've been asking myself the same things all these years. I'm hoping he'll tell me, when I find him.'

'*If* you find him,' said Freddie, 'and *if* he's alive.'

'If indeed,' said Aunt Belinda, sorrow in her voice.

'And what if he doesn't want to come home?'

'At least I will have given him the chance. That's all I can do, Freddie. And besides, of *course* he'll want to come home; he belongs on Earth, not Drumendus.' Nodding as if to convince herself she was right, she added, 'One moment of madness doesn't define a person forever.'

'Fair enough. And *whatever* happens, we're the first kids in space. Not a bad start to the summer holidays!'

'Now, time to rest, you two,' Aunt Belinda said. 'You'll need all your strength if you're to help me find my brother.'

𝄞

Ella slept for so long that the first thing she heard when she opened her eyes was Aunt Belinda chiming, 'Two hours to go before landing!'

The glistening orb of Drumendus hung proudly in the darkness ahead, its cloudy atmosphere peppered with jagged bursts of purple light. The surface of the planet remained hidden.

Ella floated over to her aunt, who was listening to a song about some blue suede shoes. 'I didn't know you liked *this* type of music,' she said.

'Just goes to show,' Aunt Belinda said, swaying from side to side in her seat, 'we can all like *any* music we want to! There are no rules. Me, it depends on my mood – right now, it just had to be Elvis.'

Ella looked back out at Drumendus. 'Where are we touching down?'

'On the edge of the Hidden Lands – the precise hill the Leopold landed on. From there, we can begin our hunt for Otto. Before that, though, there's just time for me to conduct a symphony or two.'

'Er… conduct a *what*?'

'A symphony. You know, those big pieces of music played by an orchestra? You'll play your trombone in them one day, I'm sure. Now, I think I fancy Beethoven's Fifth. One of my all-time favourites.'

Ella had a vague recollection of listening to some disco music at school that apparently used the same tune as this mysterious Beethoven's Fifth.

Aunt Belinda fiddled around with her music player and found the right track. 'One more thing.' She unlocked a container under the dashboard that housed a random collection of musical instruments. With a triumphant look in her eyes, she pulled out a thin stick with one end shaped like a teardrop. 'You know what this is, don't you, Ella?'

'Sort of. You wave it around to keep everyone in time, don't you?'

'Yes. This, Ella, is one of the greatest objects in all music.'

'Ah, yes, er… that too,' said Ella, trying not to sound bemused.

'A conductor's baton,' Aunt Belinda added. 'It helps keep the music in time, yes, but it's so much *more* than that, in the right hands. It focuses minds, it draws out meaning, it brings people together into one experience, it… Oh, you get the idea!'

'You're going all poetic on me! But, yeah, I know what you mean.' Ella thought back to the times Mr Pulp, the school music teacher, had waved his arms around in orchestra rehearsals, sometimes holding a pencil to make the beat clearer. He certainly hadn't used a real baton.

'In that moment of music-making, nothing else matters in the whole world,' Aunt Belinda said. 'With this baton, the power is quite literally at your fingertips.' She pressed the play button. 'Off we go. Enjoy!'

And with that, the music began.

*Da da da daaaaaa! Da da da daaaaaa!*

Aunt Belinda closed her eyes and waved the baton through the air with a sudden swish. Side to side, up and down, whooshing and swirling, she conducted the music as if she were performing an elaborate dance whose moves only she knew, her face mirroring the music's changing emotions. Ella laughed at first but soon became mesmerised by the combination of music and movement. The baton did have a mysterious power, in the hands of her eccentric aunt.

A couple of hours later, long after the conducting dance had finished and the baton was safely tucked away, Aunt Belinda called over. 'Right, let's get you two strapped in! Drumendus is waiting for us.'

Ella's knees wobbled, and she glanced over at Freddie.

'Keep your eyes *open*, Ella,' Freddie said, staring out of the window and grinning. 'You'll regret it otherwise!'

'Eyes open, eyes open, eyes open,' Ella panted.

The Hammerklav crunched in on itself a little as it hurtled into the thick, swirling atmosphere of Drumendus. The frame groaned under the strain, and various dials on Aunt Belinda's dashboard flicked back and forth. She laughed and pressed a few buttons, then tapped her Mozart mascot on the head.

'Come on, my dear,' she said to her beloved spaceship. 'Behave yourself, and get us down safely.'

Nothing could have prepared Ella for the descent to the surface. No theme-park ride, no rocket simulator, nothing. The purple planet had complete control for a few minutes, sending the Hammerklav lurching to one side, then the other... rattling it... clattering it... jostling it through shifting pockets of air and cloud.

'Descent rockets activated!' Aunt Belinda yelled. 'This will slow us down to the surface.' A few vicious lightning forks zipped past the window, and the Hammerklav veered off course. 'Vivaldi's vest! We're not going to land where I thought we would. This Drumendus weather is far worse than last time.'

Ella's eyes watered as she struggled to keep them open. She was certain she was about to disintegrate in a ball of purple flame, never to be seen again.

At last, the storm eased and the Hammerklav

broke through the clouds into clear air below. Freddie burst into spontaneous applause, and Ella joined in as they caught sight of the planet's surface for the first time.

'Worth the bumpy ride after all!' Aunt Belinda said, expertly guiding the Hammerklav down to a flat stretch of land not far from an ocean. 'This will have to do.'

The hardy spacecraft thudded to the surface, then seemed to let out a long, relieved sigh as its tired engines shuddered to a stop.

Aunt Belinda turned around and beamed. 'Ella, Freddie... Welcome to Drumendus.'

𝄞

Ella needed a moment to take in the fact she was still alive. Freddie, by contrast, yelped in delight and eagerly unstrapped himself.

Aunt Belinda heaved open the door and lowered the steps. 'Just as I remember,' she said, as a first waft of Drumendus air touched their faces. 'Rather chilly, and rather... purple. Let's say hello, shall we?'

Freddie wasted no time in climbing down. Ella followed gingerly, like a cat being introduced to a new home. As her feet touched the ground, a strange, unfamiliar energy flowed through her. Every fibre of her being came alive as if dancing to celebrate her arrival on Drumendus. She stared around her, taking in the mysterious expanse of sea to her right, the dense forest extending away to her left, and the sharp rocks and undulating grassy plains ahead of her. A purple tint permeated every surface. Although the sky had calmed for the time being, a thick blanket of cloud bore down on them and stretched as far as the eye could see.

And the sounds...

The continually changing soundscape of Drumendus was like nothing Ella had experienced before. Nature was performing its *own* symphony, an endless tapestry of swirling breezes, distant waves and birdsong. It wasn't like the sounds back home; if they were grey, these were truly fluorescent; if they were tucked away in the background, these were central to the very fabric of the planet, grabbing your attention and not letting go.

Then there was the Drumendus drumming, which had baffled and intrigued Aunt Belinda so much on her first mission. *Finally*, Ella was hearing it with her own ears. The beating sounds filled the air with complex rhythms from near and far as the combinations constantly shifted. Occasional moments of deep silence punctuated the soundscape, at once beautiful and threatening. The extra-loud thuds, the so-called heartbeat of the planet, seemed to pulsate from deep within its core and ooze up through the soil, grass and trees at the surface.

Ella, Freddie and Aunt Belinda stood as still as reptiles, heads tilted, listening intently to this extraordinary world of sound. Eventually, Ella broke the drum planet's spell. 'This is... unbelievable,' she said. 'I can stand here in my Earth clothes, but at the same time, it feels so... alien.'

'That'd be the crazy noises and the fact that everything's purple.' Freddie chuckled. 'But apart from that, this place really *is* Earth's sibling.'

Aunt Belinda scanned the horizon. 'I need to get my bearings,' she said, her voice unsure. 'We can't be *that* far from my intended landing site.'

'Look!' said Freddie. 'Lightning – over there!'

Ella turned to see the tail-end of an enormous flash of purple light pierce the sky in the distance. Then another. And another. The ground shook with a particularly booming drumming sound shortly after each one.

'The lightning's going *up* to the clouds, not down from them,' Ella said. 'I knew Drumendus was different, but that's just… weird.'

'Hmm, I don't remember that from my last mission,' said Aunt Belinda. 'We'll investigate once I've worked out exactly where we are. Come on.' She pulled out the tatty hand-drawn map labelled *Where's Otto?* and turned it around in her hands a few times. 'Let's see. This must be the forest I explored around the Leopold.'

She strode off purposefully, and Ella and Freddie followed along behind, doing their best to avoid the hidden ditches and swamp patches dotted beneath their feet. Ella had to tear her eyes away from her surroundings to make sure she didn't land headfirst in a puddle. Even the creaks and groans of the imposing trees were musical, deep and rich in the breezy air. Nothing escaped this planet's insatiable appetite for sound.

'It's as if everything's having a conversation with everything else,' said Ella. 'And we're interrupting it!'

'Yes, that's how it feels to start with,' Aunt Belinda said, 'but you'll get used to it.'

The air cooled as they ventured into the forest, and the canopy blocked out much of the purple light.

Ella stopped in her tracks. 'Do you know where you're going?' she said to her aunt. 'It's just... the trees all look the same.'

'To *you*, they all look the same,' said Aunt Belinda, squinting down at her map in the semi-darkness. 'To *me*, they all look... the same, yes.'

Ella laughed awkwardly. She felt unease creep into her stomach. 'We shouldn't go too far from the Hammerklav... should we?'

'Of course we should,' snapped Aunt Belinda. 'I'll guide us back, don't you worry.'

'Are you sure? It's just—'

'*Yes*, Ella!' Aunt Belinda shrugged and added, 'Honestly, I thought you two would be *thrilled* that you're the first children to set foot on Drumendus in the history of the universe! The *first* children!'

'That's not true,' came a voice out of nowhere.

# CHAPTER 7
# DRALIENS?

**E**lla and the others froze.

'Who goes there?' Aunt Belinda barked, ushering Ella and Freddie behind her. She sounded like a castle gatekeeper.

'Do not move!' said the unfamiliar voice. 'That is your first warning, lady from space.'

Ella was sure her heart had never beaten so fast, even after cross-country at school.

Aunt Belinda managed a dubious laugh. 'You stowed yourself away in the Hammerklav back on Earth, didn't you?' she said. 'It's okay. I'm not angry. Golly, *I'd* want a free trip to Drumendus if I'd known a mad retired astronaut was building a spaceship.'

'Stay quiet,' said the voice in the shadows. 'This

is your second and *final* warning. We have traps and weapons.'

'This is clearly a silly joke. You're one of the Molto siblings, aren't you? Freddie, you must recognise the voice?'

'Er… no, can't say I do,' said Freddie.

Aunt Belinda stepped towards the clump of trees from which the teenage voice came. 'Let's get to the bottom of this, shall we?'

'I warned you!' said the voice.

'Oh, do be quiet. I just… argh!'

Ella heard something move on the forest bed. She glanced down as a rope swished through the leaves and tripped her up. Freddie and Aunt Belinda were also whisked off their feet, and they all ended up in a net a few metres off the ground, squashed together like an overfilled shopping bag.

'What on Earth is all this?' yelled Aunt Belinda.

'I think you mean, "What on *Drumendus* is all this?"' said the voice. A couple of others laughed as he spoke. 'That's what you call our planet, is it not?'

'Your planet?' Aunt Belinda puffed. 'This is outrageous! Your joke has gone too far. Nobody lives on Drumendus. You're only here because of *my* spaceship. Cut us down from your silly trap at once!'

Three youngsters emerged from the shadow of a gnarled tree. Ella's heart went from beating faster than it ever had to practically stopping. These beings were certainly *not* from Earth, and had certainly *not* hidden in the Hammerklav and landed on Drumendus half an hour ago.

'Aliens…?' she whispered. 'I mean… *Draliens*…? Purple Draliens…?' It wasn't only the land, sea and sky that shimmered with purple on Drumendus; the people did too.

Freddie tutted. 'You sound just like my dad, Ella. They're not *Draliens*; they're the Drumendus natives.'

'Er… Freddie, why aren't you petrified right now?'

'Because they're purple people, that's all.'

'You're far too calm. It's like you… *expected* to find intelligent life here?'

'Well, Drumendus is Earth's neighbour, so why *shouldn't* there be species here like ours? Or more than one species, for that matter…'

It hadn't crossed Ella's mind that there might be a population of 'people' on Drumendus. Aunt Belinda was so certain there *wasn't* after her first mission, and BASS were constantly telling the public back home not to worry about UFO invasions and planet wars.

A boy and two girls circled below the trap. They were similar in size to Ella and Freddie, but their ears glowed violet and twitched at every sound. Their wide faces revealed inquisitive expressions, and their eyes glistened a deep shade of purple. They wore the most peculiar, medieval-looking tunics and tights, which were covered in colourful circular patterns. More peculiar still, they each carried a weapon that bore a striking resemblance to a musical instrument.

'Be on your guard,' the boy ordered, his hood lowered and his tousled hair pointing in whichever direction it chose. He glanced up at Ella urgently. 'They will be dangerous. And powerful too.'

Ella was sure she'd never been labelled *powerful* in her entire life.

'I think I'm losing the plot,' Aunt Belinda said, her face drained of all colour. 'People on Drumendus? *People* on *Drumendus*?'

'There are many thousands of us,' said the boy.

'Thousands? But… there can't be…'

Ella held onto her aunt's arm to try and comfort her.

'We know you're from Earth,' said the boy. 'We saw you float down from the sky in your flying box.'

'Pah, "flying box",' chuntered Aunt Belinda, who seemed to regain her composure immediately to defend her beloved Hammerklav. 'It's a spaceship. I built it myself.'

'A flying ship? Impossible.'

'Not that sort of ship – oh, never mind!'

'Who exactly are you, Earthians?'

'Hang on a minute,' spluttered Ella, her head yet again swimming with questions. 'Is that what you call us – Earthians? And how do you speak English?'

The boy ignored her questions. 'You look just like the King,' he said, with bitterness in his voice. 'Especially *you*.' He pointed at Aunt Belinda.

'The… King?' Ella said to herself.

After a lingering silence, Aunt Belinda slumped down in the net and bowed her head. 'Mozart's mittens…' she murmured, visibly troubled. 'It can't be true.'

'What can't?' said Ella.

'The King. He looks like me.'

'And?'

'That's typical of him, just *typical*...'

Ella was becoming increasingly frustrated with her aunt. 'What's typical? Aunt Belinda, what are you *talking* about?'

'THE KING! Their King must be OTTO.'

'*What?*' Ella said, shuffling herself around in the net. 'Uncle Otto is... *King* Otto?'

'King Otto indeed,' snapped the boy below. 'So *he* says. And that's why we speak your language – he *forced* us to learn it. We have our *own* language too.' His unfamiliar accent grew stronger the more aggressive he became.

The taller of the girls, whose hair cascaded in complicated plaits, shook her head and nudged the boy. 'How does the old lady know about the King, Jacopo? She's only just arrived.'

'They've come to find him, of course. Mother said this would happen eventually – that Earthians would return here, searching for the one they left behind.'

Freddie kicked Ella in the ribs accidentally as he tried to move around inside the net. 'Excuse me,' he said to the glowing-eared trio, 'this is a lovely chat and all, but could you let us down, please? It's a *bit* uncomfortable in here.'

'Not until you tell us your names and how many of you have landed,' said the boy they called Jacopo.

Aunt Belinda sighed. 'I am Belinda, and you're right to say I look like Otto. He's my brother. We have the same cheekbones, apparently.'

Now it was the Drumendus children's turn to look

uncertain. 'The King's sister, here?' said the girl with the plaits, a frown on her angular face.

Aunt Belinda introduced Ella and Freddie, then said, 'We're the only ones here from Earth, and we've come to take Otto back home with us.'

Jacopo scoffed. 'Do continue, space-lady Belinda. You expect to take your brother home? The King?'

'I hadn't planned on him being... quite so important. But yes, I am *determined* to take him home, where he belongs, and I would advise you not to get in the way.' Ella had seldom heard Aunt Belinda talk with such steel in her voice, made all the more impressive as she was currently a scrunched-up ball in a net. 'We mean you no harm!' she shouted. 'Let us down this instant!'

Grumbling, Jacopo untied one of the ropes, and the net fell open. Ella, Freddie and Aunt Belinda landed with a thump on the mossy ground. They staggered to their feet, brushed themselves off and came face-to-face with the Drumendus trio.

'See? We're not *that* different,' Freddie beamed after a lengthy stare-off.

'Don't be so sure,' said Jacopo. 'Do *not* try anything strange, and do *not* try to escape.' He and the girls surrounded them in a tight circle. 'Mirabelle, check them for weapons and instruments.'

'What can you mean, *instruments*?' said Aunt Belinda.

'No talking!' said Mirabelle, as she patted them down and found nothing.

'I don't like Drumendus as much as I did five minutes ago,' whispered Ella.

'I'll handle this,' said Aunt Belinda, turning to the Drumendus children and forcing a laugh. 'We got off on the wrong foot – let's start again, shall we? Now, before we get to know each other properly, I need to check that we are where I think we are.' She pulled out her scrappy map and pointed with confidence at one of the corners. 'I'd say we're just about... *here.*'

The younger girl, who hadn't said a word yet, chuckled. 'You're nowhere near there,' she said with a gappy grin and rosy-purple cheeks.

'We're in Balladof,' Jacopo said, then pointed at the map. '*That* is Slorac.' He spoke with a cutting tone that betrayed a history between the two places, a rivalry, perhaps. 'You are many miles off the edge of this map. And yes, we do know about *miles*, because Otto decided we should.'

Rather than looking alarmed at the fact that the Hammerklav had touched down in a completely unknown area, Aunt Belinda stared in wonderment at the boy. 'Balladof? Slorac?' she said slowly. 'How wonderful. You name your lands, just like we do.'

'Obviously. We may be a little purple, but we're not savages.'

'No, no, of course not,' Aunt Belinda laughed. 'I've just never heard those names. We call this side of Drumendus the Hidden Lands, and we know almost nothing about it – even with our telescopes and satellites.'

The plaited girl named Mirabelle tapped Jacopo on the arm with her strange-looking weapon. 'Otto's people will be here soon. We should go.' Jacopo nodded. 'What shall we do with *them*?'

Aunt Belinda let out another nervous chortle and pocketed her map. 'You're going to tell us where I can find my brother and then let us go on our way, aren't you?' She put her arms around Ella and Freddie. '*So* nice to have met you all; quite a surprise, as you can imagine.' The Drumendus trio didn't move. 'Just tell us where Otto's house is… please?'

'I don't think so,' growled Jacopo. 'And it's not a house, it's a *palace*. Otto's the King, remember?'

'Very well,' said Aunt Belinda. 'If you're not going to help us, we'll head for the purple lightning. There's clearly something going on over there. Cheerio, then! Come on, children.'

She tried to lead them past Jacopo, but her path was blocked with a swift arm movement.

'You're coming with us,' he said. 'Tie their hands, Mirabelle.'

Mirabelle did as she was told, then grabbed Ella and lined her up behind Jacopo. She went to do the same to Freddie, but he wriggled free and hissed, 'Don't you dare push me. I'm perfectly capable of lining *myself* up.'

'This is highly irregular,' shouted Aunt Belinda as she and the others were led along a dark path into the depths of the forest. 'I *demand* to see my brother. We are not your prisoners!'

Jacopo turned and smirked from the front of the line. 'It looks that way to me.'

# CHAPTER 8
# PROPER TREE HOUSES

Ella, Freddie and Aunt Belinda followed the Drumendus children tentatively through the trees. Jacopo and Mirabelle kept their weapons drawn, but the younger girl seemed far more relaxed, walking alongside Ella and whistling snippets of a carefree tune.

'I cannot *believe* it,' the girl said, turning to Ella.

'What?'

'I can't believe I'm walking with a… real-life Earthian! Otto is the only Earthian we've ever known.'

'Well, *I* can't believe I'm walking with a real-life… *Drumendite* – I guess that's what we'd call you. I didn't even know Drumendites existed. And now we're speaking English together! AND… my uncle is the King! How has my head not exploded already?'

They both laughed, and the girl took Ella's hand and swung it as they walked. 'I'm Ursula,' she said, her grin as broad as ever.

'Ella.'

'How is it possible that Earthians don't know about us, if you can fly here through space?'

'The purple clouds keep you hidden. We don't see a thing.'

'I've seen Earth a few times,' said Ursula. 'Mother has taken us to the highest mountain peaks in Balladof, where the clouds are thin. You can catch a glimpse of Earth, floating there peacefully. Such a beautiful planet.'

'It is,' said Ella, a fleeting pang of homesickness catching her off guard. 'Not exactly peaceful, though.'

'What does Drumendus look like to you, back on Earth?'

'Purple. Very pur… wait a minute! Don't you have your *own* name for Drumendus?'

Ursula rolled her eyes. 'Of course we do. But Otto renamed the planet when he became King, so that's all I've ever known.'

Ella plunged her free hand into her pocket. 'I know Otto's my uncle, but he doesn't sound great.'

'Nobody in Gurdee likes him. *Especially* not my mother!'

'Gurdee?'

'That's where we're going. It's my home.' Yet more questions sprang into Ella's mind, but before she could ask any of them, Ursula continued, 'Gurdee is the one place the King does *not* rule. Mother's in charge there, *not* Otto. We are the rebels, Mother says – and proud of it!'

A while later, Jacopo turned to Ella and the others, a self-important look on his wide face. 'Otto is the enemy in Gurdee,' he said. 'So *you* are the enemy too. Don't expect a friendly welcome.'

'We wouldn't dream of it,' blustered Aunt Belinda, who had been deep in thought up to this point, 'the way you've treated us so far.'

Ursula whispered to Ella, 'My brother always tries to act tough, but he's not so bad. You should see my mother – she *is* tough.'

'Great,' muttered Ella.

The path through the forest widened and became more downtrodden, and the trees soon gave way to a clearing and a colourful wooden fence that stretched away in both directions. The faint sound of music wafted through the heavy air towards them.

Jacopo ran on ahead and stood in front of the main gate, which looked like a gigantic metronome. He put his hand to his mouth and sang a series of short, sharp notes.

'They sing instead of using a doorbell?' Freddie said, making Ella smile.

The bar above the entrance swung over to the other side, and the gate into Gurdee opened. Ella gasped as she took in the sight in front of her. Five vast ropes stretched across the clearing, attached to tree trunks at different heights. A line of oval-shaped buildings hung from each of them, connected by an intricate system of rope ladders and walkways.

A few metres behind was another set of ropes and suspended buildings, and more behind that.

'Wow,' said Ella, wide-eyed. '*Proper* tree houses.'

'Better than our efforts in the Racket Lodge garden,' Freddie chuckled, his eyes sparkling in amazement as he looked at the hanging settlement swaying in the breeze.

'My goodness,' said Aunt Belinda. 'Just when I was starting to think we'd been kidnapped by barbarians, they show you this. Quite extraordinary. And really rather beautiful.'

Circular wooden signs hung over the four biggest buildings, with pictures carved into them that looked like those on the Drumendus children's clothes. Ella turned to ask Ursula what they meant, but instead of seeing her new friend's smiling face, she was met with a fierce glare from a group of Gurdee teenagers who had gathered to see what was going on. Ursula had been steered away by Mirabelle.

'Wait here and do *not* move,' Jacopo ordered. 'Everybody is watching you.'

Ella's eyes darted around Gurdee. She spotted people peering out of windows, gathering on walkways and climbing halfway up rope ladders to get a better view. A man wearing red trousers with tassels was perched near the top of an enormous tree, tying a rope to its trunk. He stopped what he was doing and stared down at her. Groups of musicians dotted around the settlement stopped singing and playing their strange-looking instruments and made their way closer. Some drew their weapons; in fact, their instruments *became* their weapons.

The uneasy sound of raised voices drifted out of one of the hanging buildings, and moments later, a fiery-haired lady appeared at the entrance.

'That *must* be Ursula's mum,' Ella said to Freddie.

With the ease of someone who had done it a thousand times, the lady stepped onto the nearest rope ladder and slid down it in one rapid movement. Two adults followed behind her, as did Jacopo and Mirabelle.

'Finally,' said Aunt Belinda as the group marched towards them, 'someone who looks like they're in charge. Now, two extremely important things before we get properly acquainted: firstly, I am a *peaceful* soul, and secondly, I could really do with a sit down and a cup of tea.' The lady stopped in front of Aunt Belinda and looked her up and down suspiciously. Ella was sure there was fear in her eyes too. Aunt Belinda forced a laugh. 'Ah, perhaps I should introduce us all first. Here we have my niece, Ella – hmm, perhaps you don't have such things as nieces on Drumendus… Anyway, I am Belind—'

'I know who you are,' said the lady. 'And I know why you're here. Jacopo told me.' She stepped in closer to Aunt Belinda. 'Yes, you do look like *him*. Same face shape.'

'Of course I do,' bumbled Aunt Belinda. 'That is, if you're talking about my *brother*, Otto Crinkle.'

An unexpected smile flooded the lady's face, and she turned to her people and declaimed, 'Otto

*Crinkle*! He's never told us his other name. He prefers the grander title of King Otto of Drumendus!'

Laughter rippled through the assembled crowd.

'Now, look here,' said Aunt Belinda, 'I know you weren't expecting us, and, to be quite honest, we weren't expecting you either. Nor was I expecting that Otto would be… King.'

'Your brother is the reason Gurdee exists,' said the lady. 'He's the reason we had to leave our homes and build this settlement! He took over our lands many years ago and banished us from our own city. We're the only ones left to stop him.' She looked around her, then locked eyes with Aunt Belinda again. 'I am Isolde,' she said, with the air of a queen. 'I lead the fight against your brother. We *will* take back what is ours.'

The crowd, which had formed a tight circle around them, cheered and raised their fists. Their ears glowed brighter the more agitated they became.

Ella tugged on Aunt Belinda's sleeve. 'I don't like the sound of that,' she muttered.

'Perhaps you're here to join Otto,' Isolde continued. 'Well, know this: we will resist *anyone* who tries to rule Drumendus the way he does – *especially* people from Earth!'

The noise became deafening as whoops and shouts rang around Gurdee.

Aunt Belinda shook her head in astonishment. She leaned down to Ella and Freddie and whispered, 'I memorised the route we took through the forest earlier. I'll get us out of this mess.' She turned back to Isolde and the restless Gurdee locals. 'You've got the wrong end of the stick. All of you. In fact, you've got the wrong stick altogether!'

Isolde's supporters exchanged blank looks. 'Why is she talking about sticks?' one of them said.

'I *mean*, we're *not* here to take over! We're here to take Otto *home*!'

Isolde didn't look convinced. 'Otto is wielding his Earthian powers to rule Drumendus,' she said.

'I'm sorry?'

'His sound and music powers, of course. He has harnessed them here too.'

Aunt Belinda glanced at Ella, who glanced at Freddie, who glanced back at Aunt Belinda. 'What *are* you talking about?' she sputtered.

'You heard. His *sound* and *music* powers.'

Ella frowned, and Freddie piped up with, 'Like... *magic* powers? Ha – I don't think so!' He turned to Ella. 'Imagine, an uncle of yours in a cape? *Super Otto* – the musical superhero!' Dozens of unsmiling faces stared at him, so he added, 'We... er... don't have magic on Earth, that's all I'm saying.'

'We've witnessed it ourselves,' shouted an onlooker.

'Otto's powers get stronger every day!' another said to murmurs of agreement from the crowd.

Aunt Belinda flung her arms in the air. 'I've never heard such utter codswallop in all my life! Sound magic indeed? Rubbish! I'm his sister, and I've known him since we were in nappies – he doesn't have a magic bone in his body!'

'You mean... you've never seen his powers?' Isolde said, her tone sceptical.

Aunt Belinda shook her head, clearly exasperated. 'And you don't have sonorance yourself?'

'Sono-*what*?' said Aunt Belinda, letting out an involuntary laugh.

'Sonorance. That's what Otto calls his sound powers. And nobody finds this funny, Belinda. It gets worse, in fact: he is passing on these powers to his soldiers.' Her commanding voice bounced around Gurdee. 'Your brother's sonorance is the biggest threat to our existence!'

Sheer bewilderment covered Aunt Belinda's face. 'I'm starting to wonder if this is all a dream. Perhaps I'll wake up in a moment back at Racket Lodge...'

Isolde exchanged a few hushed words with her brightly-clothed advisors, then turned back. 'You will stay in Gurdee while I decide what to do with you,' she said.

'But—'

'Take the Earthian children up to Twangbuzzer Hall,' she barked.

'*Twangbuzzer Hall?*' Ella said to Freddie as they followed a guard through the intimidating crowd. 'Doesn't sound much fun.'

'Provide refreshment for them,' added Isolde. 'But do not let them out of your sight. And be wary – they may yet have sonorance.'

'We've just told you we *don't* have sono-whatever-it-is!' Freddie protested over his shoulder.

'What about Aunt Belinda?' said Ella, unwilling to break up the trio.

'Your aunt is coming with me. I want to hear *everything* about this mission of yours.'

'No! WAIT!' Ella yelled, but Aunt Belinda was already out of sight.

# CHAPTER 9

# SINGING STEW

Ella's legs started trembling; being taken to some sort of hanging prison on an alien planet was even *worse* than playing her trombone in school assembly. When she had jumped onboard the Hammerklav back at Racket Lodge, she had imagined a very different mission to Drumendus, one in which she would have a good old explore of her favourite planet for a day or two, then fly home with enough memories for a lifetime.

What she had *not* expected were Draliens and a magic King-uncle!

Jacopo led the way to Twangbuzzer Hall. 'Up there,' he said, clearly enjoying the power trip. 'Climb.'

Ella and Freddie wobbled their way up three rope ladders. A procession of Gurdee locals followed, including Ursula and Mirabelle. Ella hoped that Twangbuzzer Hall was not a code name for a dark cell with bars on the windows and rats in the corner. Along the wooden walkway, they reached the largest of the egg-shaped lodges. An instrument a bit like a violin was carved into the circular sign above the entrance.

She peered inside. To her relief, Twangbuzzer Hall was the very opposite of what she had imagined. Its walls were covered in multicoloured musical instruments. Ornate harps and guitars hung down neatly in size order, and each corner housed shelf upon shelf of what looked like mini pianos and old-fashioned keyboards, all immaculately decorated.

'It's like a museum,' said Ella, sitting on a rug by the window as instructed.

Freddie smiled, looking around him. 'Funny thing is, their instruments are their weapons too.'

'Not funny, really,' came Jacopo's gruff voice behind them. 'We've been forced into arming ourselves like this to defend Gurdee from Otto and his soldiers. Don't get any ideas; you wouldn't know how to use the instruments anyway.'

'Hmm, I dunno,' said Freddie, in a familiar cheeky tone. 'I reckon my violin-playing's probably bad enough to hurt someone.'

Ella chuckled, but Jacopo clearly didn't see the funny side, asking instead, 'What's a *violin*?' Before Ella could explain, Jacopo had turned to Mirabelle. 'Fetch the Earthians some food,' he said. 'They are people, after all… supposedly.'

Ella looked over at the inquisitive crowd of Gurdee folks who were gawping in, as if she and Freddie were fairground curiosities.

Ursula, the cheerful girl she had met in the forest, pushed her way to the front. 'Let me in,' she said to Jacopo, who had taken up position guarding the door. 'One of them's my friend. She's called *Elsa*.'

Ella blushed at being called the wrong name, and Freddie smirked next to her.

Jacopo refused to budge.

'You're such an *annoying* brother,' Ursula said, 'always trying to look tough in front of everyone.' It was strangely comforting to Ella to see that Drumendus children could have disagreements and find each other irritating too. Ursula barged past Jacopo and plonked herself down between Ella and Freddie on the rug. Mirabelle edged her way in, carrying a huge pot on a tray. A glorious smell filled the room, and it was only then that Ella realised how ravenous she was. The stew inside the pot seemed to babble a happy tune.

'Does *everything* have to be musical in this place?' Freddie said. 'Even the food?'

'You mean, Earthian food *doesn't* sing?' Ursula said.

'Er… not the last time I checked.'

'How strange.'

'Yeah, we're the strange ones,' grumbled Freddie, tucking into the stew. After the meal, he edged over to Ella and whispered, 'They can't just keep us here.'

'I know, but let's wait and s—'

Freddie had already jumped to his feet and stormed over to Jacopo. 'Where is Belinda Crinkle?' he said, his voice as stern as he could make it. 'I… I *demand* to know!'

'You're in no position to *demand* anything, Earthian!'

Freddie's fingers clamped into fists as he edged closer. 'Where's Belinda?'

Ella jumped between them. 'Stop it, both of you!'

Suddenly, Isolde appeared at the doorway and walked calmly to the middle of the room. Her presence commanded the attention of everyone. 'Your aunt is quite safe,' she said, as Freddie and Jacopo backed away from each other. 'We have spoken at length, and I am satisfied that she is not another *enemy* from Earth, and you are not her spies.'

Freddie scoffed. 'Me and Ella – spies? That's just—'

Isolde raised her hand to stop him talking. 'There is much *good* in Belinda. I struggle to see how she and Otto can be brother and sister – they're so different.'

Ella really didn't like the sound of Uncle Otto. Not one person had a good word to say about him.

'Jacopo, take Ella and Freddie to Dingringer Hall to see Belinda. They can all rest there for the night.'

'*Dingringer? Twangbuzzer?*' Freddie muttered. 'What *are* these names all about?'

'They're our consorts, of course,' Ursula said, as they followed Jacopo out onto the maze of walkways.

'Con-*what*?'

'Don't tell me you have no consorts on Earth?'

Shaking his head, Freddie said, 'I know, I know, aren't we strange – you don't have to say it again!'

'Consort?' Ella said, vaguely recognising the word from Mum's music-making back home. 'Like – groups of musicians?'

'Exactly!' Ursula replied. 'Whatever our favourite instrument, that's the consort we belong to. There are four consorts, and they each have their own hall. Twangbuzzers play anything that has strings. Dingringers play anything that dings or rings – obviously.'

'Okay...' Freddie said, trying not to look bemused.

'But *I* am a Whackboomer! We play drums of all kinds.'

'Cool,' said Ella. 'Instruments that BOOM.'

'Yes!' Ursula said, clearly thrilled at Ella's interest. 'Whackboomers are the *best* consort, everyone knows that.'

Jacopo turned his head abruptly. 'I don't think so.'

'Which consort are *you* in, then?' Freddie asked Jacopo, his voice aggressive.

Jacopo stopped in front of another impressive egg-shaped lodge. 'I'm an Airwhoosher. This is our hall.'

'Let me guess,' said Ella, looking inside at yet more instruments arranged in impeccable rows on the walls, some of which looked a bit like flutes and recorders. 'Airwhooshers play instruments that use air?'

'Yes. *And* we have the best singers too. So *we* are, of course, the best consort.'

Freddie tapped Ella on the arm. 'Congratulations, Ella. You're not just a trombonist, you're an Airwhoosher.'

'Thanks! And you're a Twangbuzzer. Even if the strings you play are hidden inside a piano!'

Freddie laughed, and to Ella's surprise, he said, 'This consort thing is all a bit stupid, though. Don't you think?'

Ursula put her hand on his arm. 'Do be careful, Freddie, our consorts are very precious to us.'

Jacopo wheeled around, anger etched on his face. 'I'll be less kind than my sister. DO NOT speak about our consorts in that way... EVER AGAIN.'

Although Freddie looked startled by Jacopo's threat, he held his stare and didn't step backwards. 'Fine,' he said through clenched teeth.

A figure appeared alongside them, seemingly out of nowhere. Ella recognised him as the man perched high in the trees earlier. Without saying a word, he beckoned for them to carry on towards Dingringer Hall, a smug grin on his pockmarked face.

'Who is *that*?' Ella said to Ursula, scuttling ahead so the man was out of earshot.

'Scarp, one of Mother's helpers,' said Ursula. 'He won't talk to you – at least, not unless he *really* has to, and most people ignore him. But Mother finds him quite useful. He helped build Gurdee, and he's always high up in the trees, building secret walkways and rope routes nobody uses.'

They caught sight of Dingringer Hall after negotiating a few more precarious rope ladders. A sturdy man with a bushy moustache stood guard outside.

'What about *him*?' Ella said.

Ursula tutted. 'That's Figaroon.' She didn't try to hide the disdain in her voice. 'He *thinks* he's in charge. Always disagreeing with Mother. I do *not* like him. A *scoundrum!*'

Figaroon stood aside and let the children into Dingringer Hall. 'Touch nothing,' he growled.

Aunt Belinda was at the far end, admiring a rack of musical oddities. Ella ran over and flung her arms around her.

'Ooh, goodness me!' Aunt Belinda laughed, teetering forwards. 'I do hope that's Ella!' Turning around, she said, 'First things first, have you and Freddie been fed?' Ella nodded. 'Good, good. Have you seen these wonderful, exotic instruments?' She pointed to a display case of what could have been xylophones. 'Simply marvellous. And those triangles – they're *square*! Astonishing!' Much to the bewilderment of the Gurdee onlookers, she circled the room again and again, staring at the plethora of instruments that you could hit, scrape or ding. 'Who knew such things existed?'

Ella and Freddie shared a puzzled expression. 'Er… Aunt Belinda,' she said, 'you seem so… jolly.'

'Very jolly indeed. This is instrument heaven! Come over here.' She looked around the room, then leaned in and whispered, 'I *hate* being held prisoner just as much as you. I'll get us out of here tomorrow, and we'll be back on the Hammerklav before you can say square triangle. *With* Otto!'

'But—' Ella started.

'Everybody out!' Figaroon yelled from the entrance. 'Except the Earthians – they stay here. Mirabelle, guard the door.'

Within seconds, Ella, Freddie and Aunt Belinda were alone in Dingringer Hall. They wandered to a window and stared out as an extraordinary sight unfolded in front of them. Scores of people emerged from their lodges and formed groups on the walkways. As the light faded from the purple sky, and the shadows grew among the trees surrounding Gurdee, they started singing and playing their instruments.

'Isolde told me about this musical ritual,' Belinda said quietly. 'Every evening, they gather, and one of the consorts leads the music. It's their offering to Drumendus. They call it the Musing.'

Ella was transfixed. Some of the music was thankful, some joyful, some sad, some prayerful. Gazing out across Gurdee, she tried to make sense of everything that had happened that day, despite countless uncertainties swirling around her head. It was mind-bending enough that Uncle Otto was King of Drumendus, but did he *really* have magical powers too? And how did he get them? And what was Aunt Belinda's rescue plan for tomorrow? And…?

As the Musing came to a close, Isolde sang a beautiful song in her own language. Although Ella didn't understand the words, she could tell it was a song filled with longing. Perhaps longing for a life of freedom for her Gurdee followers. A life without Uncle Otto…?

Isolde's haunting voice made Ella's eyes heavy. She glanced over at Freddie, who had moved to a corner and was resting his head on a cushion. Even Aunt Belinda, who had been staring out at the ropes, walkways and ladders, looked tired.

Ella lay down and allowed her eyes to close. She was asleep in an instant, but her dreams were restless, with hazy images coming and going to the sound of incessant drumming. She awoke with a jolt a few hours later, as the first hints of daylight eased into Dingringer Hall. She checked to her right; Freddie was asleep under a thick blanket. Turning over to face the window, she expected to see Aunt Belinda curled up beside her.

Cushions lay scattered across the floor.

Aunt Belinda was gone.

# CHAPTER 10

# FIREBIRDS AND A FOOTPRINT

Ella glanced around Dingringer Hall, but there was no sign of Aunt Belinda. Mirabelle was slumped by the entrance she was supposed to be guarding, snoring robustly.

'Freddie,' Ella whispered, shuffling over to him. 'Wake up!' Freddie stirred with a grunt. 'Aunt Belinda's gone!'

'What?' said Freddie, gradually emerging from his dream, his voice ever louder. 'Who? Gone? GONE? WHAT?' He straightened up and rubbed his eyes, looking around him. 'Oh… sorry, I forgot that we're… on another planet. I was just dreaming about talking microphones…'

Ella yanked the blanket off him. 'We need to find Aunt Belinda. Come on!'

Freddie didn't look impressed. 'Well, she can't have got far,' he muttered. 'She was definitely here last time I checked.'

They headed to the entrance and stepped over Mirabelle. Outside the hall, the wooden walkway swayed in the breeze, and the birds merrily sang their good mornings to each other. There was no sign of Aunt Belinda.

'What are *you two* doing?' came an excited voice behind them, piercing the silence of the hanging village.

'Ursula!' Ella spluttered, jumping in fright and grabbing the handrail to avoid toppling off the walkway altogether. 'We're just—'

'I did wonder if you'd try to escape,' Ursula interrupted, her tone kind but firm, like Ella's form teacher back home.

'We're not trying to—'

'If you're going on an adventure, I'm coming with you!'

'We're *not* going on an—'

Freddie stepped between them. 'Belinda has disappeared, Ursula. See for yourself. We don't know if she's escaped, or if she's wandered off around Gurdee, or…' He shrugged as his sentence tailed off.

'If your aunt is still here,' Ursula said, 'I'll find her. I know Gurdee better than anyone.'

'But—'

'Back soon.'

Ursula darted away and shimmied down a couple of rope ladders and out of sight. Ella and Freddie waited in the shadow of Dingringer Hall, not far from Mirabelle, who was drooling in her sleep. A minute later, Ursula was back, as if out of nowhere.

'No sign of Belinda,' she said, barely out of breath. 'I checked the halls, the walkways and the other main lodges. I don't think she's in Gurdee.'

Ella shook her head. 'Strange. What if she's been… captured?'

'Impossible,' said Ursula. 'Nobody from outside Gurdee could get up here without being seen or heard.'

'But why would she leave without us?'

'It must be part of her plan,' said Freddie. 'Remember last night, she said she'd get us out of here? *And* she was staring out of the window for ages – maybe she was working out the escape route.'

'So there *is* an escape plan!' Ursula said. 'But… why?'

Freddie sighed. 'Much as we love it here, we don't plan on staying forever.'

'But—'

'We need to find Belinda before it all goes wrong.'

'*But*—'

'I know this isn't what your mum had in mind for us, but it looks like Belinda's taken matters into her own hands. So right now, either you're with us, or you're not.'

'Of course I'm with you,' Ursula said, clearly irritated at being constantly interrupted. 'You're my new Earthian friends.'

'Good. Because… we could really use your help,' Freddie added, more kindly.

'Aunt Belinda must have gone looking for the Hammerklav,' Ella said. 'Ursula, could you lead us through the forest to where you caught us in that trap?'

'Yes, easily.'

'Brilliant. Then we can try and retrace our steps from there.' The three of them stared down at the guards below, who prowled around in pairs, checking every corner and every shadow of Gurdee, their weapons glinting in the early-morning light. 'What about them?'

Ursula tiptoed to the nearest rope ladder. 'They won't see us if you follow me and stay close.' She looked thoroughly proud to be taking charge of their escape from Gurdee and leading the hunt for Aunt Belinda. 'This way.'

They snaked their way down to the ground, then rushed through the shadows, sometimes crouching and waiting for Ursula's command, sometimes sprinting as fast as they could to avoid being seen.

'Quickly, behind this tree!' Ursula hissed as two guards stomped into view.

Ella pinned herself against the ancient trunk, desperately trying to catch her breath. Her insides tightened as the guards' footsteps came and went. Eventually, Ursula gave the all-clear and beckoned the others to follow her.

On her very first step, Ella's foot crunched into a pile of fallen leaves.

The guards wheeled round and edged back towards the tree, their peculiar weapons drawn.

'In there,' Ursula whispered, pushing Ella and Freddie down towards the base of the trunk.

'Wait, what are you doing?' Ella protested. Certain she was about to collide headfirst with the solid mass of wood in front of her, she squinted and prepared for impact. At the last moment, though, she spotted a gap between two exposed roots and managed to slide her way in. '*Now* I get it. You could've warned us, Ursula.'

'Sorry – no time! The adults *cannot* know about our secret tree dens.'

Ella and Freddie crouched in the darkness, but there was no room for Ursula, who instead grabbed a branch over her head, wrapped her legs around it and climbed. In an instant, she was tucked away among the dense leaves.

Ella's palms clammed up as she heard the guards inch nearer and circle the tree. Their tatty boots came within touching distance, and one of them seemed to growl as he breathed. He stooped down for a closer look at the roots.

'Oh, no,' Ella mouthed silently. She knew it was only a matter of seconds before she and Freddie would be snatched out of the den. The plan to find Aunt Belinda was scuppered already!

Or was it…?

Before the guard could poke his head in, a pair of clumsy birds with oversized wings flapped down towards him. He and his friend jumped backwards, and the birds squawked in their faces and flew off at speed between the hanging buildings.

'Stupid firebirds!' one guard yelled, and they both ran off in pointless pursuit.

Ursula swung down from the tree, a broad grin on her face.

'Are those birds friends of yours?' Ella laughed.

'Not exactly – they were just annoyed to see *me* on their branch and decided to fly off, that's all. I didn't encourage them… much.'

Ursula led them to another huge tree that formed part of the fence around Gurdee. She dived into one of the gaps between its twisted roots and shouted for Ella and Freddie to join her.

'A person can't fit in there!' Freddie chuntered, squeezing himself through the insides of the trunk. 'There must be an easier way than this.'

Ella followed close behind, and they emerged into the gloom of the forest outside Gurdee. 'I'm guessing the adults don't know about this escape route either?'

'No,' Ursula said. 'And I intend to keep it that way.'

Ella and Freddie ran behind Ursula as she ducked and weaved between trees and bushes. It was a struggle to keep up, but true to her word, Ursula led them straight to yesterday's trap. The tangled net still lay on the floor.

Ella surveyed the area around her. 'I'm sure the Hammerklav's that way,' she said, pointing. 'Let's go!' A few paces later, though, she screeched to a halt. 'Look!'

Freddie ran into her back. 'Hey! What are you doing?'

Ella pointed to a patch of mud. 'Is that Aunt

Belinda's footprint? It's got zigzag patterns. I don't think the locals have them.'

Ursula leaned down and traced her finger around the edge of the print. 'These tracks are not from Gurdee shoes, that's certain. Who has patterns on the soles of their shoes?'

Ella decided not to point out that Ursula's *clothes* were covered in patterns, as were the Gurdee instruments, weapons, even walls. 'Come on,' she said, breaking into a jog, her spirits lifted by the sight of the footprint. 'Aunt Belinda can't be far away.'

Her enthusiasm wore off quicker than she had expected, and she started to wonder if the trail would ever end. Despite dawn breaking, the murky atmosphere under the forest canopy unsettled her.

'We're coming to the edge of Libera Forest,' Ursula said.

'Nice name,' muttered Freddie, sitting heavily on the ground.

'This is the end of our territory. If we go any further, we are officially on Otto's land.'

'We have to keep going,' Ella said. 'The Hammerklav can't be far.'

'A quick rest first?' Freddie harrumphed. 'We haven't even had breakfast. By this time back home, I would've had a couple of bowls of cinnamon-flavoured cereal—'

A flash of purple light whizzed over their heads, and a drumbeat echoed through the trees.

The friends froze.

# CHAPTER 11

# CHASE

'What… was… that?' Ella stammered, her body rigid like a totem pole.

Ursula pulled her and Freddie behind a thick clump of bushes. Another burst of light surged through the air, then another, accompanied by strange twanging sounds in the distance. Rhythmic drumming and whistling bounced around the trees too. It was the eeriest thing Ella had ever heard.

'That… was sonorance,' Ursula said theatrically.

'Sonorance?' gasped Ella. 'The magic power?'

'Yes. You didn't believe my mother when she told you yesterday, remember?' added Ursula, a hint of bitterness in her voice. 'Well, there it is, right in front of you.' A small cannonball flew over their heads and slammed into a tree trunk. 'This is near enough for us. Follow me.'

She went to lead them away, but Ella couldn't take her eyes off this astonishing, powerful magical display. Without thinking, she found herself jumping up and rushing through the undergrowth *towards* the sonorance, to get a better look and listen.

'ELLA!' Freddie said. 'What are you doing?'

She ignored him and darted through the forest until she was only metres away from the unfolding sound and light show. Crouching behind a tree, she looked on, slack-jawed. A fierce, deafening battle raged between a group of Gurdee rebels and Uncle Otto's soldiers.

The Gurdee fighters rushed from tree to tree, some firing arrows from bizarre-looking bows, others blowing tiny pellets out of multicoloured flutes. Ella recognised a few of them from yesterday: a man with a shield and a pointed beard dived into a bush a few steps away, and a short woman with curly hair yelled instructions to everyone around her. They defended themselves as best they could, but there was no sign of any mysterious magical powers coming from their musical weapons.

Uncle Otto's soldiers couldn't have been more different. They used *their* instruments to mount the most extraordinary assault on their opponents, harnessing the magical power of sonorance with ferocious intensity. They were fewer in number and wore ornate, gilded helmets and stripy uniforms with curious green sleeves. Some carried small drums that made the ground shake every time they were played, upending whoever was standing there. Others twanged their harp strings, firing potent streaks of light at the enemy, while others still blasted out shockwaves by playing loud notes on their trumpets – at least they looked like trumpets.

'So it's true...' Ella whispered to herself. 'Sonorance is real!' Every fibre of her being danced in excitement and terror as the battle continued all around her in full stereo. She wanted to know more. She *needed* to know more!

A line of missiles shot out of a soldier's beater, with a dramatic trail of purple light zipping along behind. They thudded against a branch just above Ella's head, then dropped to the ground and disappeared with a hiss.

'But how...?' she said, reaching down to search for the missiles in the brushwood but only picking up handfuls of wet leaves.

'Ella!' called a breathless voice nearby. 'There you are!' It was Freddie, with Ursula close behind. 'We have to get out of here – it's far too dangerous.'

Ella felt a sharp wrench on her sleeve but didn't budge. 'Wait,' she said. 'I... need to see some more.' She could *not* drag her eyes away from the incredible sonorance spectacle.

'ELLA! Let's go!'

Still she didn't move. 'Just... wait...' Eventually, she managed in a trembling tone, 'Which one is... Uncle Otto?'

'Oh, he won't be here,' Ursula said scornfully, 'now that he's worked out how to give sonorance to his soldiers. No, this battle's *far* too small for him.'

Ella frowned. '*How* does he give the soldiers sonorance?'

'No-one in Gurdee knows,' said Ursula, ducking as a stray arrow screamed past.

'But—'

'I'd love to stay and talk,' Ursula interrupted, 'but if you don't want us to be captured or hurt, we need to leave, NOW! We'd be no match for the King's soldiers if they see us.'

The sounds of the battle all but engulfed them as fighters from both sides moved closer. Arrows, missiles and flashes of light raced past their ears, and the ground shook violently. Even Ella realised, in her state of utter awe and wonderment, that it was time to leave.

Two soldiers bounded past the hedge, firing their weapons and shouting as they ran. Others followed, only inches from the hiding place. Ella tried to shuffle away before she was trampled underfoot but ended up slipping backwards down a bank.

Instinct took over.

She reached out for Freddie and Ursula and dragged them down the hill into a muddy puddle.

'Owwww!' she yawped as her friends flattened her a moment later.

Freddie wiped the muck off his clothes and tutted. 'Well, if you would pull us down here, Ella—'

'Stop!' a gruff voice bellowed from the top of the slope. Ella turned to see a soldier who looked like a giant staring down at them. A huge whistle hung around his neck on a cord.

'He's *definitely* not on our side!' shouted Ursula, making off nimbly through the undergrowth. 'This way!'

The three friends sprinted beside a stream at the foot of a narrow valley, trying not to look behind them. Ella was sure she heard a tune coming from the flowing water, to help them along their way. The sounds of the sonorance battle died away, and the valley merged into open land on the edge of Libera Forest.

'Look!' said Freddie, pointing at two old-fashioned carts parked nearby. He ran towards them but stumbled to a clumsy stop as a couple of animals wandered out of the trees. 'Woah!'

'I don't believe it!' said Ella, approaching the creatures carefully. 'They have horses on Drumendus?'

'Er... not exactly – look at their faces.'

Ella stared in amazement at the delightful creatures. 'Their heads look like...'

'Dolphins!' she and Freddie said together.

Ursula approached the animals with a calm confidence, and sure enough, they greeted her with a gentle clicking sound, just like that of dolphins. 'These are galops,' she said, stroking the side of their heads.

'Galop, as in... gallop?'

'Not GA-lop, but ga-LOP!'

'Rrrrright,' said Freddie. 'Ga-LOP.'

'Exactly. I recognise these two.' Ursula led one of them to a cart. 'They're from Gurdee. This one's Tull. Isn't he beautiful?'

A yell from the woods made them jump in shock. The giant soldier with the whistle appeared in the trees.

'Quick!' Ursula said. 'Help me attach Tull's harness to the cart.'

Ella and Freddie did as they were told. They lifted the shafts into the loops, and Ursula buckled up the straps and patted Tull on the mane. They all piled into the rickety old cart, and Ursula grabbed the reins.

'Do you know how to drive this thing?' Ella said.

'I've seen others do it all my life.'

'Very reassuring…'

'Yah!' Ursula shrieked, and Tull responded with a jolt forwards along the track. 'Good start!'

The soldier charged at them and blew his whistle sharply. Ella's hair stood on end as she felt the might of sonorance surround her once again. The air around them whipped up into powerful gusts, and the wheels of the cart lifted off the ground.

'Steady!' Ursula said, hanging on for dear life as the cart threatened to tip them all out.

The wheels bounced back down after what felt like an age, but the furious soldier played again, his long, piercing notes sending the air into tumultuous windy blasts that blew Tull and the cart in all directions.

This was the soldier's undoing. The more Tull veered off the track, with the cart careering one way then the other, the less accurate the soldier's sonorance attack became.

'He's tiring!' Freddie said, looking back at the running giant. 'He can't keep this up forev—'

The soldier let out a frustrated growl, dropped his whistle and leapt forwards, stretching out his gangly arms to grab the back of the cart. His huge feet dragged along the ground, and his fiery eyes were consumed with rage.

'We have to get him off!' yelled Freddie.

To her own surprise, Ella reacted first. She prised the soldier's gnarled fingers off the cart one by one, but he snatched her wrist and pulled her towards him. She screamed and tumbled over the edge of the cart. 'Help!'

Freddie grabbed her ankles, but she was left dangling, eyeball to eyeball with the infuriated soldier.

'If *I* fall, Gurdee girl, *you* fall with me.' He laughed, clearly failing to notice in the chaos that Ella wasn't purple.

'She's not a Gurdee girl,' Freddie roared behind her. 'She's an EARTHIAN!'

He heaved Ella back inside with an enormous grunt. The soldier's grin turned to horror, then pain, as Ella accidentally kicked him in the face as she rolled back into the cart. He fell away and came to an undignified stop in a patch of prickly weeds.

'That'll show him!' said Freddie. 'Nice work!'

'Thanks… though I… didn't mean to do that!'

Tull sped away from the stricken soldier. Libera Forest dwindled behind them, and for the first time, Ella realised how far they had come across the undulating plain. It wasn't long before the forest on the *other* side came into view. Ursula tried to slow down the flimsy cart, but Tull was having none of it.

'He is *not* impressed,' Ursula said. 'I can't get through to him.' She tried again, but Tull ignored her, galloping as fast as he could towards the forest, clicking as he went. 'Galops are known for their stubbornness. I don't know what to do.'

Tull hurtled through an unfeasibly narrow gap in the trees. Trotting through the darkness, he ran out of steam and came to a weary stop, to everyone's relief.

The silence was overwhelming.

'I've never been in here,' Ursula said, her voice quivering. 'This is Crumhorn Forest... and we are lost.'

# CHAPTER 12
# A RUMOUR IN THE FOREST

This forest felt different to Libera Forest. Very different. The tree trunks weren't as thick but were so densely packed that it was almost impossible to see further than a few metres in front, let alone try and guide a disgruntled galop in a particular direction. The air was close and unforgiving, and although occasional shafts of light sneaked down to the forest bed, they were mere spotlights in an atmosphere of gloom and threat. Tull's agitation grew, and he reared up on his hind legs and tried to wriggle free of the harness. The cart lurched around in circles, but Ursula eventually calmed him with a few soothing words.

'What *now*?' Ella said, stepping out of the cart with the others and surveying her surroundings.

'We get back to the plain, that's what,' said Freddie. 'I don't like this place.'

'I can't believe we've ended up so far from anywhere useful! We didn't even come close to finding Aunt Belinda. That's the whole reason we're out here! What were we thinking? We're totally lost and—'

'Hey!' Freddie said, swinging around to face her. 'Stop it!' He paused, then added quietly, 'We'll find Belinda. First, we need to get out of this forest, okay?'

'Yeah, er... okay,' Ella said, shuffling her feet through some fallen twigs, embarrassed at her outburst. 'Let's... do that. It's this way, isn't it?' She pointed.

'No,' said Freddie, 'it's definitely *this* way. I remember that weird-shaped branch over there.'

'I don't think so. I remember this tree.'

'What are you talki—'

'I thought you two were best friends!' said Ursula, smirking. 'Is this how best friends act on Earth?'

Ella and Freddie stopped bickering and looked at each other. 'Pretty much, yeah.'

They all laughed, then Ella reluctantly agreed to go in Freddie's direction, as Ursula also had a vague recollection of the odd-shaped branch.

Ursula led Tull and the empty cart between the crowded trees, and Ella and Freddie trailed behind. The further they walked, the more uncomfortable Ella became. Worse still, she had the strange sense that they weren't alone.

Her patience ran out as her shoe nearly came off in a slippery mud patch. 'Argh!' she yelled, running in front of Ursula and putting her arm out. 'Look around you! *All* these trees have weird branches. *There's* one shaped like a submarine! See?'

Freddie glanced around him, and Ursula groaned and said, 'I'm not sure we came this way after all. Sorry, Ella.'

'Just keep going,' blustered Freddie. 'We're bound to get out soon.'

'No! This isn't the way. I knew it!' Ella shouted. 'Freddie, I wish you'd listen to me more often, and not be so… stubborn all the time!'

Although he couldn't bring himself to apologise, or even defend himself, Freddie bowed his head and muttered, 'It can't go on forever… the forest, I mean.'

'Of course it can, if we go round in circles!'

Time wore on, and the exasperated trio ended up tearing their way through clumps of thick undergrowth. Poor Tull looked utterly fed up.

Just as they were all about to collapse in a heap, something caught Ella's attention. 'Down there,' she said to Freddie, pointing to a shallow ravine.

'Is that what I think it is?'

'If you think it's a person carrying an instrument-weapon thingy, then yes,' said Ella, more sarcastically than she had intended.

'*Two* people and *two* instrument-weapon thingies, actually.' Freddie motioned his head towards another figure in the small clearing.

Ursula let go of Tull and stepped forwards. 'But… we're in the middle of the forest,' she said, her tone flustered. 'Why would there be anybody here, especially *soldiers*? I… Wait a minute.' She gasped. 'I know what this is!' She tried to speak but instead had to stifle a squeal of excitement.

'Don't keep us in suspense,' said Ella, feeling her eyes broaden. 'What is it?'

'Look beyond the soldiers. What can you see?'

Ella and Freddie scanned the area intently. Through a tangle of branches, a mysterious entrance emerged, carved into an ancient rock formation. Strange markings and patterns adorned the border of the arch-shaped opening.

'A cave!' said Ella, her heart leaping. 'But what could be so precious in there to need guards?'

Ursula gulped. 'I've overheard whisperings about this in Gurdee. But I didn't think they were *true* for one moment!'

'*What* whisperings?' said Freddie impatiently.

'There are rumours of a remote cave, hidden deep in the forest, that has… magical powers of its own.'

'Like… sonorance powers?'

'Yes. According to Mother's spies, only Otto and a few of his soldiers know where the cave is… until now!' She leaned in close. 'Some in Gurdee believe that Otto received sonorance in there and *didn't* bring it with him from Earth!'

'Well, *yeah* – that's what we've been saying all along!' Ella laughed. 'Believe me, I wish we *did* have sonorance on Earth, that would be seriously fun. But… we don't.'

'Yes, I believe you now! And Otto's soldiers must have visited the cave too, to receive *their* sonorance.'

The trees on either side of the cave bent inwards towards it, and Ella noticed an eerie purple shimmer hanging in the air around the entrance. Even the sounds of the forest were amplified into a dramatic, ever-changing chorus in the ravine. It was the most other-worldly, mesmerising bombardment of the senses.

'It's… awesome,' said Ella, taking in every detail of the cave. Was this really the *source* of the incredible sound magic that had changed Drumendus forever? A terrific, deep drumming boomed up from the depths, as if tempting Ella to go inside and discover its secrets.

Freddie looked at her, a gigantic grin daubed across his face. 'Are you thinking what I'm thinking?'

Ella nodded and readied herself to sprint down the hill towards the cave, unable to resist its lure, even with the threat of armed guards nearby. 'Let's go.'

A figure sprang out of the bushes behind them. 'Not so fast!'

Ella reeled around and shrieked. She was about to plunge down the slope when the man reached out a sinewy hand and pulled her upright.

'Scarp!' said Ursula. 'What are you doing here?'

'I should ask you the same question,' Scarp said in a gravelly voice. He took a rope that was hanging off his belt and tied Ella's hands together in a matter of seconds.

'Let my friend go!' said Freddie, but Scarp grabbed his hands too and bound them in one confident movement before he could pull away.

Ursula shook her head but did not try to resist Scarp tying her wrists together too. 'Wait until Mother hears about this.'

Scarp's face changed to a grimace that must have been as near as he could get to a smile. 'Yes, wait indeed. She'll hear everything.'

'You've been following us?' said Freddie.

'And stopping you doing something *very* foolish, it seems,' he said, checking the knots were tight and ordering them into the cart behind Tull. 'You couldn't outsmart those guards down there – even if you are *Earthians*.'

'But the cave,' Ella started, still full of knee-trembling wonder at being so close to the origin of sonorance. 'That's the cave where—'

'Enough. We leave for Gurdee at once.' Scarp jumped into the driver's seat and flicked the reins, and Tull weaved off through the trees until they reached the border of Crumhorn Forest. Another galop waited obediently on the plain, and Scarp tied it to the cart alongside Tull. They raced towards Libera Forest, Scarp constantly glancing from side to side, checking for enemies.

'Can you slow down?' Ella pleaded, after the wheels lifted clear off the ground on a particularly sharp bend.

'No,' came the coarse response.

Ursula tutted and turned to Ella and Freddie. 'Typical. This is such a Scarp thing to do.'

'What do you mean?'

'He follows people around and reports everything

back to Mother. He's always watching and listening from up in the Gurdee trees. He's such a loner... Still, Mother seems to like him.'

'Er... why?'

'He's loyal to Gurdee. Mother cherishes loyalty above all else.'

At the edge of Libera Forest, a group of brightly clothed people appeared on the path from Gurdee, some on foot and others riding galops. Isolde led the way.

'Mother!' shouted Ursula.

'Oh, there you are, my child!' said Isolde, dismounting her galop and rushing to the cart to hug her daughter. 'We've been searching for you!' Her voice betrayed both relief and frustration. 'Where have you *been* with the Earthians?' She pulled back and held Ursula's cheeks in her hands. 'Don't you know the danger out here?'

'Mother, I—'

'You could have been hurt – all of you! There was a battle today in the forest. Tybalto was struck in the chest. He's lucky to have escaped.'

'We know... We saw it.'

Isolde gasped at her daughter. 'You were there?'

'Yes,' said Ursula, who proceeded to tell the story of the escape from the battle scene, the galop chase across the plain and Scarp finding them in Crumhorn Forest.

'I cannot believe such recklessness!' Isolde said, staring at Ella and Freddie too. She turned to Scarp, who lifted his gaze. 'Of course, *you* would be the one to find them. Excellent work, Scarp.'

A stocky man with an unkempt moustache stomped over. Ella recognised him as Figaroon. '*You* stole the cart, Ursula?'

'Yes,' she said, her head bowed. 'I'm sorry.'

'I was nearly captured by Otto's soldiers looking for that cart,' Figaroon growled. 'So was Tybalto, who was already hurt. We had to crawl on our bellies through the mud to escape! What if—'

'And we're very thankful you did escape, Figaroon,' Isolde said firmly. 'Calm yourself.'

'But these children—'

'*Calm yourself.* And remember with whom you speak.'

Ella stood up in the cart, trying not to wobble. 'This is all my fault.'

'Yes, I expect it is,' said Isolde coldly.

'*I* asked Ursula to help us. And we didn't mean to take Tull and the cart, but this giant soldier was chasing us. And then we lost our way and saw the—'

'Wait,' Isolde said, just as Ella was about to tell her about the cave. 'Belinda is not with you. Where is your aunt?'

'We don't know!' said Freddie. 'That's *why* we left Gurdee – to look for her! Ella and I woke up in Dingle-Ringle Hall, or whatever you call it, and Belinda was gone!'

Ella knelt down towards Isolde from the cart. 'Can you help us find her? Please?'

Isolde didn't answer.

Ursula took her mother's hand. 'I can lead us to where we found the Earthians yesterday,' she said.

'That's near where they landed in their flying space box… I mean, space-*ship.*'

Isolde sighed. 'Very well,' she said. 'We should find Belinda before Otto does. Show us the way, Ursula.'

Beaming, Ursula joined an irritated-looking Scarp in the driver's seat of the cart. She grabbed Tull's reins and directed him through the trees. Isolde followed keenly behind with the others. 'We'll track the forest border around to the south-eastern path,' Ursula said as they reached the vast expanse of the plain. 'It's not far!'

They never made it to the south-eastern path.

## CHAPTER 13
# A FACE BETWEEN THE BARS

A company of Uncle Otto's soldiers rushed out of Libera Forest directly towards them. To Ella's surprise, only two of them rode galops; the other four matched the speed of the majestic creatures but followed on foot.

Ursula seemed to guess what Ella was thinking. 'The runners have mastered speed sonorance. That's how they travel so fast.'

'Epic!' said Ella and Freddie at the same time. 'How do they do it?' Ella added.

'No idea – I don't have sonorance, do I?'

Uncle Otto's stripy-uniformed soldiers fanned out in meticulous formation, their helmets shining in the morning light. The two at the back carried a chunky crate of some sort, mounted on long poles.

The others drew their sonorance weapons, poised for attack.

Isolde led her galop to Ursula's cart. 'Do not move, children,' she said, her eyes fixed on her opponents. 'These fighters are capable of anything.'

A tense standoff unfolded, with weapons at the ready but neither side flinching. In the distance beyond Uncle Otto's soldiers, Ella spotted the strange purple lightning from yesterday that streaked up towards the clouds. For the first time, the hazy shapes of a settlement emerged on the horizon.

'What's that over there?' she whispered, tapping Ursula.

'That is our city – Stradbow,' Ursula said, smiling.

Freddie leaned forward in the cart. 'Isn't Gurdee your city?'

'Gurdee's where we live until we take back what's ours. Mother and her followers were banished from Stradbow when Otto became King.'

Still nobody moved a muscle in the standoff.

Ella looked again at Stradbow. Imposing walls encircled the city, and a bright white building shimmered on raised ground in the middle. From this distance, it looked like an oversized armadillo. 'That *has* to be the palace?' she said.

'Plectrumm Palace, yes. Mother will reclaim it when the time is right.' There was a steely determination in Ursula's voice.

The deadlock was finally broken when one of Uncle Otto's soldiers nudged his galop forwards. 'The famous Isolde,' he said with disdain. 'So *far* from Gurdee, with so few followers?'

'I have everyone I need, Squeelo,' said Isolde, her tone cold, her stare unblinking.

'King Otto would be *thrilled* if you were to come with us to Stradbow.' When Isolde didn't answer, he continued, 'This can proceed in one of two ways: you can come with us peacefully, or we can take you by force.'

'Fighting talk,' Isolde hissed, her ears glowing brighter.

The man called Squeelo laughed. 'You forget, we have sonorance on our side.'

'But we have *heart*!'

Squeelo waved his arm, and his soldiers moved into a tighter attacking formation. The bizarre crate two of them were carrying came into view, and Ella realised that the sides were not made of wood, but metal bars from top to bottom.

'A cage,' she murmured, her heart racing. 'There's… someone in there.' A familiar face appeared between the bars. 'AUNT BELINDA!'

'ELLA!'

A formidable mix of fury and elation tore through Ella, on seeing her dear aunt cooped up like a savage criminal. She felt her legs spark into action, and without thinking, she vaulted out of the cart and bounded towards the cage.

Isolde reached down from her galop and grabbed Ella, but she wriggled free easily. 'Stop, Ella! You don't know who you're up against!'

It didn't matter to Ella. She was determined to release her aunt from that horrible mini-prison. Freddie appeared alongside her, and they jumped up and grabbed the cage bars.

The soldiers were quick to react – this was the perfect excuse to attack their enemy. The front line unleashed a fervent barrage of sonorance against Isolde and her followers, forcing them to retreat and scatter. The sheer might of the magical energy flying in all directions took hold of Ella again, and although she did her best to focus on the cage, everything merged into a confused blur of yelling and beating and stamping. She could do little more than hang there, her grip on the bars slowly weakening as volleys of missiles and streaks of light zoomed past.

One Stradbow soldier moved so fast that she whipped up a trail of purple smoke as she leapt from her galop and sprinted towards the cage. She yanked Ella to the ground far harder than was necessary.

A second later, Ella felt herself being carried away at great speed, and a strange buzzing noise filled her ears. It was as if she were being swept along in a flying dream. 'What's… happening?' she spluttered.

'Let me go!' she heard Freddie yell nearby, though she couldn't see him in the confusion of the battle.

Through her fear, one potent thought crystallised in her mind:

Ella wanted sonorance… no, Ella *needed* sonorance, more than anything in the universe.

𝄞

The ground whizzed by in a vague smudge below Ella. Chilly air rushed past her face, like it did when she cycled downhill at top speed. As the fraught noises of battle faded into the distance, the only sounds left were the rapid sonorance footsteps of the soldier holding her and the peculiar buzzing noise that came and went, like a persistent fly in her ear. The soldier had scooped up Freddie in her other arm, but despite carrying a couple of children, she ran so fast that the same wispy cloud of smoke trailed along behind her.

She reached the striking city walls of Stradbow in no time and swept through the gates. Two other soldiers followed her in at the same breakneck speed and skidded to a clumsy stop in a circle around Ella and Freddie.

'I've *never* run so fast with speed sonorance,' panted one of them, an excited look on his young face. He stared down at his long legs as if astonished to have kept them under control.

'Me neither,' said the other soldier, turning to the lady who was still holding Ella and Freddie by their waists. 'How do you run so fast, Major Castanex?'

'Hours and hours of practice, of course,' the lady said. 'The faster you wish to go, the more practice you need to do. That's how sonorance works – you know that! You two are nowhere near ready to harness the full power of speed sonorance.' The way she spoke about it fascinated Ella yet more.

'Er... excuse me, *Major Castanets* – or whatever your name is,' said Freddie, still hanging from the lady's arm like a towel on a washing line, 'could you have your chat about your magic powers *after* you've put us down, please?'

Ella smirked, and her worries eased for a moment, knowing that her best friend was alongside her, albeit upside-down.

Castanex dumped her dangling prisoners by a wall. 'Watch them until the others return with Belinda Crinkle,' she said to the two soldiers. 'Do *not* try out your sonorance on them. Do you understand?'

The long-legged soldier loped forwards. 'But what about King Otto's rule? We're permitted to use sonorance on prisoners to improve our skills. I have some new mind-control spells I've been practising on my pianarack. Could I at least *try* them on the Earthian invaders?'

'I don't like the sound of that,' muttered Ella.

Freddie nodded. 'I don't like the sound of a *pianarack* either – sounds too much like *anorak*.'

The soldier's friend, a young lady who was as short as he was tall, piped up with, 'Major Castanex, I can assure you, there would be no harm to the Earthians. Trebble has practised on me, and I can safely say that he is terrible at mind control!' She let out a thunderous laugh and looked over at Ella, as if she should agree. 'And he doesn't even have his pianarack here. Useless!'

Trebble's face crumpled, and he seemed to have shrunk from embarrassment. 'Watch out, *Cloff*,' he mumbled. 'Otherwise I'll... I'll... drop my pianarack on your foot!'

'ENOUGH!' Castanex bellowed. 'You pathetic drumskulls are a disgrace to the King's army.'

'Drumskull…' said Ella under her breath. 'I'll have to remember that one.'

'How King Otto *ever* allowed either of you to receive sonorance is beyond me,' Castanex spat as Trebble and Cloff skulked away. 'The Earthian children are valuable prisoners, just like Belinda Crinkle.'

Ella laced her fingers together and gazed around her. Here she was in the famous Stradbow, the centre of her uncle's kingdom, the city Isolde and her followers were so desperate to take back and call home again. Guards patrolled the thick walls, which curved off in both directions. On higher ground in the middle of the city, Uncle Otto's spectacular Plectrumm Palace dominated the skyline, a constant reminder of who was in charge.

'Did you hear that weird buzzing noise when Castanex was carrying us?' Ella said, her mind inevitably returning to sonorance.

'Yeah,' said Freddie. 'No idea what it was.'

'I reckon she was making it herself, to do the speed sonorance.'

'What? Castanex, buzzing like a bee? Haha!'

'It sounded more like "zzzzmmmm" than "bzzzzzz",' she chuckled.

'O-kay…' Freddie grinned. 'Look!' He pointed to a group of Stradbow children loitering on a street corner. 'They're singing.' He glanced the other way. 'And *they're* playing instruments!' He flung his arms towards the purple sky. 'Of course they are – this is Drumendus!'

Just like in Gurdee, music and sound were at the heart of Stradbow. Musical symbols, which looked like distant cousins of those from home, were carved into every wall. Dozens of melodies, drum patterns and songs floated across the city in the breeze, merging into one mysterious but captivating soundscape.

The soldiers carrying Aunt Belinda's cage swept through the city gates, followed by the man called Squeelo, who trotted in on his galop, his face muddied.

Ella and Freddie sprang to their feet. 'Aunt Belinda!'

'Ella!' came a voice from within. 'There you are.' She peered through the cage bars at the city stretching away in front of her. 'Well, I never. A city on Drumendus! Hidden away from us all this time.'

'SILENCE, Earthians!' Squeelo bawled, then waved his arm at the soldiers. 'Take them all to Plectrumm Palace.'

Castanex shunted Ella and Freddie side by side, flanked by Trebble and Cloff. 'Follow the cage,' she said. 'And keep up!'

Ella and Freddie did as they were told. Before long, crowds had gathered and were jostling to get a better view. The soldiers even began a marching song:

*'We are proud to march in time,*
*We are soldiers in our prime!*
*We will serve and fight,*
*Whether day or night,*
*And we love to sing in rhyme!*

*Make way, make way,*
*Make way for Stradbow's finest!'*

'Woah, the army is popular here,' said Ella, startled at the growing crowd. 'Everyone's desperate to catch a glimpse.'

'They're here to see us, not the army!' Freddie said. '*We're* the star attraction, Ella – the first Earthian kids on Drumendus!'

The road narrowed and became riddled with eager people. An insistent man shoved Freddie and shouted, 'Who *are* you?', and another jumped in front of Ella and tried to shake her hand.

'Get off me – er, please,' Ella said, her breathing shallow as anxiety took over yet again.

The crowd responded with a boisterous cheer and surged closer with ever greater force. Trebble and Cloff tried to make space around them with vague threats and weak arm gestures, but the panic on their faces was a clear sign that they had lost control. Ella heard Castanex yell, 'This is all *Squeelo's* fault! He should have put the Earthian children in cages too – that's what *I* would have done!'

Someone buffeted Ella into the deepening crowd, and for a terrifying moment, she saw nothing but manic, unfamiliar faces, ogling at her from every direction.

A girl leapt out of nowhere, grabbed Ella's T-shirt with pinpoint precision and whisked her through the mob into a side alley.

# CHAPTER 14

# SEREN, ADE AND THE MUSICAL WONDERLAND

'Hey!' Ella shouted, off-balance. 'What are you doing?'

'Rescuing you!' said the girl, leading her by the wrist along a slender alleyway.

'I don't *need* rescuing!' Ella looked over her shoulder at the raucous crowd stumbling past – they clearly hadn't noticed that she and Freddie had disappeared.

The girl laughed. 'I think you do; you were about to be swallowed up.'

Moments later, a boy hauled Freddie into the same backstreet. This time, though, some of the crowd did seem to notice, and a band of shadowy figures charged towards them.

'AFTER THEM!' boomed a gruff voice.

'Follow us,' said the girl.

'But my aunt's back there!' Ella said. 'I *cannot* lose her again. We need to—'

'You already *have* lost her!' the girl said, leading Ella away just before the charging mob swamped them.

They sprinted along the narrow alley and were soon deep into the crooked streets of Stradbow. There was no time to look back, such were the never-ending twists and turns of these tiny lanes. The Stradbow children made it look effortless, negotiating the maze with ease – they were obviously used to running off after causing mischief.

At a busy junction, they hid behind a chunky wooden gate to catch their breath.

'I didn't think it could be *true!*' the girl said, grinning from ear to ear and stepping back to stare at Ella. 'Earthian children in Stradbow?'

'And you've kidnapped us,' muttered Freddie between deep breaths. 'Thanks for that.'

'Saved you, more like,' said the boy triumphantly. 'We're friends of Earthians. I'm Ade.'

'And I'm Seren,' said the girl. 'We're—'

'Twins!' Ella said, noticing how similar their purple-tinted faces looked. 'I'm Ella and this is Freddie. Er… nice to meet you, and all, but my aunt is in that horrible cage, and she's all alone – again! I've no idea *what's* going to happen to her when she sees Uncle Otto.'

'We can help you,' Seren said. 'Don't wor… wait a minute! Did you say, "*Uncle* Otto"?'

'Er… yeah.'

'Incredible!' the twins said at the same time.

'Our father works for the King,' said Ade. 'He's *extremely* important. We overheard him telling Mother that Earthians had landed, but he didn't say you were the King's *family*!'

'We should bow to you,' said Seren. 'You're royalty!'

Freddie smiled. 'Ella is. I'm not.'

'Princess Ella!'

'Don't give her ideas!' said Freddie. 'Anyway, how does news travel so fast on Drumendus? We only landed yesterday, and we were taken straight to Gurdee!'

'King Otto discovers everything. You two will be the talk of the city!'

A barrage of angry footsteps tramped into earshot. The same gruff voice yelled instructions, and the twins peered through holes in the gate as the mob rushed past.

Ella's heart thumped against her chest. 'What now?'

'No idea,' Freddie replied.

'It's okay,' said Seren, 'they've gone.' Raising an eyebrow, she added, 'I do have one question.'

Ella sighed. 'Let me guess: why aren't we using our sonorance?'

'Yes! You are Earthians after all!'

'We just don't fancy it right now,' Freddie said, prompting a nudge from Ella.

'Father says that everyone on Earth is dangerous

and powerful, just like King Otto. But you don't seem... either of those things.'

'That's because we're not – we're just normal kids!' said Ella. 'Uncle Otto – I mean, *King* Otto, probably says we're all dangerous to keep you in line. We don't have son—'

'Look!' Ade interrupted, his eyes suddenly ablaze with excitement. 'Over there in the shop window!' He pointed down one of the long, winding roads that led away from the gate. 'I've wanted that instrument forever!'

The road was lined with muddled stone buildings and tightly packed entrances.

'Music shops,' Ella said, bursting into laughter. 'So many music shops!'

'Music shops, libraries, workshops,' Seren said. 'This is the oldest street in Stradbow – the Hubbub. You can borrow, buy or swap any instrument you like. *Everyone* plays and *everyone* sings here.'

'Fantastic!' Ella said, just as a tambourine-shaped clock attached to the wall started chiming overhead.

They darted over to a rundown shop whose rusty sign hung above the door at a most peculiar angle. It read:

*Mandoleena's Musical Wonderland*

'Who's Mandoleena?' Ella said.

'The most legendary shop owner in the Hubbub!' Seren said. 'When she was younger, she won the city music competition – the Stradtacular – *eight* times!'

'Cool.'

Ade gazed through the window and yelped. 'That is the *exact* mipe I need to complete my collection!'

'Mipe?' Ella said, staring into the dingy room at some hollow cylinders laid out on a table.

'Yes. Mouth pipe – mipe! They hang on a chain from high to low around your neck, and you blow into them to play them.' He pointed at the smallest one. 'I'll have twenty-four with this one – a complete set!'

'Ade *loves* his necklace,' Seren mocked, rolling her eyes. 'Shame he can't actually play the mipes.'

'Who cares?' snapped Ade, heading inside. 'They look *amazing* around my neck!'

A kerfuffle up the road caught Ella's attention, and she turned to see two soldiers marching towards her, ordering groups of harmless-looking musicians out of their way. 'Uh-oh,' she muttered. 'Quick – go in!' She nipped into the cramped shop and crouched in a corner with Freddie. Seren kept a watchful eye on the soldiers from the doorstep.

Ade bounded over to an elderly lady whose back was so hunched that she looked headless at first glance. 'Hello, Mandoleena,' he said, holding out the mipe he had picked up from the display. 'I'd like to buy this, please, to complete my collection!'

'Of course, Ade.' Mandoleena lifted her head and closed her eyes, as if listening intently to something. 'And something for your friends, perhaps?' she said out of the blue. 'I can hear them over there.' She gestured towards Ella's hiding place. 'I remember the sound of everyone who has ever set foot in my shop, and *they* sound different. *And* they must have been running, with all that heavy breathing.'

Ella and Freddie stared at each other, bewildered.

Ade shuffled on the spot. 'Er, I'm not sure what you m—'

'My eyesight may be failing, young man, but my hearing is as sharp as ever!'

A rack of miniature trombone-type instruments sat in Ella's eyeline, and when Ade glanced over at her, she pointed at the most colourful one without really thinking.

Ade trundled over and picked it up. 'Okay – this trombolino, please.'

'An excellent choice,' said Mandoleena.

Ade gave Ella the trombolino and paid for both instruments.

'Thank you!' Ella whispered, a grin opening across her face.

Freddie prodded her. 'Look.'

To their horror, one of the soldiers had stormed into the shop, tripping clumsily as he entered. Seren followed behind sheepishly.

'Major Chirrupp! What a pleasant surprise,' Mandoleena said, not even looking in the soldier's direction. 'I'd know those footsteps anywhere. Welcome.'

'Father!' said Ade. 'What are you…?' He shot Seren a piercing look.

'I tried to distract him,' Seren murmured. 'Didn't work.'

The twins' father immediately spotted Ella and Freddie huddled in the corner. 'I should've known,' he said. 'The Earthian children are supposed to be at Plectrumm Palace, with the King himself!'

'Earthians?' said Mandoleena. 'In my *Wonderland*? Well, I really have heard it all now!'

'Father, we were—' started Seren.

'…about to bring them up to the Palace,' finished Ade.

Major Chirrupp's severe look softened, but that didn't stop him barking, 'Follow me, now!' at the twins.

Ella slipped the trombolino into her trouser pocket without him noticing.

'I'll make sure you two get to the Palace this time,' Chirrupp said to Ella and Freddie, tying their hands. He looked over his shoulder and added, 'Mandoleena, my apologies for the trouble my offspring and their new *friends* have caused.'

'Oh, no trouble at all,' said Mandoleena. 'This is the most exciting thing that's happened in the Hubbub for twenty years!'

Chirrupp and the other soldier marched the four children through the disorderly streets of Stradbow. A while later, they arrived at a spectacular pair of golden gates, guarded by soldiers in familiar stripy uniforms and green sleeves.

'This is *our* neighbourhood,' Ade declared as the gates swung open to reveal a line of opulent houses, stretching up the hill. He pointed to a tall building next door to Plectrumm Palace itself. 'That's where the soldiers' families live. But Seren and I explore the Palace all the time!'

'Our building is the *biggest* in Stradbow,' said Seren proudly, 'apart from the Palace, obviously. When we were little, Father taught us a song to help us remember how to get to our living quarters. Do you want to hear it?'

'Er, I… suppose…' muttered Ella.

Chirrupp looked over at Seren. 'This is no time to start singi—'

The beaming twins ignored him and launched in with full gusto:

*'In through the fourth door,*
*Up to the third floor,*
*Down the second corridor,*
*First left, home!'*

Ella wasn't sure she had heard an actual tune, but the twins' commitment was certainly impressive. 'Great song – thanks for that…'

Seren pretended to bow. 'We've a song for everything. Singing is one of our favourite activities.'

'I can… tell…'

A constant stream of curious people came out of their homes to gawk at Ella and Freddie. Some wore elegant cloaks with hoods, others strange hats shaped like seashells. Uncle Otto's grand Palace loomed over them, its walls curving upwards in perfect symmetry.

'Keep up,' said Chirrupp, as they reached the

Palace grounds. 'The King does *not* like waiting, and you're already late.'

Once inside, they wound their way along endless corridors and passed through numerous empty halls. Ella couldn't help noticing how eerie it was. 'There's no-one here,' she said, leaning in to Freddie.

'That's what *you* think,' said Ade, pointing to a dark corner of the hall they were crossing. 'The King's spies are watching you this very moment.'

Through a slender gap in the wall, a pair of eyes stared at them unblinkingly. Behind the next door, a guard stood statuesque in the shadows, and along the corridor after that, a lone figure darted out of sight at the far end.

'This is getting creepy,' Freddie said.

'They use a network of hidden passages that we don't know about,' Ade chuckled.

'That's enough of that, thank you, young man,' Chirrupp said. 'Walk with me at the front.'

Seren smirked as her brother skulked forwards. 'Father is *terrible* at being strict,' she whispered to Ella and Freddie. 'He's always telling us things we shouldn't know – by accident, of course.'

'Sounds fun,' said Ella. 'Does your father have sonorance?'

Before Seren could answer, Chirrupp stopped and knocked on a thickset door. This wasn't just a standard knock; this was a complex rhythm that needed both hands and, by the look on his face, serious concentration.

'That's Father's knock-motif,' said Seren.

'Knock-who?'

'Knock-*motif*. His knock pattern. All the King's soldiers have one. Father's no good at rhythms – that's why his is so simple.'

'*Simple?* You are joking, aren't you?'

'Of course not. You should hear Major Squeelo's. That's the most complicated knock-motif of all!'

Chirrupp turned around, a stern look on his face. 'Get ready. King Otto is behind this door.'

# CHAPTER 15

# A DRAMATIC CREATURE

The door swung open with a tuneful creak to reveal a hall twice the size of any they had yet encountered. An elegant table stretched out in front of them, and a man with long dark hair cascading down his shoulders sat at the far end.

Ella stood and stared. There he was, her uncle, Otto Crinkle, one of the most famous people on Earth, and now King of Drumendus! It was almost too much to take in.

'We found the Earthian children, Your Majesty,' said Chirrupp, bowing and ushering Ella and Freddie forwards with an ungainly shove. 'They were with the twins!' he added, letting out a nervous squeaky laugh.

'You need to get control of your children, Major Chirrupp,' Uncle Otto replied. His voice sounded as though he were forcing it lower than was natural, but its tone was undeniably that of a Crinkle.

'Yes, Sire… Sorry, I—'

'You and the twins can leave,' Uncle Otto said, waving them away dismissively. He turned to a guard who had been lurking in the corner. 'Bring in our other guest.'

As Chirrupp, Ade and Seren backed out of the hall, another door creaked open and Aunt Belinda was led in. Her tentative footsteps echoed around the impeccable stone walls. On seeing Uncle Otto, her face transformed into an expectant grin, and she rushed over to the table.

'My brother,' she said warmly, looking him up and down. 'I'd recognise that jawline anywhere!'

Uncle Otto didn't answer, choosing instead to fix his sister with a stare and tilt his head. His expression was confident but suspicious, and his thin mouth was curved into a joyless smile.

Aunt Belinda didn't look fazed at all. 'I'd like to say you haven't changed a bit, Otto, but that would be rather a fib!'

Uncle Otto gestured for her, Ella and Freddie to sit at the table, where identical places had been laid in front of countless dishes of food. They duly obliged.

'I must say,' added Aunt Belinda, 'I'm *not* impressed that I was put in that ghastly cage, but I'm willing to let that pass now that we're finally in the same room. Who'd have thought, the two finest astronauts in history reuniting after all these years? And on Drumendus itself!'

'Astronauts?' Otto scoffed, finally answering his sister, disdain flashing across his face. 'I'm a King now, Belinda, not an… *astronaut*. I have powers here that you can only dream about.'

'I think an astronaut's a cool thing to be, actually,' said Freddie out of the blue.

Otto shifted his gaze, his face unchanged apart from a disapproving upturned lip. 'Freddie, I presume?'

'Freddie Molto, yeah. Ella's *best* friend.'

'I see.' Uncle Otto finally looked at Ella, and quite unexpectedly, his face opened up into a warm grin. He looked just like Aunt Belinda for a fleeting moment. 'Ella Crinkle,' he said. 'Belinda's rising star, so I hear.'

'Er… hi,' was all Ella could manage through the nerves.

'A lifelong drumgazer?' When she nodded, he continued eagerly, 'So was I, Ella, *so was I*. I expect it's rather different here than you pictured. Your Uncle Otto, the *King* – and you thought I was dead!'

'How… how do you know that?'

'I know a lot of things, Ella. I hear whisperings in the streets of Stradbow, from across the plain, even from high in the trees.' He turned to Aunt Belinda, and the kindness in his eyes disappeared instantly. 'This is my planet – *including* that makeshift village of tree houses.'

'Gurdee's a lot more than that,' said Freddie, clearly unafraid to take on the King.

'Really? Well, Libera Forest can't protect it forever.'

'Now then, Otto, enough of that,' said Aunt Belinda, knocking on the table as if bringing a meeting to order. She looked at her brother and beamed. 'I've imagined this moment a thousand times – seeing you again after so long. Never in a trillion years did I picture you as King… nor did I picture you as some sort of magician! But never mind, here we are.' She leaned over and patted his hand. 'I'm here to take you *home*, Otto. Back to Earth, where you jolly well belong! Think of it as some long-overdue sisterly love. The Hammerklav – my spaceship – is ready and waiting, so let's—'

'You have *never* shown me sisterly love, Belinda!' Otto interrupted. 'And now you come here as my saviour, to whisk me back to Earth?'

Leaning back in her chair, there was hurt in Aunt Belinda's eyes. 'That's not good form, is it, Otto? I… I admit, it's been hard these past twenty-five years, to show any love – but you've been on another planet!' She caught her breath, then ploughed on. 'It was your choice to stay here, remember?'

An unsettling silence engulfed the hall as Uncle Otto sat there, thinking. 'My choice?' he muttered eventually.

'Yes! Surely you remember? I *begged* you to climb aboard the Leopold before take-off, and you just stood there!' Uncle Otto didn't move. 'And… in fact, what could be *more* of an act of sisterly love than me flying back to Drumendus, to take you home?'

'How little you understand, Belinda. How very little.' He stared at his sister's bewildered face, then looked around the table at Ella and Freddie. 'Pick up your knives and tap your glasses and plates.'

Ella glanced at Freddie, whose eyes were scrunched up in confusion. She picked up her knife and tapped the glass and plate in front of her. Freddie and Aunt Belinda followed. As they did so, the most intense, irresistible bell-like sounds rose into the space above them and hovered there in a tapestry of a thousand musical combinations, then gradually softened and disappeared into the silence from which they had begun.

'What *is* it with the sounds here?' said Ella as her nerves evaporated and a feeling of wonder enveloped her yet again. 'It's like I'm being hypnotised.'

'Yes!' said Uncle Otto, standing up. 'That's precisely it, Ella. Every noise, every note, every whisper has a *purpose*. The sounds on Drumendus have the most breathtaking power and beauty. You've felt it since the moment you arrived here, haven't you?'

Ella nodded.

'Wonderful,' Uncle Otto said, another genuine smile covering his face. 'We're not all that different, Ella, you and I.'

'Er... okay...' said Ella, unsure how to respond.

'You've felt it too, haven't you, Freddie?' he said.

Freddie shrugged and nodded.

'Well, let me tell you – there's lots more where that came from.'

'That's still no reason to stay here, Otto,' snapped Aunt Belinda.

Uncle Otto ignored her and picked up his glass.

'I've harnessed this power in unimaginable ways. Let me show you.'

Before Ella could tell him that she already knew about sonorance, and even where it came from, he began tracing his finger around the rim of the glass in rapid circles. As each note sounded, a jet of purple water burst across the room and exploded like a firework against the wall. Each explosion was more forceful than the last, and Uncle Otto's expression became increasingly wild. He dropped the glass and jumped onto the table, sending plates of food smashing to the floor. 'Look what I can do!' he bellowed. '*Here!* On Drumendus! Nowhere else!'

Ella lifted her hands to her cheeks and looked on, her eyes nearly popping out of her head in amazement. 'More! Do MORE!' she found herself calling out, to Aunt Belinda's obvious shock.

Uncle Otto duly obliged. He grabbed a drum that was dangling around his neck and struck it with a beater from his robe pocket. The rhythms were rapid and complex, and missiles of all shapes and sizes flew across the hall, some perilously close to Ella's head. A few even formed groups mid-air, then ricocheted against whichever wall Uncle Otto commanded.

'Stop it, Otto!' Aunt Belinda yelled. 'You could hurt someone!'

'I'M NOT FINISHED YET!'

He flung his beater to the floor and stamped on the table, flying high towards the ceiling then landing with a thud. Again he stamped, and again he flew. It was the most mesmerising display – Uncle Otto really did look like an invincible superhero.

He stood in the centre of the table and banged the drum with his hands, shouting manically to the rhythms. The plates shook, and the floor rumbled. The Palace walls looked as though they were alive, pulsating in and out as Uncle Otto unleashed his unstoppable sound magic. The guards were thrown across the floor from the sheer power of the shuddering all around them, and Freddie and Aunt Belinda clung to the table for dear life.

Wave after wave of excitement tore through Ella, such was her desire to obtain sonorance. Nothing in her life had *ever* wielded such power over her, or made her feel so utterly alive. There and then, sonorance was the *only* thing that mattered.

To Ella's disappointment – but no-one else's – Uncle Otto snapped out of his magical frenzy and hopped off the table as if nothing had happened. The effects of his sonorance wore off instantly, and the guards struggled to their feet and crept back to their posts.

'That is just the beginning,' Uncle Otto said, grabbing what looked like a purple carrot and biting into it with a satisfying crunch. 'My sonorance is growing every day. I practise for hours and hours. I push the limits, seeing where it takes me next. Drumendus is calling me. It *wants* me to harness its power.' He turned to Ella and waved his half-eaten carrot at her. 'You understand, don't you, Ella? I *know* you do. I can see it.'

'Well, I'm appalled, Otto,' said Aunt Belinda, preventing Ella from agreeing with him. 'I always knew you were a dramatic creature who craved attention, but this?'

Uncle Otto grimaced. 'Tell me, sister,' he said, 'why would I want to leave a place where I am both King and master magician? Hmm?' There was no response. 'Exactly. I'll *never* return to Earth.'

Aunt Belinda tutted. 'Really, Otto, I don't recognise you when you talk like this.'

'Of course you don't – you haven't seen me as King before! All you know is the unruly older brother, always in your shadow. The *second* person to walk on Drumendus.' His voice teemed with resentment. 'Well, *that* Otto died years ago, but *King* Otto is very much alive.' He stood up and swept towards a set of double doors leading onto a balcony overlooking Stradbow. 'Let me show you something.'

Ella was first to follow him outside, and Freddie and Aunt Belinda trailed behind warily. From the balcony, the view of this densely packed city, its myriad alleyways snaking in every direction, was truly breathtaking. Far beyond the city walls, Ella spotted the borders of the two forests, Libera and Crumhorn, on either side of the vast plain. The tops of distant mountains shimmered on the horizon, some obscured by angry swirls of purple cloud. And the famous deep drumming of Drumendus emerged from within the planet every few seconds and reverberated around the city.

'Ah, the planet's heartbeat,' said Uncle Otto, somehow knowing what Ella was thinking. '*I* came up with that name, by the way. Well, over there, I've added the *King's* heartbeat.' He pointed down the hill to an area just past the Palace walls.

'What are *they*?' said Freddie.

'My biggest triumph so far: marvelodrums. The largest drums ever made, and the loudest. Watch!'

They stared in silence at the two remarkable contraptions. Giant beaters attached to levers dropped onto the drumheads, and lightning bolts shot up to the sky and pierced the purple clouds in a dazzling blaze of light.

Freddie put his hand to his forehead. 'So *that's* the lightning that goes the wrong way! We saw it as soon as we landed.'

'But… how?' Ella stuttered. 'The beater's moving on its own… and where does the lightning come from… and…?'

Freddie sighed. 'It's called *sonorance*, Ella. Surely you've worked that out by now!'

A self-satisfied grin crossed Uncle Otto's face. He was clearly thrilled at their astonishment. 'This is my most advanced sonorance – so far, at least. I practised constantly, with as many drums as I could find. Each one produced a different lightning effect. I learned to shoot out flashes far into space, but it took an age to get them fully under my control. Still, there's been quite a light show in recent weeks.'

'That's what we've seen from Earth,' Freddie said eagerly. 'And it's been *you* all along!'

'What do you mean?' Uncle Otto said, raising an intrigued eyebrow.

'It's headline news. Everyone's terrified of the purple Drumendus lightning – it's made the whole planet glow brighter! Some people think it's the end of the solar system as we know it, but most think it's just the weather going crazy.'

'The *weather*?' Uncle Otto laughed. 'Little do they know.' He seemed more pleased with himself than ever, knowing that his actions were affecting people on Earth too. Was there no end to this man's appetite for power? 'The skies are angrier indeed, thanks to me, but my sonorance is far more potent than any weather pattern. I wouldn't expect Earthians to understand.'

'But you *are* an Earthi—'

'This is all rather farfetched, Otto, I must say,' Aunt Belinda said with a shake of the head. 'First your *performance* in the hall, and now this? I—'

'*And*,' Uncle Otto said, cutting her off, 'the marvelodrums beat twenty-four hours a day; I don't even need to be there. They only stop on my command. *Nobody* on Drumendus can do this sort of sonorance, not even my best soldiers. Do you know *why* I keep the marvelodrums beating? To protect my kingdom from spying eyes.'

'I beg your pardon?'

'I've seen the satellites from Earth, desperately trying to get a better look at this side of the planet… the side *you* all thought couldn't possibly be inhabited. Well, the lightning from the marvelodrums turns to purple clouds in the sky. It's my shield, and it gets thicker every day.'

'So *that's* what this is all about,' Aunt Belinda said.

'Protecting Drumendus? What are you so afraid of, Otto? Nobody from Earth is planning to come here and take over. Golly, no-one even knows there are people here! And all *I* want is to take you home.' Her voice had become exasperated. 'Come back to Earth with us! I won't ask again, I promise – as long as you say yes.'

'Stop!' said Uncle Otto, banging his fist on the rail. 'There's no hope of that! Earth is not my home anymore.'

Freddie raised his hand as if he were back at school. 'Er, Mr Otto – wouldn't it be cool if you came back to Earth, 'cos you'd be the only one who could do sonorance, so…? Not that you should, obviously… I mean, you'd probably go to prison, but still, you could escape… and—'

'Not helpful,' muttered Ella.

'Who knows whether sonorance would work on Earth?' Uncle Otto said. 'Drumendus gave me my powers when I arrived here – nothing whatsoever to do with Earth. And now everyone knows it – thanks to the trio of Earthians who have appeared without so much as a hint of magical powers between them. Until yesterday, everyone on Drumendus thought that everyone on Earth had sonorance!'

Freddie, clearly irritated by Uncle Otto's mocking tone, piped up with, 'You shouldn't have told lies about it, then, should you?'

'I did not tell lies! I just didn't correct the locals when they found me. They *decided* that my powers had come from Earth. Can I remind you, Freddie Molto, that you are addressing the King?'

'You've reminded me enough times already, thanks.'

Ella didn't know whether to applaud Freddie's fearlessness or curl up in a ball of embarrassment, so she did neither, instead choosing the safe option of looking into the middle distance and scratching her ear.

'As long as the *King* has the most formidable sonorance, that's all that matters,' Uncle Otto growled, clearly taken aback at being spoken to so directly, especially by a child. 'I even have the power to give sonorance to others, if I so wish.'

'Well, that's not true, is it?' Freddie said, not finished taking the King of Drumendus to task. 'That cave in the woods gives people sonorance, not *you*.'

Uncle Otto swung around with such fervour that Ella nearly toppled over the balcony rail. 'WHAT DID YOU SAY?' he roared.

Freddie stepped back at the sudden outburst. 'Er… the cave… that's all – we saw it in Crumhorn Forest. Obviously we couldn't get in, with all the guards protecting the entrance, but…' His voice trailed off.

Uncle Otto's face transformed from a look of fury to one of disbelief, and his cheeks turned a deep shade of red. 'Guards! Take these three to the dungeon.'

'Dungeon?' said Aunt Belinda. 'We're not criminals.'

'You will stay under lock and key until I find out *everything* you know,' he yelled, storming back inside and leaping across the hall with a single sonorance stamp. 'And I will find out EVERYTHING!'

# CHAPTER 16
# A BREAK IN THE CHAIN

'Nice one, Freddie,' said Ella, as the guards jostled them out of the hall towards a spiral staircase.

'What did I say?'

'Oh, I don't know, maybe telling Uncle Otto that we know his biggest secret?'

'Everyone'll find out about the sonorance cave in the end.'

Aunt Belinda turned around, her face troubled. 'What's all this about a cave?'

Ella told her of the mysterious guarded entrance in Crumhorn Forest, and of Ursula recalling the rumours of a magic cave that was the true source of sonorance.

'Vivaldi's vest!' said Aunt Belinda, then smiled knowingly. 'So, Otto wants to hide the cave's existence from everyone except his closest soldiers, to keep the power in *his* hands, and to make his subjects think that *he's* the special sonorance-giver! That's why he's so angry you discovered it.'

At the bottom of the gloomy staircase, a guard led them to a row of old-fashioned prison cells with bars from floor to ceiling.

'You two, in there,' he barked at Ella and Freddie, then turned to Aunt Belinda. 'You, in there.'

'The cheek of it,' she blustered, trundling into her cell.

Many wearisome hours later, three trays of leftovers from Uncle Otto's feast were brought down to the prisoners. Freddie devoured his food in a matter of seconds, then stood up and wandered over to the cell door. 'I think I preferred it upstairs,' he said, wrapping his fingers around the bars.

'We wouldn't be down here if it wasn't for you,' Ella said.

'What?'

'You heard.'

'I just told the tr—'

'Stop it, you two!' came Aunt Belinda's voice from the other cell. 'Just remember, *I'm* the one who brought you to Drumendus, even if it was slightly by accident. If you must be cross with someone, be cross with me. I'm old enough to take it… I think. Now, get some rest.'

Ella closed her eyes and dropped into a shallow sleep. Her dreams were a whirlwind of magical images and half-formed battle scenes, and she startled herself awake a few times in the night.

'Psst!'

Someone was trying to get Ella's attention in her dream.

'*Psssst!* Ella!'

Or was it in real life?

She rubbed her eyes and eased them open. The faint purple light of the early morning seeped into her cell through a slit in the wall. She pushed herself upright, her entire body aching from lying on the thin straw mattress. 'Who is it?'

'Seren and Ade,' came an urgent whisper. 'We've come to rescue you!'

The twins' beaming faces peered through the cell bars. Ade's set of miniature musical pipes hung proudly on a chain around his neck.

'How did you get down here?' said Ella, her voice hoarse.

'Through a secret passage, of course,' said Seren. 'Father knows most of them, so we do too – he has no idea how much we follow him!'

'But the prison guards – they'll catch you!'

'I wouldn't worry,' Ade said. 'Fast asleep. Look.'

Two guards were slumped over a table behind the twins, snuggled up to each other and snoring gently.

'No way,' said Ella, recognising them straight away as the arguing nitwits from yesterday. 'Those two, again?'

'Trebble and Cloff, yes.'

Ella noticed a set of keys dangling out of Trebble's tunic pocket on a cord. 'Quick!' she hissed. 'Try and get them without waking him up.'

'Easy,' whispered Seren.

'WHO'S THERE?' Freddie's voice boomed around the walls from his bed.

Seren sighed as the noise died down. 'At least, it *would* be easy... if your Earthian friend kept quiet...'

'WHO'S THEEEERE?' Freddie yelled again. His arms flailed around, but his eyes stayed tight shut.

'Great time to have a bad dream,' grumbled Ella.

His outburst set off a chain reaction of confused sleepy mutterings. Aunt Belinda mumbled something from the other cell about cooking scrambled bongo drums for breakfast, then, rather more alarmingly, Cloff started warbling a tune that was much too high for her vocal range. This woke up *Trebble*, who stood up and grabbed a pair of what looked like sharpened xylophone bars from the table.

Seren and Ade pressed themselves into a shadowy corner, and Ella jumped back onto her bed and lay as still as she could.

'What's all this shouting?' grumbled Trebble, stomping towards the cell. 'Be quiet in there!' He didn't notice the twins.

'I... must have had a nightmare,' Freddie said, ruffling his hair.

'Earthians,' Trebble tutted, trudging back to the table.

Ella spotted Ade shuffling around in the corner.

'My necklace!' he chuntered. 'It's stuck!' He squirmed again, this time more panicked.

Ella darted over to the cell bars and strained her eyes to see what had happened. Ade's precious chain had become caught on a rusty old nail underneath his armpit. The more he struggled, the tighter it knotted itself. The twenty-four hollow mipes clunked together as he shook.

'Help me!'

Seren looked at her brother and said gently, 'There's only one thing for it, Ade.' She grabbed his necklace with both hands. 'Sorry.'

'No! It's my favourite! Do *not* break it—'

His plea fell on deaf ears. Seren grimaced and pulled the chain apart. The mipes clattered together in a confused cacophony of sound, and the necklace fell to the stone floor as Ade wriggled free.

Trebble leapt to his feet but banged his head on a beam, having clearly forgotten how long his legs were. '*What* is going on?' he thundered, rubbing his head. 'Who's there?'

Ade stared down at the mess on the floor. 'My necklace! My mipes!'

'Forget the mipes!' said Seren, trying to pull him around the corner. 'We need to get out of here. We'll come back for you, Ella…!'

Trebble tore after them, barely in control of his limbs as he ran. Cloff followed, and the four of them collided with a thump in the semi-darkness. In the chaotic scuffle that followed, Ade unintentionally kicked the necklace towards Ella in her cell. She grabbed it and tucked it under her mattress before anybody noticed.

'We should have known it was you two!' Cloff yelled as the twins wriggled free and sprinted away. 'Just wait until your father hears about this!'

Trebble went to try some speed sonorance but then gave up and sidled back towards the cells. 'If you're planning something, I *will* find out. Understood, Earthian girl?' He tried to sound threatening, but his voice ended up more like a toad with a sore throat.

Ella nodded and sat on her mattress.

'After breakfast, I feel like practising my sonorance on the prisoners,' Cloff jeered from the table. 'Do you agree, Trebble?'

'Oh, yes, *yes*, I do,' Trebble answered with glee.

Ella tried to lie down, but the uncomfortable lumps from Ade's broken necklace prodded her in the back. She eased it out from under the mattress with great care, making sure that the mipes didn't clunk together. She allowed one of the finely decorated tubes to slip off the end of the broken chain and land softly beside her. Freddie ambled over and picked it up. Then, quite unexpectedly, he placed it on the stone slabs and rolled it around with the sole of his foot.

'What are you doing?' frowned Ella.

'Do you still have that mini-trombone thingy?'

She reached into her pocket. 'My trombolino? Yeah…?'

'I have an idea to get us out of here.'

# CHAPTER 17
# A FAMOUS EARTHIAN ANIMAL

Ella and Freddie slipped all twenty-four mipes off Ade's chain. 'I hope this works,' she whispered, checking that Trebble and Cloff weren't looking – they were busy tucking into a hearty breakfast and having a vocal-range competition between mouthfuls.

Freddie kept watch as Ella stretched her arm through the bars and rolled the mipes along the floor, one in front of the other, forming a line between the cell and the guards' table. With the last mipe in place, she sat back to admire her handiwork.

'Time to play your trombolino,' Freddie said. 'As loudly as you can.'

Ella fetched her instrument. 'I haven't actually played it yet. I don't know how it's meant to sound.'

'There's only one way to find out – go for it! And the worse it sounds, the better.'

'Huh?'

'The more shocked the guards will be!'

Ella lifted the trombolino to her lips, breathed in as deeply as she could and blew into the mouthpiece. A high-pitched squeal pierced the air, and the poor instrument shook as she played. She moved the miniature slide forwards and backwards with her other hand, and the note she was playing snaked higher and lower, as if an emergency siren was going off in the cell. Freddie smiled and gave her a thumbs-up, then put his fingers in his ears.

Trebble and Cloff dropped their food and staggered to their feet in utter confusion. Trebble bear-hugged Cloff in fright, and they scampered towards the cell, straight into the trap. As if in slow motion, their boots slipped on the rolling mipes, upending them in perfect harmony. They yelped mid-air and thudded to the ground by the cell.

'It worked!' said Ella, stuffing the trombolino in her pocket and grabbing the keys attached to Trebble's tunic. 'We did it!' With shaking hands, she reached around and turned the key in the door.

'You clever pair!' Aunt Belinda laughed as Ella rushed out and unlocked her door too. 'I saw the whole thing. That'll teach those two buffoons.'

'Let's go,' said Freddie, stepping over Trebble and Cloff towards the exit.

A hand shot out and grabbed Ella's ankle.

'You do *not* escape on my watch,' snarled Cloff

from the floor, her glowing ears quivering in fury.

Unfortunately for her, Ella's fumbling fingers dropped the heavy set of keys straight onto her forehead.

'Owwww!' Cloff screeched.

'Sorry, I—'

'You'll regret that, Earthian!'

Ella shook her foot free and accidentally kicked Cloff in the ear.

'Owwww!' Cloff yelled for a second time, clutching the side of her face.

'Oops, sorry again, I didn't mean to—'

'Stop apologising, and run!' Aunt Belinda said behind her.

To Ella's dismay, Trebble regained consciousness and lunged at her aunt's legs, rugby-tackling her to the floor.

'Go, you two!' Aunt Belinda bellowed, facedown against the rough stone slabs. 'RUN!'

Ella hesitated. 'I can't leave you again!'

Freddie dragged her towards the dungeon door, which was ajar. 'We have to go *now*. It's our only chance!'

Ella groaned in frustration as Trebble bundled Aunt Belinda into her cell. 'Back soon,' she called. 'I promise!'

She sprinted after Freddie along a damp corridor and up a spiral staircase towards ground level. Creeping into a courtyard, they tiptoed past a group of sleepy galops and even sleepier soldiers.

'That's the road we came up yesterday to the

Palace,' Freddie whispered as they reached the other side. Stradbow stretched away in infinite detail below them, and beyond the city walls, the misty plain unfolded towards the forests and mountains on the horizon. 'Come on.'

A soldier lying a few metres away snorted in his sleep. His leg twitched as if he were dreaming of his favourite dance. A scrunched-up bag that was perched on his lap toppled over, revealing some bread rolls and peculiar-looking purple fruit inside.

Without thinking, Ella slinked across and went to take some food.

'What d'you think you're doing?' Freddie hissed.

'Nothing… I just…'

Trebble burst into the courtyard. 'AFTER THEM!' he roared.

The drowsy soldier jolted upright, and for a strange moment, he and Ella ended up nose to nose. 'What's going…?' he started. 'Are you stealing my…?'

Ella grabbed the bag, again not thinking, and bolted down the hill with Freddie. Without daring to look back, they practically galloped past Uncle Otto's marvelodrums and the ornate buildings lining the street.

'Do you… have an… escape plan…' wheezed Ella, nearly losing control of her legs as the descent became steeper, 'by any… chance…?'

'Of course…' panted Freddie.

'Good!'

'You didn't let me… finish! Of course… NOT!'

The gold-painted gates leading to the sprawling streets of Stradbow loomed large ahead of them.

'Any bright ideas?' said Freddie.

'Just one,' Ella puffed, spotting a small door built into the right-hand gate. A young chap was guarding it, his expression vacant. 'Worth a try.' She fetched the trusty trombolino from her pocket and attempted to summon up some courage. 'Hey, you!' she shouted, rushing towards the teenage guard. 'Open this door NOW!' She lifted the trombolino to her lips, as if ready to play right in his face. 'We're... dangerous.' She regretted saying that as soon as the words had left her mouth, and she didn't dare glance over at Freddie, who must have been smirking at her efforts to act tough.

The befuddled guard flung his arms in the air and stumbled backwards against the gate.

Ella felt a steely determination rise up inside her. 'Open the door, or I'll... I'll *trombolino* you with this... magic trombolino!' She wasn't exactly sure what she was talking about.

The guard gasped. 'You have sonorance? Everyone is saying you don't.'

Ella tried to lie but instead found herself answering, 'Well... do you want to find out?'

'No, no, no!'

The guard fumbled around with his keys and unlocked the door. Ella couldn't help saying a quick 'Thank you' on her way past as she and Freddie darted through.

Many minutes later, after lots of wrong turns and a scattering of arguments, they collapsed in the shadow of the curved city walls to catch their breath. The heavily guarded gates leading out of Stradbow stood a stone's throw away. They hid behind a line of carts and wolfed down a bread roll and some purple fruit.

'Every soldier in Stradbow will be hunting for us,' Freddie said, sliding to the floor. 'What now?' Ella didn't answer. 'Ella?'

'Oh, sorry. I can't stop thinking about what happened earlier. I don't even *have* sonorance, but that guard was a terrified wreck. Just shows... even the *thought* of it is crazily powerful!'

The purple dawn over Stradbow lit up the Palace walls on the hill. People emerged from their houses and got on with their day as they always did, with no idea that they were metres away from a couple of weary Earthian fugitives. Ella and Freddie watched as supplies came and went in carts through the gates.

A soldier marched straight towards the cart they were hiding behind. Ella recognised him as Major Squeelo from yesterday. 'Crumhorn Forest, leaving now!' he shouted over his shoulder. 'Two carts with supplies to the Rain Cavern.'

'Did you hear that?' Ella said, as quietly as her excitement would allow. 'The Rain Cavern. That *must* be the sonorance cave in the forest!' She jiggled her arms up and down. 'This is our chance!'

'Where is Minor Kazoodle?' Squeelo barked. 'He's supposed to be driving the other cart.'

The same teenage soldier Ella had terrified with her trombolino a few minutes earlier rushed down the road. 'Sorry, Major,' he wheezed, 'I was guarding the other gates, and then—'

For a dreadful moment, Ella was sure he was about to blurt out that she and Freddie had escaped, but Squeelo interrupted with, 'Get into your cart, Kazoodle!'

'But, Major, the Earthi—'

'You've already made us late!'

Kazoodle lowered his head in embarrassment and jumped in.

Ella grinned at Freddie. 'This is our departure,' she said, imitating the voice of a train manager. '*Cart number two to Crumhorn Forest, calling at the Rain Cavern.* Come on!' She climbed carefully into Kazoodle's cart and hid, beckoning for Freddie to do the same.

'Another cart ride,' Freddie huffed under his breath. 'Brilliant!'

'At least Scarp isn't driving.'

'True... but this had better work. My stomach can't take many more of these.'

The city gates groaned open, and the galops cantered through and sped out onto the plain. It didn't take long to reach Crumhorn Forest.

In the neighbouring cart, Squeelo boasted to his friend about his speed sonorance and combat skills. He called over to Minor Kazoodle. 'What about *you*? What sonorance can you do? If any at all?'

'Oh, I've been practising,' said Kazoodle with a nervous laugh. 'The King likes my voice – he says it sounds like a famous Earthian animal. What did he call it, again? Ah yes, a *sheep*. My voice is like a sheep's voice – I can only imagine what sort of magnificent creature that is. Such an honour! I've been working on my chanting sonorance.'

'And what does that sonorance actually *do*?' Squeelo said, his tone laced with contempt.

'I can move things towards me… I think. I'm… not totally sure yet—'

'Chanting?' mocked Squeelo. 'That's not *real* sonorance.'

'It… it certainly *is* real. I'm still discovering it, that's all. You'll see.'

Something inside the bag Ella had snatched from the sleepy soldier at the Palace was digging into her thigh. She pulled out a hefty carved drumstick and rested it in the palm of her hand. She had never seen such care and craftsmanship.

'I didn't mean to… steal this,' she whispered to Freddie. 'Just some fruit and bread… that's all…'

The cart lurched to a halt, and they heard the soldiers jump to the ground. Freddie tucked the drumstick into his back pocket. 'I'll look after it for now, okay? Seeing as you've got the trombolino?'

'Sounds fair,' said Ella, a resolute smile spreading across her face. 'Let's get us some sonorance, shall we?'

# CHAPTER 18

# FOLLOW THE DRUMS

Squeelo, Kazoodle and the other soldier ambled over to the entrance of the Rain Cavern and exchanged words with two others, one of whom shouted at them for being late. Ella recognised her as Major Castanex, the super-strength speed-sonorator from yesterday.

Ella and Freddie eased out of the cart and hid.

'Now we just have to get in there,' Freddie murmured. 'A distraction?'

The soldiers' arguing escalated into a scuffle, and it wasn't long before Castanex had shoved the timid Kazoodle into a bush.

'They're doing pretty well at distracting themselves,' said Ella with a scoff. 'Come on.'

As they tiptoed towards the carved entrance, a

guard bounded out of the cave and jumped straight into the melee with the other soldiers. A sprawling mass of bodies writhed and grunted on the floor, with punches thrown and kicks landed completely at random. There was no sign of any sonorance, but Ella wasn't keen to stay and find out if there would be.

'I think that's our cue,' she said to Freddie, and they edged unnoticed through the archway of the hallowed cave.

Echoey drum sounds filled the damp air inside the cave, sending Ella's senses into overdrive. The same rhythm repeated itself again and again, as if calling the two explorers down into the depths of Drumendus. They followed a pinched passageway, dimly lit by wall torches, until they came to a fork in the path.

'Right or left?' said Freddie.

Ella stopped and listened intently. 'Definitely right.'

'Er... how do you know?'

'Follow the drums.' She led them into the heart of the cave network, her confidence growing with every step. The curving path split into one final fork. 'Through here,' she said, shuffling along a passage whose low ceiling brushed against her hair. 'We must be close.'

They clambered down some uneven steps and stopped as the passage opened out, their backs pressed against the lumpy stone walls.

Ella gasped in impossible excitement. 'The Rain Cavern!'

A vast cave stretched away in front of them. Its ceiling was peppered with a million stalactites, and its walls were covered in jaw-dropping patterns, grooves and markings, interweaving and overlapping like a giant underground art installation. This beauty, this detail, was surely not the work of people but the work of Drumendus itself, over thousands of years. And yet, so much seemed familiar to Ella as she stared around her; there were patterns that looked like people singing, there were shadows in the walls that resembled musical instruments and there were countless markings that could have been notes on a page or other musical symbols she knew from home.

She stepped forwards, but Freddie grabbed her and yanked her back against the wall just in time. 'Wait! It's a lake.'

Ella looked down and noticed the gentle ripples lapping up against the stone shore. 'Thanks,' she said. 'That could've been... chilly.'

They stood in silence, looking, listening, as the drumming continued from directly below them. To Ella's surprise, a fountain of water whooshed upwards after each set of drumbeats, like a great cymbal roll in an orchestra. The water then rained down onto the lake's surface with a playful pitter-patter, and an expectant pause completed the cycle before the drumming started once more.

*Drums, fountain, rain, silence...*
*Drums, fountain, rain, silence...*
*Drums, fountain, rain, silence...*

Ella and Freddie were transfixed, rooted to the spot as the sequence repeated. This was the source of the never-ending heartbeat of Drumendus, the drum pattern that echoed across the whole planet in all its simplicity and might, the drum pattern that even Aunt Belinda heard on her mission, twenty-five years ago.

'Now we know why it's called the Rain Cavern,' Freddie said. 'Any ideas about what to do?'

Ella smiled. Her breathless anticipation had given way to a deep sense of contentment. She felt completely at home in the Rain Cavern. And she knew *exactly* what to do.

'Over there,' she said, pointing to the far side of the lake.

A lone rock rose out of the murky water, a majestic underground stage. Each time the fountain erupted, most of the water cascaded down onto the rock's perfectly smooth surface. At first glance, it appeared to be an island, reachable only by swimming through the lake, but in fact, a slender stone pathway led to the rock from the opposite shore.

Ella walked around the lake confidently, with Freddie scampering close behind. Without a second thought, she climbed over to the rock, stood centre-stage and waited.

For a few seconds the only sound was the thump of her heartbeat.

*BOOOOOOM! First drum from the deep.*

She squeezed her eyes shut.

*BOOOOOOM! Second drum from the deep.*

The rock quaked beneath her.

*WHOOOOOOSH!*

A jet of water shot up from the lake.

She stretched out her arms and lifted her chin. Freezing water rained down on her face and drenched her from head to toe. Only it wasn't freezing… it was warm! And it didn't just warm her on the outside; it warmed her on the *inside*. The warmth intensified under her skin and spread out across her entire being, energising every cell and sharpening every sensation. The contentment she had felt on entering the Rain Cavern had transformed into sheer joy, and for the first time in her life, tears of happiness spilled down her cheeks.

'I have sonorance,' she whispered. 'I have *sonorance!*'

She took an enormous breath, rubbed her eyes and shinned down the rock to Freddie.

'How do you… feel?' said Freddie, his face unsure.

Ella patted her clothes and laughed in shock. 'Dry!'

Freddie joined in, then said, 'And… are you still Ella… if you know what I mean?'

'I think so. But I feel… incredible.'

'Goose bumps, that sort of thing?'

'Times that by a *million*, and you might get close,' Ella said, elation still coursing through her veins. 'I could be Super-Ella from now on, just to warn you.'

'Well, that's hardly fair,' said Freddie, scrambling over to the rock. 'My turn.'

Ella watched as her best friend stood and waited for the sequence to begin again. The first drum boomed out across the cavern, then the second, and the spectacular fountain surged up to the ceiling, then fell in a million droplets onto the lake, onto the rock and onto Freddie.

He wiped his eyes and jumped down to Ella, punching the air in delight. He too was bone-dry. 'I see what you mean! I feel A-MA-ZING!'

They high-fived each other and hurried back around the lake.

Before they could reach the steps, though, the sound of angry voices echoed through the vast underground space.

'In there!' Freddie said, pointing to a crevice in the rock that neither of them had spotted earlier.

Ella shook her head. 'We can't fit through there!'

'Of course we can. We've got sonorance now.'

'Er, yeah, but how's that going to make us shrink—'

'Earthians! Don't move!' bellowed a vaguely familiar voice.

Ella looked around to see Castanex closing in. There was no choice but to follow Freddie into the narrow passage. 'I *refuse* to get stuck…' she muttered, breathing in and squeezing herself through with an undignified grunt.

To her relief, the crevice was mercifully short, and once they cleared it, they ran as fast as they dared in the dingy torchlight, ending up in a small chamber after going around a corner that seemed to last forever.

'Agh! More water!' Ella said, running knee-deep into a pool, then springing backwards.

They glanced around the peculiar cave, desperately looking for a way out. Three small rocks poked out of the pool in a line, and Freddie prepared himself for a running jump.

'Wait!' Ella yelled, spotting a faint ray of purple light coming from a jagged archway. 'That *must* be from outside. Let's go.'

They had run out of time. Castanex tore into the chamber and lunged at Freddie.

'No!' Freddie shrieked, thrashing around as Castanex wrestled him to the damp stone floor. 'GET OFF!'

Ella gulped and reached into her pocket.

It was time to test her sonorance.

She pulled out the trombolino and put it to her mouth. Blowing into it, she *thought* as hard as she could about forcing Castanex off Freddie, blowing her away with a magnificent burst of sound magic.

Sure enough, the note she played was high enough, and piercing enough, to bounce around the cave walls and distract Castanex into sitting upright. Freddie even managed to wriggle one arm free.

But there was no sign of sonorance.

Ella focused her mind and played another note, her intention so strong that she was sure her brain was about to explode. This time, Castanex let out a grunt and writhed around on top of Freddie, as if she had been given an electric shock.

Ella lowered the trombolino, her eyes bulging in astonishment. 'It... worked,' she smiled.

'Do it again!' said Freddie, still pinned down by Castanex's sturdy body. 'AGAIN, Ella!'

Ella obliged, and again Castanex jolted fiercely for as long as the note sounded. The trombolino shock was so powerful that she rolled off Freddie and plopped into the pool with a neat splash.

'I can't believe I've done sonorance!' said Ella, her fingers trembling as an irresistible sense of pride took over. 'I just *thought* really hard about getting her off you, and... This is crazy... I've never felt anything like... I can do ANYTHI—'

'Yeah, tell me later!' said Freddie, peering over at the soggy, spluttering Castanex. 'And thanks, by the way.'

'Guards!' roared Castanex, waist-deep in water. 'SEIZE THE EARTHIANS!'

Kazoodle appeared out of the darkness and crashed straight into Ella. He grabbed the trombolino and tried to prise it out of her hands.

'Freddie!' Ella said, losing her grip. 'Do something!'

Freddie took the drumstick out of his pocket and waved it in the air like a wand towards the soldier. Nothing happened. 'It's not working!' he yelled. He tried again, but there was no dramatic flash from the end of the stick, nor did a missile shoot out of it. 'Stupid thing!'

'Hit something with it!' gasped Ella.

'*Hit something with it,*' Freddie repeated. His eyes darted around the cave and settled on Ella's head. '*Hit something with it.* Right...'

For a moment, Ella was certain he was going to wallop her in the face. She couldn't work out why, but he *must* have had a good reason, so she shut her eyes and prepared for impact.

It didn't happen. Instead, a drumbeat thwacked perilously close to her ear. She opened an eye and saw what Freddie had seen: a drum hanging down from Kazoodle's neck on a string. Freddie was using Kazoodle's drum against him as he wrestled Ella for the trombolino!

'Take *that*, Mister *Kaboodle*!' screamed Freddie. 'And that! AND THAT!'

Sonorance missiles flew out of the centre of the drumhead and bounced around the chamber chaotically. Some splashed into the pool, and one ricocheted off Castanex as she tried to climb out, which simply enraged her yet more. In the confusion, Kazoodle loosened his grip on the trombolino, and Ella yanked it back towards her and sent him hurtling into the wall. Freddie rushed over and gave Kazoodle's drum one last almighty whack, so hard, in fact, that the drumstick flew out of his hand and disappeared into the water.

The sonorance ball pinged off a stalactite and collided with Kazoodle's bottom. 'OUUUUCH!' he yelped, clutching his behind and collapsing to his knees.

'That's what you get for attacking my *friend*!' Freddie snarled.

'Nice work,' Ella beamed. 'Let's get out of here.'

# CHAPTER 19
# PRACTICE MAKES SONORANCE

Ella and Freddie followed the light out of the cave and sprinted towards the trees. In the clearing, they passed a mumbling heap of semi-conscious guards, who had clearly come off second best in the earlier squabble with Castanex.

'We should take their instruments,' said Ella.

Freddie shook his head and pointed to a groggy soldier who had woken up and was reaching for his weapon. 'Come on! We got what we came for, didn't we?'

Ella frowned, then remembered. 'Oh, yeah, sonorance! That'll take some getting used to. Magic powers? *Me?*'

Freddie laughed as they nipped through the trees with a new-found spring in their step, their eyes peeled for any unwelcome attention.

'I don't know about you,' said Ella, scarcely out of breath as they reached the border of Crumhorn Forest, 'but I feel so… light. And alive!'

Freddie perched on a tree stump. 'Me too.'

'We've barely eaten, we've barely slept—'

'We've barely washed!' added Freddie.

'Speak for yourself!' Ella chuckled. 'I cannot believe we did some sonorance back in the cave – and it worked!'

'Yeah! Though… I wasn't sure what I was doing, really.'

'I noticed,' Ella chortled. 'Do you remember what the guards said about sonorance back in the cart?'

'Something about practising…'

'Uncle Otto mentioned it too, *and* Castanex when we first arrived in Stradbow.'

'Urgh! I'm not a fan of practising.'

'Freddie, to learn some actual magic, I think you can make an exception, can't you?'

'I suppose so,' Freddie harumphed.

'And by the way, the only reason you're really good at the piano is because you *do* practise!'

'Okay, okay, I get the idea! I'm sure you do four hours a day on your trombone.'

Ella ignored him. 'Let's start, then. We've a lot to learn before we go back to Stradbow to rescue Aunt Belinda.'

Shrugging, Freddie made another harrumphing noise. 'It's okay for you, you're a trombonist!'

'So?'

'So doing sonorance on the *trombolino* must be

DRUMENDUS

easy! *And* you'll be good at those other instruments we saw in Gurdee. What are they called again? *Airwhoosher* instruments, that's it.'

Ella thought back to the peculiar names the Gurdee folks used to describe their instruments and music groups. 'Yeah, but—'

'I'm a *twangbuzzer*,' he interrupted, 'who only plays piano. How can sonorance help me? Unless there happens to be a pianarack hanging around, or whatever it's called—'

'You're forgetting what you've seen,' Ella said, trying to calm him down. 'It's not all about the instruments. Sonorance is musical magic *and* sound magic, right?'

'Mm-hm. And?'

'And we can both make sounds, can't we?'

'Obviously. Get to the point, Ella.'

Again, she ignored his tetchiness. 'Let's try!'

She jumped up and started clapping, clicking, tapping and stamping with such enthusiasm that she forgot to focus on anything in particular.

Nothing magical happened.

'Yeah… that made you look *really* magical,' said Freddie, whose sulky face had changed to a bemused grin. 'Maybe slow down a bit? It's all jumbled up at the moment.'

'Ah, yeah,' said Ella, trying again, this time just clapping. Still nothing happened. 'Hmm. I'm sure we can crack this. We just need to *think*.'

Freddie jumped up. 'That's it!' he said, his negativity seeming to evaporate, as it so often did with him. 'We need to *think*. Remember what you said back in the cave, you *thought* really hard about getting Castanex off me?'

'Yeah…?'

'Then you gave her that trombolino shock!'

'Yes!' Ella said, glad that her best friend was back to his cheerful self. 'So… we need to practise, *and* we need to think the right thoughts.'

'Exactly! Let's try clapping again.'

Ella nodded and clapped her hands 'Er… what I am supposed to be thinking?'

'Okay, let's work it out. Why do we clap?'

'To congratulate each other. But saying well done to the grass isn't really magic.'

'Hmm. Why else?'

Ella cast her mind back to school. 'The teachers clap to get our attention, if we're being noisy. That happens to a kid called Drawl in every *single* lesson.'

'Worth a try.' Freddie walked a few steps into the forest and stood with his back to Ella. 'Get my attention. Turn me around.'

Ella clapped again, her eyes fixed on Freddie. She cleared her mind except for one thought: to make him face her. It took a few seconds, but slowly he turned his head. Ella sped up her claps, her hands brimming with the sonorance she was creating. Even the branches and bushes surrounding Freddie began leaning in.

'I… can't… resist…' gasped Freddie, his body trembling as he tried to fight the magic. 'Argh!'

With a final burst of sonorance clapping, Ella

DRUMENDUS

spun him towards her. Not only that, his feet left the floor and he whirled around in a mid-air blur. The branches catapulted back into position as soon as she stopped, and Freddie landed with a dazed grunt.

'Cool!' she said, staring down at her burning hands.

Freddie leapt up and stormed over, a furious look on his face. 'Ya, ya, YA!' he yelled, punching the air in front of him.

To Ella's astonishment, the air punches landed on her chest and shoulder, as if Freddie was right in front of her. 'Ouch! What are you doing?'

He snapped out of his rage as quickly as he had started. 'Oh, sorry, Ella. I… don't know what I was thinking.'

'It's… okay,' she said, rubbing her arm.

'You had *control* over me when you were clapping, and that was… frightening. My brain told me I had to fight back.'

'I knew you were green belt, but I never thought you'd use it on me!'

'Blue belt, actually!'

They both laughed, and Freddie went over to a tree and practised a few more air punches and kicks. Sure enough, they all thudded against the trunk when he shouted, 'Ya,' but didn't when he punched silently. The nearer the tree he went, the firmer the impact.

'This is fun!' he said, skipping back over to Ella. 'What else can we try?'

'I've a few ideas…'

For the next hour, Ella and Freddie let their

imaginations run wild. Ella had never felt more exhilarated in her life, or more *powerful*, and it was clear Freddie felt the same.

Eventually, they collapsed in a heap at the bottom of a hollow. Spying a tiny stream, Ella knelt down and drank some water with a cupped hand.

'Break time, *Super-Freddie*,' she said.

'Okay, *Super-Ella!*'

They sat cross-legged side by side, watching the water meander its way past in gentle song.

'So... now that we're *definitely* superheroes,' Ella said, 'let's check what we've learnt so far.'

They made a list:

1. *Clapping and clicking – grabs the attention of people and things*
2. *Air punches and kicks – produces real punches and kicks (don't forget the 'Ya')*
3. *Cooing like a dove – sends people to sleep*

'This is just the start,' Freddie said. 'I can't wait to try out more stuff and... I can't *wait* to practise!'

Ella giggled. 'That's quite a change from earlier!'

'Just shows what a bit of magic can do, eh?'

'This is such a crazy adventure!' Ella hesitated, then added, 'As long as we get back home...'

'Of course we will,' replied Freddie, but his eyes revealed a sense of doubt, 'once we've rescued Belinda. You'll see. Much as I like it here, I still think I prefer Earth. Purple's cool 'n' all, but seriously, does *everything* have to be purple?' He got to his feet, brushed himself off and ran up to the nearest ridge. 'Let's try stamping. I want to make the ground shake.'

Ella made sure her trombolino was tucked safely in her pocket, then joined him. They stamped as hard as they could.

The earth didn't shake.

'Try at *exactly* the same time,' said Freddie. 'And *really* picture the ground shaking. One, two, three, STAMP...'

Still nothing happened.

'Wait,' said Ella. 'The ground only shakes from drumming. Remember Uncle Otto's soldiers outside Gurdee?'

'Oh, yeah.'

'And Uncle Otto *himself* on the table yesterday! His drumming made the whole room shake! Hmm... stamping must do something else.' She set off for a running jump. 'Let's try this.'

Reaching top speed along the ridge a few seconds later, she noticed Freddie waving his arms above his head.

'I've just remembered!' he called. 'Otto stamped yesterday, which made him—'

'FLY... AAAAARGH!' Ella stamped and leapt high into the air, her limbs flailing as if she had been pushed off a diving board. Misjudging her landing, she thumped back to the ground and rolled along the grass, coming to an ungainly stop at Freddie's feet. 'Did I... fly?' she said.

'It wasn't pretty,' said Freddie, sheer admiration covering his face, 'but it was flying!'

'YES!' Ella yelled, clambering to her feet and dancing a made-up jig on the spot. 'Again! You do it too!'

Freddie obliged, and they sprinted and stamped in tandem, flying above the grassy plain without a care in the world. They even managed a sonorance leap from a standing start, as long as the stamp was loud enough and the thought clear enough. Landing was the tricky part, and Ella picked up dozens of bumps and bruises along the way. But she didn't care one iota.

For these two ecstatic Earthians, there was no time, there was no place. There was only sonorance, this *beautiful* sonorance.

They ran towards an isolated clump of trees and leapt up to an overhanging branch, swinging back and forth, whooping with glee.

'We need to try speed sonorance!' said Ella, turning her head. 'You know, the *zzzzmmmm* noise Castanex was making?'

'Oh yeah. That's going to be so fun.'

From her swinging position, Ella noticed that they had strayed far across the plain, in completely the wrong direction. 'Er, Freddie?' she said. 'Stradbow's miles away. Look.' She glanced over her shoulder, her hands getting tired from hanging onto the branch. 'But Libera Forest is just there.'

'Oops,' said Freddie. 'We got carried away – quite literally. We'd better get going.'

'Yep. Let's—'

'WOAH!' Freddie bellowed, startling Ella into

letting go and landing awkwardly on the ground. 'What's *that*?'

'What's *what*?' Ella snapped, rubbing her elbow.

Freddie jumped down and pointed. 'THAT.'

In the distance, a sinister ball of smokey light was rolling across the plain.

# CHAPTER 20

# JUMBLE IN THE HUT

Ella scrunched up her eyes to try and see the ball of purple light more clearly. 'I have *no idea* what that is,' she said, her heart pounding into overdrive.

'Otto's soldiers,' shouted a vaguely familiar voice behind them. 'And they're heading straight for you!'

Freddie grabbed Ella's wrist and they wheeled around in fright.

'It's okay,' Ella whispered, relieved that she at least recognised the figure. 'It's Jacopo from Gurdee, remember?' She stared at the teenager with the patterned hood and tousled hair who had caught them in the trap moments after they had landed on Drumendus. 'But be careful. He's the one who thinks he has something to prove to everyone.'

Behind Jacopo, two other violet-eared children emerged.

'Mirabelle,' said Freddie, looking at the stone-faced girl with the elaborate plaits in her hair.

'And Ursula!' Ella said to the gappy-grinned girl who had discovered the Rain Cavern with them yesterday. 'What are you doing out here?'

'I *would* ask you the same question,' said Ursula, her cheeks as rosy-purple as ever, 'but we don't have time. Otto's soldiers will be here any moment.' She looked over Ella's shoulder at the streaky smoke trails edging closer. 'The ball of light you can see is a group of them using speed sonorance. Come on.'

Ella groaned. 'But Freddie and I need to get back to Stradbow and rescue Aunt Belinda. We've got half a chance now with our sonorance.'

'Sonorance? You two have *sonorance*?'

'We sure do!'

'I am SO jealous!' said Ursula.

Jacopo scoffed. 'You can't have had it for long. I doubt you know what you're doing!'

Ella saw Freddie's fists tightening.

'I'll happily test that theory on a *drumskull* like you!' Freddie said, then chuckled unexpectedly. 'Woah – I can't believe I remembered that Drumendus insult.'

Ursula stifled a laugh, then put her hand on Ella's arm. 'It's incredible you have sonorance, and I want to know *everything*! But we have to go now, or we'll be captured – Otto's soldiers are fast. Hurry!'

Ella and Freddie reluctantly followed the Gurdee

children into Libera Forest. As they ran, Ella told Ursula all about escaping Stradbow with Freddie and returning to the Rain Cavern to get sonorance. Ursula cheered with delight on hearing of the dramatic water-fountain ritual and the cave battle with Castanex.

They stopped at the colourful Gurdee fence and stared around them. Ella noticed there was no music wafting through the trees this time. All was eerily quiet.

Freddie nudged her. 'What about rescuing Bel—' he started, but was interrupted by a piercing shout that echoed around the hanging buildings beyond the fence. Then another… and another…

Ella's shoulders rammed up towards her ears in surprise. 'What was that?'

Jacopo raised his hand. 'Shh.' Leaning his head to one side, he listened intently as the calls continued. There were no words, but each one was a different pitch and a different length, clearly a message being sent across Gurdee. 'I am needed,' he said solemnly. 'There are orders to guard the settlement. Otto's soldiers are approaching the east gate. Follow me… quickly!'

They nipped along a narrow path around the perimeter fence and squeezed through one of the secret tree-trunk entrances. 'Climb,' said Jacopo, pointing to a rope ladder that led up to a small building. 'You can stay in the Jumblehut with Ursula. You should be safe there. Mirabelle, come with me.'

Ursula tugged on her brother's sleeve. 'Excuse

*me,*' she said. 'You can't put our Earthian friends in a storage hut full of old ropes and broken bits!'

Freddie stepped between them. 'We can defend Gurdee with you,' he said. 'With our… sonorance!' He didn't sound convincing.

'Be quiet and *climb*!' Jacopo growled. 'A battle is no place for children.'

'How rude!' muttered Ursula. 'You're only a bit older than—'

'GO!'

Without another word, Ella, Freddie and Ursula rushed up the rope ladder and into the cramped so-called Jumblehut. The air was muggy and the smell fusty. The tiny slits for windows let in almost no light. Outside, people called to each other and clattered along the wooden walkways, preparing to defend their Gurdee homes.

Moments later, all was quiet, and the companions in the hut sat as still as their bodies would allow.

'We must be the only ones left at this end of the village,' said Ursula. She tutted, then added, 'I wish the King and his soldiers would leave us alone. These attacks are happening more than ever, and they get closer to Gurdee each time. I do *not* like it.' Out of the blue, she managed to force a smile. 'But Mother will keep them away. She always does.' There was little conviction as she spoke. 'And now, we have a secret weapon – *two* secret weapons, in fact.' She gestured to Ella and Freddie.

'Hmm, I wouldn't call us that *quite* yet,' Ella muttered, 'with our current skill levels…'

'You know more than you think, I'm sure of it. Ignore what Jacopo says – he's just jealous that he doesn't have sonorance. *And* he's so desperate to be seen as important. You're a threat to him, that's all. He'll see your value in the end.'

They huddled in the Jumblehut, and Ella lost any sense of time as they waited for an all-clear signal that never came. Eventually, Ursula sighed and headed to the door, easing it open to peer outside.

'Wait,' said Ella. 'What are you doing?'

'Fetching supplies. You're our guests and I will not have you forgotten about. And… I'm starving!'

Before any of them could protest, she had slipped out of the hut. She returned with a selection of patterned clothes for Ella and Freddie to change into and a basket of curious-looking food. The three of them tucked in eagerly, then lay down and waited. Ella battled against her heavy eyelids, but there was only ever going to be one winner, and she fell into a deep and dreamless sleep.

𝄞

A sliver of purple-tinged light under the door was the first thing that came into focus as Ella awoke. She tried to sit upright, but her body was as stiff as a board after hours spent lying on the lopsided wooden floor.

'Another comfy night on Drumendus,' she muttered to herself, fiddling with the oversized Gurdee tunic she had chosen from Ursula's selection.

The others were already awake, exploring the contents of the Jumblehut. Ella's early-morning brain fog lifted as she looked around her. 'Is this… a room full of instruments?'

'Yep!' said Freddie, sporting a multicoloured tunic himself. He threw Ella a slice of purple bread. 'I didn't notice the good stuff in here either. It looked like piles of junk last night.' He rummaged through a tangled mess of strings in the corner and lifted up a broken instrument. 'Look! Skinny violins!'

'They're strumalots,' said Ursula. 'Our bows and arrows. And they make a nice sound too, of course, when played by the right person! Mirabelle's an expert.'

'And what is *that*?' Freddie said, lifting up a delicate wooden instrument with keys running down one side. It looked as though it had seen better days. 'It looks like a toy!'

'That's one of our most prized instruments, Freddie: a melodonk.'

'Melo-*donk*!' Freddie guffawed. 'As in, *donk*?'

'I have no idea what you mean.'

'*Donk*. The sound a frying pan makes when you hit someone over the head with it?'

Still no reaction from Ursula, but Ella giggled at Freddie's unusual comparison.

'Anyway,' Freddie ploughed on, 'if it has keys, maybe I can play it. I play piano back home.'

'Ah, you mean *pianarack*,' Ursula said. 'That's the name of a *real* instrument.'

'Er, no – *piano*.'

'What's a *piano*? It sounds like something you eat.'

Everyone laughed, though Ella struggled to make the culinary connection.

'Let's give this melodonk thing a try,' Freddie said, facing Ella and pressing the keys.

The sound was higher than she had expected and had a dreamy feel to it, especially when Freddie played long notes. A sadness came over her as she listened, but it passed as Freddie began a more lively tune, which lifted her spirits until she was almost roaring with laughter. Freddie finished with a flurry of notes that jumped around with so many twists and turns that Ella felt her mind practically somersaulting inside her head, confusing her thoughts and making her extremely dizzy.

'Stop!' she yelled, reaching out to try and grab the melodonk.

Freddie lowered the unassuming instrument but didn't let Ella take it. 'What's wrong?'

'You just…' she panted, 'you just… controlled my *emotions* with that thing.'

Freddie's mouth widened into a mammoth grin. 'I did?'

'Yes. You made me sad… then happy… then totally confused.'

'Cool! Can I do it again?'

'No!'

Freddie turned to Ursula. 'Can I try it on you?'

'No, thank you,' Ursula said, lifting her arms in defence. 'Try it on your enemies, not your friends!'

Freddie couldn't bring himself to put it down, and

he had a strange look in his eye. 'But I need to perfect my skills. It's all about *practice*, remember?'

'Don't! Please!'

It was too late. Within seconds, Freddie had his helpless victim bawling her eyes out as he played the same sad tune as intensely as he could. Then he launched into a quick, jumpy melody. His eyes were fixed on Ursula, who stood up and attempted some outlandish dance moves on the Jumblehut floor whilst whooping and cheering uncontrollably.

'Stop it, Freddie!' Ella yelled.

'Not yet.'

'She's had enough!'

'Just a bit more,' Freddie chimed, as Ursula staggered about in a stupor, unable to resist the melodonk's sonorance. Her body looked exhausted.

Ella *had* to stop him. She pulled her trombolino out of her pocket, put it to her lips and blew as forcefully as she could. The sonorance-laced note whizzed across the hut and blasted Freddie out of the door. He landed heavily on the walkway, dropped his melodonk and groaned.

Ella sprinted outside, followed by a still-delirious Ursula. 'Woah! Freddie, I didn't mean to—'

'Uuuurrghhhh!' was all Freddie could manage.

'Sorry,' Ella said, leaning down. 'Are you okay?'

Freddie opened his eyes, and to Ella's relief, they were filled with a familiar steely twinkle. 'Do I look okay?' he chuntered, letting out a few dramatic coughs as he stood up. 'Lucky for you, I'll live,' he said, scooping up the melodonk.

Instead of amusement, Ella was surprised to feel a sense of irritation take over. 'Freddie, you went too far with your sonorance on Ursula. You should've stopped.'

Freddie turned square on to her. 'Is that right?'

'Obviously! She didn't *want* to dance any more. But *you* made her.'

The twinkle in Freddie's eye had transformed into fire, but Ella was determined not to back down.

Freddie let out a hollow laugh. 'So *you've* decided that *you're* the judge of what we can do, eh? What are you, the sonorance police?'

'No, but—'

'So sorry, Officer Crinkle,' he sneered. 'I will behave better next time, *Officer Crinkle*!'

'Don't be such a—'

'Drumskull? Yeah, that's me, a right *drumskull*!'

Ursula jumped between them, having recovered her senses. 'Ella, Freddie, calm down!'

'But—'

'It's okay. I'm unharmed. You just need to use your new-found powers wisely, alright, Freddie?'

Freddie barged past them towards the hut. 'WHAT? YOU TOO? Lecturing me? Ugh, you can all go and—'

The thudding of missiles against bark brought his rant to an abrupt end.

'Get down!' hissed Ella, throwing herself to the floor.

The others followed, and Ursula peered over the edge of the walkway, careful not to be seen.

'What's going on?' Ella whispered.

Ursula exhaled heavily. 'It had to happen in the end. The battle has reached Gurdee. Otto's army is here.'

# CHAPTER 21

# STANGNAM'S SONG

Ella struggled to see anything, her body pressed against the wooden walkway, but she heard the now-familiar sound of a Drumendus battle. The air was besieged by whooshing, calling and broken fragments of melody, all punctuated with incessant drum patterns. It was both terrifying and captivating. As she knelt up, a string of sonorance cannonballs zoomed past her cheek and ricocheted around the hanging walkways. One of them flew straight into the hallowed circular sign above Dingringer Hall and smashed it to pieces.

'No!' Ursula cried. 'They cannot do this to us!'

On the ground below, three attackers zipped in and out of the shadows and between the trees.

'I recognise him,' Ella said, nudging Freddie and

pointing to one of them. 'Down there, in the scarlet trousers.'

Freddie scrunched up his eyes as the figure sprinted under the Jumblehut towards the heart of Gurdee, with the other two soldiers close behind. 'I can't make him out.'

'Strange,' muttered Ella. 'He's not in a Stradbow uniform. No stripes or green sleeves.'

There wasn't time to ponder it. Directly below them, another ferocious duel grabbed their attention – a soldier with a bass drum chased another with a strumalot. The drumming soldier held two enormous beaters, one to thwack the drum as hard as he could and the other to fire out sonorance cannonballs. The drum itself, though, was so unwieldy that his aim was often wayward.

'He clearly doesn't practise enough,' said Freddie, finding something to smile about even in the midst of battle.

A look of panic spread over Ursula's face. 'It's Mirabelle down there – with the strumalot!'

Ella looked over the rail. Mirabelle defended herself fiercely, but the other soldier had the advantage. One of his sonorance cannonballs hurtled into her stomach, throwing her backwards into a tree trunk. Groaning, she slumped forwards into a pile of soggy leaves.

'No!' shouted Ursula. 'MIRABELLE!'

The drumming soldier turned and stared up at the terrified group. He aimed a beater at them and brought the other one crashing down onto his drum in a quick repeated pattern.

Ella ducked yet again as a volley of cannonballs whistled by overhead. 'Look out!' she shrieked.

The man grabbed the rope ladder and climbed up towards them, his grin as wonky as some of the rungs themselves. 'This hanging village of yours will soon belong to the King,' he said, scrambling to the top. 'A souvenir to remind him of the downfall of the Gurdee rebels. You can't stop us. Not even your little Earthian visitors can stop us!'

Freddie stood up and stepped over a crouching Ella, one arm tucked behind his back. 'That's what you think,' he growled.

'Freddie, what are you doing?' Ella rasped.

The soldier's laughter boomed around the trees. 'I heard about your lucky escape from Stradbow this morning, but your luck has run out. You have *no* chance against us. Not without—'

'SONORANCE?' yelled Freddie. The soldier's sneer turned to dismay as Freddie swung his arm in front of him to reveal the wooden melodonk. 'Your friends haven't told you, then? We found the Rain Cavern. WE HAVE WHAT YOU HAVE!'

The soldier was so taken aback that his arms became tangled in the straps of his drum as he fumbled around for his beater. Freddie seized the opportunity to play a few bursts of music on his melodonk, each of which was deliberately disjointed and extraordinarily fast. The soldier became increasingly agitated as Freddie's sonorance seeped into his mind, and he lurched from side to side along the walkway.

'Tricky… Earthians…!' he stuttered, edging nearer and grasping for his drum beater.

'Ella, help!' Freddie said. 'I can't play like this forever – my fingers are throbbing!'

With a deep, focused breath, Ella mustered up the courage to jump up and help her friend. 'Right then,' she said matter-of-factly, considering she was under attack from a crazed purple soldier on another planet. She channelled her power into her fingers, which tingled eagerly in response, then clicked them as hard as she could towards the soldier, hoping that sonorance would do its thing.

It did.

The nearby branches sprang to life and careered into the soldier with pinpoint precision. Astonished at her success, her confidence flourished, and she unpocketed her trombolino and blasted out some high notes, which shocked the hapless soldier into losing his balance. She even stamped and flew into the air to avoid a string of missiles he had managed to fire off whilst staggering forwards.

Could Ella dare to believe that she was becoming a *real-life* magical superhero?

Freddie certainly seemed impressed at her quick thinking and versatility. 'Nice combination sonorance!' he called over. 'He's not so smug now!'

'Thanks! Grab his drum on the way past!'

'I can do better than that,' said Freddie, who threw his melodonk over to Ella and unleashed such a forceful torrent of shouts that the air punches and kicks that followed sent the soldier headlong into the Jumblehut. He crash-landed in the corner with a whimper.

The three friends piled in afterwards. Ursula snatched his bass drum and beaters and tied his hands with some broken instrument strings.

'Great work,' said Ella, returning Freddie's melodonk. 'We make a good… team.'

'Yeah… Er… sorry about before,' Freddie said. 'I went… totally over the top with Ursula. A rush of sonorance to the head. I'll have to get used to all this power.'

Ella blushed. 'Oh… no problem. I'd… forgotten all about it,' she lied.

Ursula sprinted out of the hut and climbed down the rope ladder. 'Mirabelle!'

On the forest floor below, Mirabelle leaned against a tree trunk, rubbing her stomach. 'I'm okay,' she coughed. 'Help me up, Ursula. I… I have to keep fighting. I have to protect Gurdee.' She looked around her. 'Where's the soldier with the drum?'

'We captured him. He's up in the Jumblehut.'

'Captured him?' said Mirabelle, struggling to her feet. 'How on Drumendus did you – ah, of course, the Earthians' *sonorance*.' Even from up on the walkway, the disdain in her voice was clear to Ella. It was fair enough. After all, here were a couple of Earthians, newly arrived on Drumendus, and already *they* had more power than any of the Gurdee rebels! 'We must question the Stradbow soldier at once,' said Mirabelle, making for the rope ladder. 'We must find out everything we can about Otto's plans, his armies, *everything*! And we *must* get sonorance! We MUST!'

A lone figure emerged from the shadow of a tree. 'Yes, we must indeed.'

'Mother!'

Ursula sprinted towards Isolde and flung her arms around her. Isolde returned the hug, but then quickly pulled away and ushered the girls up the rope ladder. Her face was covered in streaks of dirt, and her fiery hair dangled in tousled knots around her shoulders. 'I became separated from the others. We held Gurdee this time, but the Stradbow army will regroup and return. They're using sonorance the likes of which I've *never* seen.' She paused on reaching the walkway, then added, 'I fear that their next attack will be our surrender.'

'No!' said Mirabelle. 'We have a loyal army here – we'll defend Gurdee to the end.'

'Yes, but Otto's soldiers are ever bolder. They know where to attack, they know our traps, they know our weapons. It doesn't seem to matter how I organise my people, they're a step ahead. I just do *not* understa...' She saw Ella and Freddie and looked them up and down with suspicion. 'I heard that you were back here.'

'Nice to see you too,' murmured Freddie.

'Your aunt couldn't escape with you from Stradbow?' she said, ignoring him. Ella shook her head, and Isolde walked purposefully into the Jumblehut. 'What is *he* doing here?' she yelled, staring at the soldier inside, who snuffled in his sleep like a toddler with a cold. 'That's Stangnam. He's one of Otto's most accomplished sonorance drummers! He would have been one of *us* in Gurdee, but Otto persuaded him otherwise with shallow promises of riches and rank.'

Ursula rushed forwards. 'Mother, I can explain.'

'Explain quickly, then!'

Ursula spoke in such breathless bursts that it was hard for any of them to keep track. As soon as she mentioned Ella and Freddie getting sonorance in Crumhorn Forest, Isolde raised a hand to signal silence.

'So, the *Rain Cavern* exists after all...' she said, her words unhurried, as if trying to process this game-changing information.

'Yes,' said Ursula. 'The rumours are true. Oh – not that I had heard the rumours, of course.'

Isolde shot her a look. 'Indeed.' She turned to Ella and Freddie. 'You two found the cave. How?'

'We hid in the back of a cart in Stradbow and were taken straight there,' said Ella. 'Then we sneaked in.'

'Surely, you do not just "sneak in" to Otto's most prized possession on Drumendus?'

'Er... *we* did.'

'But... the guards?'

'Oh, they were busy arguing amongst themselves,' Ella said, more casually than she had intended. 'We were... lucky, I guess...'

'Could you find the cave again?'

'I reckon so.' Ella looked over at her best friend. 'I don't know about you, Freddie, but I can *feel* where

179

the Rain Cavern is. Even now, I know it's that way.' She pointed to one of the walls of the hut. 'Does that make any sense whatsoever?'

'Perfect sense,' said Freddie. 'I thought it was just me!'

'The only way to beat sonorance is with sonorance,' said Isolde, her tone more urgent. 'I need to find the Rain Cavern, otherwise Otto will capture Gurdee, and that will be the *end* of Drumendus as we know it. You two will show me the way.'

Freddie stood up, clutching his melodonk. 'Wait a second – you can't just order us about.'

'This is *Gurdee*, not Earth. I can.'

'What I mean is, what can you do for *us* in return? Can you help us rescue Belinda from Stradbow?'

Isolde hesitated, then said, 'Can *you* take Otto back to Earth with you?'

'Answering a question with a question – very helpful…' Freddie sighed.

'Er… we can't really promise that, Isolde,' said Ella, remembering her uncle's crazed reaction when Aunt Belinda tried to persuade him to return to Earth. 'Uncle Otto didn't seem too keen to leave last time we checked.'

Freddie scoffed. 'Ha, understatement of the year.'

Isolde shook her head and wiped a smear of mud from her face. 'You *must* take Otto with you. We can't live with that corrupt so-called King any longer!'

'He doesn't want to leave!' Freddie said, his face reddening. 'Do you expect us to drag him out of

Stradbow, kicking and screaming? He's the most powerful person on the planet!'

In the corner of the Jumblehut, Stangnam's eyes pinged open and he stared around him.

Isolde stepped forwards, towering over him. 'I want answers,' she growled. 'When is the next attack coming?'

Stangnam grimaced through his obvious grogginess. 'I won't tell you anything, Isolde.'

'How many of you have sonorance? *How do you all know so much about Gurdee?*' Her voice shook with frustration and anger.

Still he sat there, a stubborn smirk etched across his face.

'*Tell me!* TELL ME NOW, OR—'

'Let me try something,' Freddie said unexpectedly.

Isolde stepped back and nodded. 'If you must,' she said warily. 'But be swift – there's no time for games.'

'Sonorance isn't a game,' Freddie replied, catching Ella's eye and smiling. 'I've learnt that the hard way already. It's serious stuff.'

He sat opposite Stangnam and started playing a tune on his melodonk, the same notes over and over again. Ella became transfixed, as did the others, and Stangnam's edgy smirk transformed into a childish grin. His eyes glazed over as the sonorance pierced his mind. 'Okay, Stangnam,' Freddie started, adopting a tone that reminded Ella of a firm but kind adult, 'what's Otto's plan for attacking Gurdee?'

'Must… not… talk…' Stangnam mumbled, clearly desperate to resist.

'You can tell us,' Freddie continued in a sing-song voice. 'Now, what's the plan?'

Stangnam sighed, as if giving up the fight in his mind. Then it all came out. 'That's easy,' he said, beginning a song, to everyone's surprise:

*'Today we attack,*
*And tomorrow again,*
*The next day back,*
*More women and men!'*

'What's going on?' Mirabelle said, frowning. 'Why is he singing like an incoherent child? That's not in the least bit helpful.'

Freddie ignored her. 'I love your song, Stangnam. What's the next verse?'

'That's easy,' he chimed again:

*'More and more will arrive each day,*
*With sonorance and their drums to play.*
*High to the secret walkways go,*
*Till Isolde and her people know*
*That Gurdee is the King's domain,*
*And forever that way will remain!'*

Ella couldn't help but grin. 'Who knew that Stangnam was a singer-songwriter?'

Isolde launched herself forwards, quite without warning, and grabbed Stangnam by his collar. 'What do you mean, "the secret walkways"?'

'That's easy,' Stangnam chuckled:

*'The sky-high walkways we will climb,*
*Along to...'*

A spine-chilling yell from outside shut him up and startled them all.

# CHAPTER 22

# NOT YOUR AVERAGE TUG OF WAR

Isolde rushed to the door of the Jumblehut to listen. 'Watch *him*,' she hissed, gesturing towards Stangnam.

Ella and Freddie stood over the soldier, pointing their trombolino and melodonk in his face. Ursula tilted her head to listen to the intense fragments of singing and shouting that flew across the hanging village outside.

'It's one of those messages they call to each other,' Freddie said.

Ursula raised her arm. 'Sh!'

Isolde cupped her hand around her mouth and sang a message back across Gurdee, her voice laced with palpable fear. She grabbed a tatty cloth bag and began stuffing any weapons she could find into it. 'We're surrounded, so we—' She paused, the words stuck in the back of her throat. 'So we have to get out of Gurdee. There's only one escape route, beyond Twangbuzzer Hall, but Jacopo and the others can't hold it for long.' Angry tears started streaming down her cheeks. 'I hoped this day would never come.' She fired a fierce glance at Ella and Freddie. 'I built this settlement from nothing. I've defended it with my life for all these years. And now, just as *you* arrive, Otto's army invades MY Gurdee!'

'Don't look at us!' Freddie said. 'It's not our fault this is happening.' He turned to Ella, and murmured, 'Is it?'

Ella shook her head. 'Of course not, although… us being here probably didn't *help* much.'

Isolde appeared not to hear. 'There's no other choice but to flee. I would die before being that *Earthian's* prisoner!'

Yet again, Ella was reminded that this entire war was caused by one space mission, twenty-five years ago, when the Crinkle siblings, desperate to satisfy their curiosity, landed on a planet that wasn't theirs to land on and changed it forever.

Isolde beckoned Ursula and Mirabelle over to her and hugged them. 'I'm so sorry it's come to this,' she whispered through her tears. 'We will keep up the fight, I promise.' She wiped her eyes and ushered everyone towards the Jumblehut door. 'Come on.'

A tree trunk crashed through the roof, narrowly missing Ella's head.

'WHOA!' Ella cried, her trombolino flying out of her hand and taking Freddie's melodonk with it. 'Watch out!'

The splintered chunk of wood lodged itself between Stangnam and the others, and the walls of the hut creaked, its floorboards snapping underfoot.

'GET OUT OF HERE!' screamed Isolde, scooping up the trombolino and melodonk and shoving them into her bag.

Ella ducked under a beam and ran out of the hut after Freddie and the others. She looked over her shoulder, only to see a swarm of Stradbow soldiers rushing along the high walkways and swinging down through the trees on long ropes. Stangnam yelled for help from inside the Jumblehut.

Ahead, Isolde, Mirabelle and Ursula navigated effortlessly through the hanging village towards Twangbuzzer Hall, climbing rope ladders and leaping between platforms without a second thought.

'It's like an assault course,' Ella said to Freddie, 'but higher off the ground! How are we going to keep up?'

'By now, I thought you'd be able to answer that question!' Freddie panted.

'Oh, yeah – sonorance!'

She chuckled before very nearly tumbling over the edge of a walkway that turned sharply in front of her. Regaining her balance just in time, she stomped hard and soared into the air, reaching out for a rope ladder she was sure she could grab before the ground caught up with her.

The ladder was too far away...

She would never make it…

In a flash of sonorance inspiration, she clapped her hands as fast as she could to try and catch the ladder's attention, just like she had done with Freddie yesterday on the edge of Crumhorn Forest. She only had a second or two, but it was better than plummeting to the ground face-first. She clapped as if it was the last thing she would ever do.

At the last conceivable moment, the lowest rungs of the ladder flicked upwards just enough for her to grab on.

'Good catch!' shouted Freddie from the opposite platform. 'I'll take the long way round, if you don't mind.'

'A sensible idea!' yelled Ella, climbing a few rungs and waiting for the ladder to swing back under the walkway.

It didn't swing back. Instead, it swung further *upwards*, as if being pulled by an invisible force.

'What's happening?' Ella screamed, looking around her from a near-horizontal position.

On the platform behind her, a soldier she vaguely recognised was chanting furiously, arms outstretched, luring the rope ladder towards him. The ladder groaned on its hinges under the force of his sonorance chant.

Freddie turned and sprinted back along the walkway, but a flurry of cannonballs smashed into the wooden slats between him and the soldier. A gaping hole appeared, and Freddie almost fell to the forest floor himself. 'It's the soldier from the Rain Cavern!'

he called over to Ella. 'The one who's been practising his chanting, remember?'

'Yes!'

'He's the one the others were laughing at… about chanting not being real sonorance!'

'It feels pretty real to me right now!' Ella replied. 'And why are you giving me his life history?'

'Well, he's clearly been practising! Although… he really *does* sound like a sheep!'

'Stop talking and do something! The ladder's about to *snap*!'

Without his melodonk, Freddie looked lost for a moment, but then his face lit up as he seemed to think of something. 'Oi, Minor Kazoodle!' he shrieked.

The soldier glanced over, evidently flummoxed that Freddie knew his name. The ladder dropped as his attention was momentarily diverted, but he quickly recovered and continued chanting in his peculiar bleaty voice, albeit with more urgency.

Ella was sure Freddie would try a sonorance leap over the gap to stop Kazoodle, but instead, to her amazement, he planted his feet and started singing. It wasn't exactly a recognisable tune, and the only word he used was 'Yoo-hoo', the same sound Ella's granny used to make when she called across a station platform to catch her attention. Freddie was beckoning the ladder towards him, playing Kazoodle at his own game!

'Yoo-hoo! *Yoo-hoo!* YOOOOO-HOOOOO!' He was relentless, his tone piercing and his arms outstretched, just like Kazoodle's.

NOT YOUR AVERAGE TUG OF WAR

Ella found herself in the middle of an extraordinary sonorance tug of war. Freddie versus Kazoodle. So far, it was an even contest, with her rope ladder tilting one way, then the other. Her grip began to lose strength, and she slipped down to the rung below, then the one below that. It wouldn't be long before the rungs ran out or, worse, the ladder snapped altogether…

She *had* to try something else. She emptied her mind as best she could, considering her perilous predicament, and focused on the rope ladder on the next level down. She started her own 'Yoo-hoo' song, willing the ladder up to her, so she could snatch it if she got close enough.

Kazoodle's chant became yet more frantic, as did Freddie's singing. The sonorance engulfing Ella felt so intense that it was almost unbearable, but remarkably, through this caterwaul of rival spells, her *own* sonorance was working too, and the ladder below edged upwards, defying gravity little by little.

Freddie let out a frustrated groan. 'I can't compete! Kazoodle's chant's too strong!'

One of the ropes of Ella's ladder finally gave up and snapped. She jerked down to one side, only just managing to hang on. With a last gasp of sonorance singing, she swung the lower ladder upwards. 'YOO-HOOOOOO!' It was agonisingly close to her. She reached out, straining every sinew to grab it.

She would have to jump…

The ladder Kazoodle was bewitching finally tore violently off its hinges and flew towards him as fast as a fire bolt.

But Ella was not on the ladder; she was mid-air, lunging for the *other* one.

Her fingers wrapped themselves around the lowest rung, as if in some slow-motion dream, and she found herself swinging under the walkway and up the other side, like a theme-park pirate ship in full swing.

'Ella!' Freddie shouted. His voice was so shrill that it sounded as though he were directly above her…

And indeed he was.

Freddie too was clinging to the ladder, a few rungs up!

'What…?' she started. 'How did…?'

'A sonorance jump, that's how!'

'Talking of which…' As the ladder reached its highest point, Ella roared, 'NOW!' and let go. She soared over Gurdee's brightly coloured border fence and landed in a bouncy patch of ferns, Freddie right behind her.

'OUCH!'

'OWWWW!'

'We *have* to work out a soft-landing spell,' Freddie tutted as they rose gingerly to their feet. 'At least we made it.'

They stumbled through the trees and at last found a path leading away from Gurdee. Isolde met them on the edge of the forest. Ella was relieved to see Jacopo, Mirabelle and Ursula with her.

'Were you followed?' Isolde said in a frenzy. Her whole being shook as she spoke. 'Answer me!'

'I… I don't think so,' said Ella.

Another group of Gurdee soldiers emerged, having made it away from the battle. More arrived a minute later.

'Sonorance is our only hope now,' said Isolde, pacing up and down among her followers. 'Gurdee's overrun, most of my people are captured. We have nowhere to go... except the Rain Cavern.'

She knelt down in front of Ella and Freddie, settling herself at their eye level. 'I know I've not given you two the friendliest welcome, and for that, I am sorry. But now I need you – *we* need you. Otherwise, everything we've built is lost. Otherwise... that *scoundrum* Otto will be King of us all!' She placed a hand on Ella's shoulder and the other on Freddie's. 'Will you lead us to the Rain Cavern? Please?'

For some reason, the image of Aunt Belinda trapped alone in that horrible dungeon in Stradbow forced its way into Ella's mind. 'Of course we will,' she said, seeing the desperation in Isolde's eyes, and in those of her followers. 'But Freddie and I could *really* use some help rescuing my aunt.' Her words were slow and her voice deliberate. 'Can you help us?'

Freddie grinned at her in apparent approval; here was twelve-year-old Ella, holding her own against the revered leader of Gurdee.

Isolde nodded. 'I will try...'

'Try...?' Freddie began, but Ella stopped him before he got going, knowing that this was as good as it would get from Isolde. The situation was desperate enough without pushing her over the edge completely.

Isolde glanced around her. 'Some of my closest

advisors are missing. Has anybody seen Scarp?' The group shook their heads. She asked after a few other people too, but there was no sign of them either. 'We don't have our galops,' she added, 'so we'll have to travel on foot. Let's go.'

With that, she strode to the head of the gathering and marched out of Libera Forest.

# CHAPTER 23

# WHAT OTHER COLOUR?

Isolde led everyone confidently across the plain. They dashed through shallow valleys and up over grassy banks, and little by little, the border of the imposing Crumhorn Forest edged closer. With every step, Ella felt more drawn to the trees and to the Rain Cavern nestled deep inside. The cave's perpetual drum pattern seemed to bounce around in her chest, calling her back with irresistible intensity. She knew Freddie would be feeling the same, having been soaked in the magical water of the fountain just yesterday.

In the final hollow before the trees began, Isolde looked around at her followers. 'I can see you're all weary,' she said. 'We'll rest here a moment.' She turned to Ella and Freddie and gave them back their trombolino and melodonk. 'You two will lead us to the Rain Cavern. But first, we eat.' Her face softened, and she almost managed a smile. She signalled for her grumpy, bushy-moustached advisor, Figaroon, to give each of them a couple of biscuits, and he reluctantly agreed.

'Thanks,' said Freddie, sitting down and examining the tiny replica of a musical instrument. 'Even the *snacks* on Drumendus are musical!'

Ella crunched into her biscuit and smirked. The sound of a simple bite seemed to echo around her mouth with far greater importance that it should have done. She leaned back on the grass and stretched out her tired limbs.

'How long have we been here?' said Freddie, joining her and staring up at the purple sky. 'I've lost all track of time.'

Ella counted on her fingers. 'One night on the Hammerklav, one night in Dingringer Hall, one night in the Plectrumm Palace dungeon and one night in the Jumblehut.'

'Do you think we'll sleep anywhere that doesn't have a random name?' Freddie chuckled.

'Nope.'

'This whole thing's completely crazy, if you ask me. A few days ago, I was doing a school quiz about the Singles Charts, and *now* I'm stuck on Drumendus with my best friend, trying to rescue my neighbour from her brother, who happens to be a power-hungry baddie – no offence to your Uncle Otto, by the way.'

Now it was Ella's turn to chuckle. 'None taken.'

A flash of purple lightning crackled through the sky, and Freddie sat up abruptly. 'Ella, will we ever get home?' he said.

Leaning on her elbows, she replied, 'That's up to us.'

The travellers gathered up their things and made their way into Crumhorn Forest. The lure of the Rain Cavern was so great that Ella instinctively knew the way; she could simply put one foot in front of the other, and sooner or later, they would arrive. Under the gloom of the canopy, the atmosphere intensified, and the group twitched at every branch that moved and every twig that cracked underfoot. Deeper and deeper they ventured into the forest, through thick undergrowth and steep cuttings.

'Is this really the way?' said Isolde, her face distrustful.

'Yes,' said Ella. 'We're close now.'

'How can you be sure?'

'I can *feel* it. The sonorance is so strong here that I'm actually shaking. Look.' She held out her trembling hand for all to see. 'Sonorance is part of me now, and I *have* to answer its call.' She hesitated and shook her head. 'It's… it's impossible to explain.'

'I'm glad it's not just me, then,' Freddie beamed. 'But you'll all feel it too when you get sonorance. I mean, *if* you get it, that is…'

Ella stopped and pointed to a gap in the trees that led down to a shallow ravine. 'Over there!' she whispered. The mysterious carved entrance materialised through the branches, and the same mystical purple shimmer hung in the air. Ella felt like laughing and crying at the same time. 'The most *amazing* place in the universe,' she said to herself, struggling to control the bizarre mix of emotions inside her.

She could sense that Isolde and the others were also utterly transfixed by this awe-inspiring corner of Crumhorn Forest, watching, listening, taking it all in.

'Where are the guards?' Freddie said, his voice hushed.

Ella frowned wryly. 'Taking over Gurdee, of course...'

Without warning, Isolde shook herself out of her trance and gave the signal to advance down to the cave. 'Hurry!'

'Wait!' said Ella, unable to stop her in time. 'There'll be soldiers in there... be careful. WAIT!'

Isolde tore through the scattered bushes and brushwood as if they weren't there and sprinted across the misty clearing at the foot of the slope. After a moment of hesitation, and a fearful look to each other, her loyal followers rushed after her. They pinned themselves against the stone wall by the entrance.

'WHO'S THERE?' someone boomed from the mouth of the cave.

'Uh-oh,' Ella muttered, as a group of stripy-uniformed soldiers stormed outside, Majors Squeelo and Castanex among them. 'They must've heard Isolde.'

The soldiers fanned out in the clearing and scoured the forest.

'The Earthians!' bellowed Squeelo, spotting Ella

and Freddie straight away. 'SEIZE THEM!'

'NOW!' Isolde yelled.

The Gurdee rebels leapt out of the shadows and ambushed their opponents, then disappeared into the darkness of the Rain Cavern.

'AFTER THEM!' Squeelo spluttered, and a few disoriented guards staggered to their feet and rushed inside. 'The Earthians are *mine*.'

Ella tugged at Freddie's sleeve. 'We need to go, *right now*.'

'But... Isolde... the Gurdee folks... we need their help to rescue—'

'*Forget* it, Freddie! Squeelo's coming for us... and Castanex.'

Without looking back, they sprinted up the slope and stamped hard, soaring into a tree and landing clumsily in the densely packed branches. The haunting sound of speed sonorance echoed below them as Squeelo and Castanex rushed from tree to tree, desperately searching for their prey.

'Zzzzmmmm... Zzzzmmmm...'

'This is so creepy,' Freddie mouthed.

Ella nodded and peered down between the branches, her spine tingling. Eerie trails of wispy purple smoke crisscrossed the forest floor where Squeelo and Castanex had run.

After what seemed like an age hiding in the same cramped spot, they eventually heard Squeelo order, 'Back to the cave!'

Ella turned to her best friend. 'Looks like it's just you and me – again.'

Freddie shrugged, his expression tired but determined. 'Looks like it – much as we try to build our team!'

'To Stradbow?'

'To Stradbow.' Freddie climbed as high as he dared and scanned the surroundings. 'That way,' he pointed.

They shinned down the tree and made their way to the edge of Crumhorn Forest, checking around them at every step. Once on the plain, they charged to Stradbow with a flurry of sonorance stamps. It was utterly exhilarating; Ella was sure she'd *never* get used to the feeling of flying. They even tried some *zzzzmmmm* sounds for speed sonorance, but it was much more difficult than it looked to get their legs to cooperate, and they collapsed in a heap more often than not.

Nearing the mighty city walls, they watched as groups of soldiers came and went, and galops and carts streamed in and out of the gate. As one cart passed, they hopped inside and attempted to hide under a pile of blankets but instead became tangled up in them like a pair of oversized sausage rolls.

The driver turned around and shrieked. 'Earthian children!' he said. 'So the rumours are true—'

Freddie put his finger to his lips. 'Sh, sh, shhhhhhhh!' His sounds were deliberate and rhythmic.

Ella joined in, her attention fixed firmly on the hapless man. 'Sh, sh, shhhhhhhh! Sh, sh, shhhhhhhh!'

The driver opened his mouth to protest, but nothing came out. He tried again, but all he managed was a head shake and an expression that resembled a confused goldfish. Ella and Freddie were stopping him talking with their sonorance *shushing*! Ella gestured for him to look ahead and steer the cart as normal through the gates. She then hid back under the blankets alongside Freddie and continued to shush quietly.

Once inside Stradbow, the cart seemed to speed up.

Freddie kneeled up. 'Hey! What are you doing?'

The driver swerved his galop into a bumpy patch of road, and Freddie lost his balance and tumbled out of the cart, taking Ella with him, still wrapped in a blanket. 'Leave me alone!' the driver eventually blurted, rounding a corner out of sight.

'How rude!' said Freddie, brushing the dirt off his arms. 'We were only hitching a lift.'

Ella adjusted her tunic and stood up. '*And* stopping him speaking, to be fair. Can't have been much fun! Anyway, we got into Stradbow. Let's get up to Plectrumm Palace.'

'Wait…'

'What is it?'

'Something's… different. I can't work it out.'

Ella looked up and down the street, then at the buildings around her. 'It's the silence.'

'Huh?'

'The silence. Remember when we first came here? There was music everywhere. People on every street corner. And now… nothing. Not even Uncle Otto's marvelodrums are beating.'

'Maybe everyone's been told to stay indoors because there are Earthian children on the loose!'

'Yeah, 'cos we're such scary fugitives…'

They darted along the deserted roads in the direction of Plectrumm Palace up on the hill, but each alleyway turned a corner and veered off course. Again and again it happened, and their frustration grew as the Palace remained very much out of reach.

Just as they were about to retrace their steps for the hundredth time, something caught Ella's eye. 'I recognise that!' she said, pointing to a giant wall-mounted clock that resembled a tambourine. 'That's the music-shop street.'

Freddie smiled. 'Oh, yeah, the Hubbub! Hmm, not much of a hubbub now – there's no-one here.'

'Let's ask Mandoleena how to get to the Palace, if she's there. Come on!'

The Hubbub felt completely different without the bustle of people and the jam-packed pavement displays outside each music shop. Mandoleena's Musical Wonderland looked even more shabby than last time, and the crooked sign hung yet more precariously above the entrance.

Ella pushed against the door, half expecting it to be locked.

'Ah, do come in, Earthians,' came Mandoleena's voice as the door creaked open. 'Nice to hear you again.'

Ella grinned in astonishment. How could Mandoleena know it was them?

The old lady shuffled into view. 'You've been running again, just like last time!'

'Er... yeah, we have,' Ella said. Did this lady remember *everything*?

'You two are the most wanted people on Drumendus. I'd get in such trouble if the King knew you were here. You shouldn't stay long.'

'Oh, we don't mean to—' Ella started.

'I'm too old for all this, I suppose,' Mandoleena said, waving away Ella's concerns. 'And I'm *far* too old for all these parades.'

'What parades?'

'King Otto is having yet *another* one at Plectrumm Palace. Everybody's gone up there – that's why the streets are deserted. Oh, how the King *loves* reminding us how powerful he is. At least he stops those wretched marvelodrums, so he can make his speeches and address his adoring public.' She turned away and busied herself with what looked like a pile of socks.

'What are they?' Ella said.

'Whirlsocks. They're just toys, really. Please, take one each.'

'Oh, we don't have any Stradbow money – or whatever you call it.'

'They're gifts, my dears.'

'Oh – thank you!' Ella turned the whirlsock over in her fingers. A small stone was tucked inside. 'Er... how does it work?'

'It's quite simple: you whizz it around your head. It makes quite the whooshing noise through the air at full speed. Now, what has led you to my shop, of all places? Are you lost?'

'Yes, actually,' Ella said. 'We're trying to get to the Palace, but the roads are all too higgledy-piggledy. We can't get anywhere near!'

Mandoleena chuckled. 'Stradbow has a knack of doing that to people. I'm afraid I cannot help you *directly*; that would be going against my King.'

Ella felt her heart sinking.

'But do let me sing you a line from a song I composed myself, to cheer you up.'

Frowning, Ella said, 'Oh, you really don't have t—'
'It goes:

*The colour purple fills the sky; what other colour meets the eye?'*

'Er… thanks,' said Ella. 'That was—'
'Off you go, then,' Mandoleena interrupted, ushering them out onto the street. 'The *road* awaits.'

She disappeared back into the shop and clinked the door shut behind her.

'What was she on about?' said Freddie.

Ella shrugged. '*What other colour meets the eye?*' she repeated a few times. 'There are loads of colours everywhere.' She stared along the street, thinking as hard as she could.

'*The road awaits…*' Freddie pondered. 'What could she mea—'

'There!' Ella yelled, making Freddie jump.
'What? Where?'

'I've been staring at it the whole time! Look down. *What other colour meets the eye?*' Before Freddie could answer, she blurted out, 'The red stone built into the road! There's another one there... and there!'

'Oh, yeah!' Freddie said. 'How did we miss them?'

'We follow the stones to get to Plectrumm Palace – that must be it! Worth a try, at least.'

In a fit of excitement, Freddie swung his new whirlsock over his head.

Ella looked on in bewilderment as the whirlsock whirred into life. 'Freddie – you seem... taller!'

He glanced downwards. 'Er... that may be because my feet are off the ground!'

'I think you've found our soft-landing sonorance!' She tried it herself and floated a few feet off the ground, landing with a graceful knee bend. 'I feel like Mary Poppins – all I need is an umbrella!'

They scurried through the empty streets of Stradbow, following the red stones like a couple of eager detectives. A few minutes later, the magnificently decorated golden gates leading into the Palace neighbourhood came into view, complete with stripy-uniformed soldiers ambling up and down in front of them.

'Open up!' yelled a bearish voice behind them. 'Make way!'

The gates swung open, and the guards moved aside.

Ella's jaw dropped as she saw what was being wheeled towards them.

## CHAPTER 24
# A VERY SPECIAL GUEST

'The Hammerklav!' Ella gasped, pulling Freddie into the shadows. 'Here, in Stradbow?'

'Mozart's mittens!' said Freddie, a confused look flashing across his face. 'I mean… unbelievable!'

Sure enough, Aunt Belinda's most successful invention, her beloved grand-piano-shaped spaceship, was being hauled up the hill towards Plectrumm Palace on a huge wheeled platform. It looked in surprisingly good condition, considering the battering it had taken on the voyage from Earth, with just a few scorch marks on the lower panels and a small emergency hatch hanging open at its base. Further down the road, a procession of carts followed, each carrying important-looking soldiers and citizens, dressed in their most ostentatious outfits.

'This must be the parade Mandoleena was telling us about,' Freddie whispered. 'But how did they find the Hammerklav?'

'Aunt Belinda must have told Uncle Otto.'

'Or was forced to tell him...'

Ella felt an uncomfortable jolt in her chest. How *had* Uncle Otto treated her aunt? What was he capable of? From what Ella had seen of his unpredictable behaviour, it didn't look too promising. 'We *have* to get Aunt Belinda out of the Palace,' she said. 'But how are we—'

'Watch out!' Freddie interrupted as the edges of the enormous wheels scraped along the walls of the narrow alleyway. 'It's coming straight for us.' He scrambled onto the platform and made for the Hammerklav's open hatch. 'Come on, Ella, or you'll be crushed... or worse, you'll be *seen*!'

'Not sure I follow your logic,' she muttered, following her friend reluctantly onto the platform. She pulled herself through the hatch into the spaceship, a split second before the alley opened out again towards the gates. 'That was close...'

They sat back to back as their eyes slowly adjusted to the darkness of the cabin. Everything looked the same; Uncle Otto must have forbidden anyone to go inside.

'I wasn't sure we'd ever see in here again,' Ella said, 'I mean, if... the rescue plan... went wrong...'

Freddie tapped her on the hand. 'We don't *have* a

rescue plan, Ella,' he said. 'How could it go wrong?' Yet again, Freddie had lifted her spirits, as only *he* could, despite their stay on Drumendus feeling ever more perilous.

They peered out of the smudged cockpit window. The crowds lining the hill up to Plectrumm Palace erupted in cheers and chanting as the Hammerklav rattled past on its platform. Eventually, it came to a halt alongside the towering marvelodrums. Uncle Otto himself appeared on a terrace high above them, in the shadow of the spectacular Palace. There he was, Ella's uncle, dressed in robes and a crown. He raised his arms to greet the crowds, who whooped and clapped and broke into song, their ears glowing as violet as ever.

*'Oh, there's no King like Otto,*
*That's our motto!*
*A blessing for Drumendus,*
*He really is stupendous!*
*Both powerful and kind,*
*He rules with us in mind,*
*He is the greatest King,*
*To him we proudly sing!'*

'I bet Otto wrote that himself,' sneered Freddie. 'Honestly. *Kind?* If he's kind, then I'm a glockenspiel!'

*'Oh, King Otto does amaze,*
*His spirit is ablaze!*
*His music and his parties...'*

'What, *another* verse?' Freddie said.

As the lengthy tribute came to a raucous end, Uncle Otto lifted his arms again, this time to quell the self-congratulatory cheers. When all was silent, a nearby guard stepped forward and presented him a drum beater on a cushion. Uncle Otto lifted it above his head and threw it at one of the marvelodrums with a fearsome 'Yaaah!'. It spun through the air and hurtled into the heart of the gigantic drumhead. A burst of coiled lightning crackled into the sky above Stradbow, then exploded in the clouds like New Year fireworks, throwing the crowd into yet another adoring frenzy.

'That's a new one, lightning fireworks,' said Freddie, shaking his head. 'Your uncle does love being dramatic, doesn't he?'

A shadowy figure was led out of the Palace, shoulders hunched and head bowed, as if the *last* thing they wanted was to be standing in front of thousands of people.

'May I present a *very* special guest!' Uncle Otto said, swaggering around the timid-looking figure. 'A close family member, in fact.' He guided the figure to the edge of the terrace. 'My sister, Belinda! FROM EARTH!'

Ella tried to speak but simply spluttered instead.

Aunt Belinda…? Up there…? She looked like a helpless slave being exhibited to a baying crowd. What was Uncle Otto thinking?

The masses cheered again, and some clapped a complex rhythm. To Ella's surprise, Aunt Belinda herself raised a hand and gestured for them to be quiet. They responded in an instant, clearly curious to hear what she had to say… as was Ella herself.

'Well, er… hello, everyone,' she started in her usual unassuming manner, her unkempt hair blowing around in the breeze. 'This is all rather… unexpected. As you've no doubt heard by now, I flew to Drumendus in a spaceship.' She pointed down to the Hammerklav. 'That one there, in fact.' Ella instinctively ducked, even though she knew she was too far away to be spotted. 'We landed miles away from Stradbow, but my brother's soldiers found the spaceship and pulled it here.'

'You see?' gloated Uncle Otto, wafting his robe around as he paced the terrace. 'You see what *Earthians* are capable of? We can build machines that fly through space and visit other planets. To those of you who *still* doubt how I got here twenty-five years ago, this is all the proof I'll ever need.'

A rather more muted cheer rippled through the onlookers, and Uncle Otto nodded for Aunt Belinda to carry on.

'My niece came along for the ride, and her friend,' she said. 'They're not here… at the moment—'

'*Ella* and *Freddie* are their names,' interrupted Uncle Otto, his voice turning edgy with irritation, 'and they *must* be brought back to me – as soon as possible. I'm sure we will *all* help to bring them in safely.' He cast his eye over the now-silent crowd and glared at the groups of soldiers dotted around, who looked back sheepishly. 'They cannot go missing *again*,' he growled.

'I do hope Ella and Freddie are okay,' Aunt Belinda continued. 'I know they've had quite an adventure since arriving here, then escaping, then...' Uncle Otto whispered something at her, and she added, 'Ah yes, yes, I'll get on with it. Now, I came here to rescue Otto and take him back to Earth.' Hushed tones of intrigue spread around the crowd. 'But finding out that he's King changed those plans somewhat.' She attempted a laugh, but no-one responded. 'So Otto's staying put, you'll be pleased to hear, and...' She glanced at her brother. 'And... I have decided to continue *my* adventure and... stay on Drumendus!'

She raised her arms in an awkward gesture of triumph, and a look of genuine joy crossed Uncle Otto's face. He grabbed another drumstick from an unsuspecting guard and hurled it down at the marvelodrum next to the Hammerklav with a 'Yaaah!'. Once again, the drum released a twirling flash of light skywards over the delighted Stradbow gathering.

Ella slumped to the floor of the Hammerklav. She was numb all over, apart from her legs, which had resorted to their familiar tremble. She hardly heard the celebrations outside. Her mouth was dry and her throat choked up. She looked at Freddie, who seemed equally stunned. After a moment, she managed, with a shudder, 'Aunt Belinda... staying on... *Drumendus*?'

'That's what she said. I'm sorry, Ella.'

'But... it can't be true? It just... can't!' She clasped her hands together and rubbed her fingers, as if trying to warm them up even though they weren't cold. 'What about the rescue…? What about… our *life* back home?'

'Ella—'

'*What about—*'

'ELLA! Stop it, or I'll… I'll use my melodonk on you! Okay?'

Freddie's threat was unintentionally comedic enough to snap her out of her growing agitation. 'Sorry,' she muttered. 'I just—'

Uncle Otto's gloating voice rang out from the terrace. 'A new era is beginning in Stradbow, with my sister by my side. And… I have saved the best news till last.' He allowed the silence to linger for an uncomfortably long time before declaiming, 'My soldiers have captured Gurdee! The last rebel stronghold is ours!'

The rapturous crowd roared in delight yet again.

Freddie tutted in disgust. 'How convenient. He's missed out the part about Isolde and the others escaping to the Rain Cavern. Unless he doesn't know, of course…'

Ella wasn't listening. She stared up at her aunt in the distance, still in utter disbelief about her staying on Drumendus.

Just as Uncle Otto reached a final crescendo in his victory speech, lapping up the glory until he was full to the brim, Aunt Belinda tapped him on the arm and said, 'May I add another word or two?'

Uncle Otto tried to shoo her away, but she was having none of it. 'If you must,' he snapped, 'but keep it brief. I'm peckish.'

Aunt Belinda stepped to the edge of the terrace. 'Ella and Freddie, if you are hiding down there somewhere, do come and join us in the Palace.' She cleared her throat as if trying to hide the emotion building up in her voice. 'It's up to you. The power is quite literally at your fingertips.'

Uncle Otto stepped in front of his sister as a scattering of confused whispers swept through the crowd. 'Yes, well, thank you, Belinda, that's all very enlightening,' he said. 'Time to go.'

Two guards hastily ushered her back towards the Palace, and the bumptious Uncle Otto extracted one last cheer from the crowd before striding off looking self-satisfied. Everyone dispersed, and the eager chatter faded away as families returned to their homes, workers to their shops and music groups to their rehearsals. Three soldiers took up position at the base of the Hammerklav platform, looking as bored as ever once the streets had emptied.

Ella couldn't contain the fury rushing through her. 'I just don't buy it,' she spat.

'Buy what?'

'Uncle Otto *made* Aunt Belinda do this. She'd never *choose* to stay! He's persuaded her.'

'Well, whatever happened up there,' Freddie said, 'it's our job to *un*-persuade her.'

'How, exactly?'

'By getting into the Palace and getting her *out* of it, before it's too late.'

'Like I said, *how* exactly?'

'I need to think, Ella! And maybe you could too, that would be helpful…'

Ella's mind surged from one vexed thought to another. How could she and Freddie possibly get out of this mess? She tried to breathe but ended up simply huffing and puffing, which she knew would irritate Freddie no end. Fiddling with one of the Hammerklav's many levers, she muttered, for no apparent reason, 'Stupid spaceship.'

'Don't take it out on the Hammerklav,' Freddie said.

'*Who*, then?'

Freddie knelt down by the semi-open hatch door. 'Who do we know who loves exploring Plectrumm Palace more than anything?'

It took Ella a second to remember. 'Seren… and Ade?'

'Exactly. The twins say they know every corridor and every secret passageway. With them, we'll find Belinda in no time.'

'*And* we know where they live!' Ella said. They nodded at each other and prepared to leave the Hammerklav. 'Ready?'

'Ready.'

# CHAPTER 25
# A PIGGY'S BACK?

Ella and Freddie poked their heads through the hatch of the Hammerklav until it was safe to jump out. The guards traipsed up and down with barely a glance towards Uncle Otto's new showpiece; they chose instead to sing to each other and make jokes about strumalot players. It was all too easy for Ella and Freddie to slip away unnoticed, without giving sonorance a second thought.

'Let's follow the Palace walls,' Ella said, sprinting away from the Hammerklav. 'That should lead us to Seren and Ade's place—'

Four singers appeared out of nowhere, laughing as they brushed past. They were so engrossed in their song that they didn't even notice the pair of startled Earthians.

Ella watched as they danced out of sight. 'It *is* kind of cool here, don't you think?' she said. 'Despite everything?'

'Don't go falling in love with Stradbow, will you, Ella?' Freddie said, pulling her behind a cart as another group of carefree musicians wandered by, playing tunes to each other, as if in conversation. 'We don't have time for that!'

'I know, but… all the sounds, the playing, the singing… it's part of *life* here!'

'*Life* is exactly what you're risking if you don't snap out of it. Come on!'

They continued around the edge of the Palace walls until they reached the imposing building that housed the soldiers' families. It soared upwards towards the purple clouds, with dozens of identical entrances neatly lined up along the road.

'We'll never find Seren and Ade in there!' Freddie moaned.

Ella cast her mind back to their first encounter with the daredevil twins. 'Wasn't there a song they sang about getting to their living quarters?'

'Oh, yeah.'

'How did it go again?'

'Don't ask me! That feels like a million years ago.'

Ella strained her memory to try and recall a few fragments at least. Ade's enthusiastic vocal efforts had stuck in her mind much more vividly than the song itself. 'There were numbers in the lyrics, weren't there?'

Freddie's mind seemed to click into gear. 'Yes! The fourth *door* and the third *floor*, that's it!'

They dashed over to the correct door and slid through it. Inside the chilly entrance hall, they tiptoed up a spiral staircase to the third floor.

'*Down the second corridor,*' said Freddie, leading the way, 'then—'

'*First left, home!*' shouted a voice over their shoulder.

Ella felt herself being pulled backwards into a room, and she toppled to the floor in a heap alongside Freddie.

The door slammed shut. A figure stood over them.

'Ella! Freddie!' said Ade. 'You remembered our song!'

Freddie glared up at him. 'No need to grab us like that!'

Seren appeared and helped them to their feet. 'You came back!' she said. 'The prized possessions of Stradbow! Finally, some *excitement*. We've been banned from leaving home.'

'Banned?'

'Yes. Ever since we helped you escape from Plectrumm Palace. King Otto was *furious*. And so was Father.'

'Grounded on Drumendus,' Freddie chortled. 'Who knew that was a thing here?'

'What's *grounded*?'

'Oh – never mind,' said Ella. '*Anyway*, first of all – thanks for trying to help us escape from the dungeon yesterday. And *second* of all… we need your help… again.'

'I was hoping you'd say that,' said Ade, his voice squeaking in delight. 'It's been so *boring* around here! What can we do?'

'You can show us the way to the dungeon, where we'll rescue my Aunt Belinda – simple as that.'

'She won't be in the dungeon! She's the King's *honoured* guest now; she'll be in the special rooms behind the Pyramidee Stage.'

'The *what*?'

'The Pyramidee Stage – it's one of the concert stages outside the Palace. The King's guest rooms look out onto it… I shouldn't know that, of course.' There was such joy and pride in everything Ade said that Ella couldn't help but smile.

'This *rescue* of yours,' Seren said to Ella, her eyes full of intrigue. 'Will it involve your… sonorance?'

'Sonorance!' Ade echoed, barely able to contain himself.

Ella beamed. 'I'm twelve years old, and I have magic powers – what do *you* think?'

The four of them laughed and sat down in a circle to plan the rescue mission. Ade threw around farfetched ideas until his imagination had run dry, and he sang snippets of songs and rhymes that made little sense to Ella and Freddie. At one point, he even reeled off a list of important 'landmarks' in the Palace to look out for, including a painted gong and a wall of old portraits. Seren kept reminding them that their father, Major Chirrupp, would be home for lunch soon, as would hundreds of other soldiers in the building, so it was a huge risk going out into the corridor, let alone back out onto the street. After a bite to eat to calm rumbling stomachs, they settled on something resembling a plan, with high-fives all round, much to the twins' bemusement.

The plan went wrong in seconds.

'Hello!' a woman's voice called from the entrance hall.

'It's Mother,' Ade rasped. 'She should be at choir practice!'

Seren ushered Ella and Freddie behind the door.

'What are we going to do?' Ade whispered in fright.

'Erm… Sing something,' said Ella, surprised at her own quick thinking. 'Freddie and I'll do the rest!'

The twins' mother walked in and dumped some baskets of food on the floor. 'My rehearsal was cancelled after the big parade,' she said. 'King Otto's sister was there, and—'

'Mother!' Seren interrupted. 'We have a song for you… if we may?'

'Oh… Yes, alright… that would be… lovely.'

The twins opened their mouths and started singing two completely different tunes, their eyes darting around with uncertainty and alarm.

'Well, that's… an interesting… song,' their mother said, clearly trying to show support for their wayward musical efforts. 'Perhaps you could add some words… after you've worked out the tune, that is?'

From their hiding place, Ella and Freddie joined in, cooing like doves. The sound of the four of them was utterly strange, but the effect was almost instantaneous.

The twins' mother sat down to listen, then yawned and rested her head on a cushion. 'What peaceful… music…' Her eyelids dropped, and she fell fast asleep.

'Incredible!' said Ade. 'I want sonorance!'

'I don't know how long she'll be asleep,' said Ella. She scampered to the window that faced the Palace walls and peered outside. 'Back to our plan. We'll piggyback you over the wall with a sonorance jump, then you lead us through the Palace.'

'Simple!' Seren said.

Ade ran on the spot in excitement. 'I can't wait to fly!'

To Ella's surprise, a concerned look flashed across Freddie's face. 'Can't we think of something else?' he murmured, looking down at two soldiers guarding a gate.

'Such as?'

'I… dunno.'

'Freddie, what's wrong?' Ella said, unable to work out his sudden wariness.

'I'm just… not sure I can jump the distance with someone on my back.'

Whilst it felt strange for Ella see him hesitate like this, she was also reassured to know that even Freddie had the occasional doubt.

She patted him on the arm. 'You totally *can* jump it!' she said, attempting to sound confident. 'Think how high you jumped out on the plain.' He didn't look convinced, but there wasn't time to mull it over. 'By the way,' she added, 'I'm glad it's not just me who worries every now and again!'

Below them on the street, a formation of soldiers marched down the hill, chanting as they went. Their tone was aggressive and their steps purposeful.

One of the guards at the gate walked alongside the last line. 'What's happening?' he said. 'This isn't the normal marching time.'

'A disturbance at the Rain Cavern,' came the gruff reply. 'The rebels are causing trouble again. The King is sending reinforcements, but our unit doesn't even have sonorance – it must be a *big* disturbance.'

'Typical!' the guard said. 'When will those Gurdee tree-dwellers realise they're defeated? I'm sure you'll crush them.'

Ella's mind turned to Isolde and her followers. Had they made it to the main chamber? Did they have sonorance?

Her resolve strengthened, and she smiled to herself. 'Piggyback time.'

She and Freddie crouched down in front of the twins, who climbed on. Ade clasped his arms around Ella's neck so tightly that she struggled to breathe for a moment.

'Careful,' she coughed.

'Sorry!' Ade said. 'I just *love* the word *piggyback*!'

'WHAT IN THE NAME OF DRUMENDUS IS A PIGGY'S BACK?' thundered an ominous voice from the doorway behind them.

# CHAPTER 26
# UP TO A B

Ella and Freddie lurched around, with Seren and Ade clinging to their backs.

'Father!' said Seren.

Major Chirrupp, the twin's rangy father, stomped forwards and pointed. 'What are these two doing in my home?'

'None of your business!' Ade blurted out. 'And by the way, it's not "piggy's back", it's *piggyback*!'

'Careful, young man. This is no time for jokes.'

'I'm not joking! And we're leaving!' He dug his knees into Ella's sides, as if she were a horse that needed giddying up. 'Jump, Ella. Jump out of the window – I want to fly! NOW!'

Chirrupp stepped forwards. 'Oh, no you *don't*. Get down from there!'

'Stay where you are, *Chirrupp!*' snarled Freddie. 'We know sonorance that you couldn't master in a million years!'

The venom of Freddie's outburst clearly caught Chirrupp off guard, and he blundered around the room, reaching for any musical instrument that hung on the wall. 'I... I know sonorance too...' he stammered, unable to unhook a circular contraption. 'Now, how does this thing work again? If I can only remember what to do—'

'He never was good under pressure,' muttered Seren, and Ella almost laughed at Chirrupp's sheer incompetence. How could one of Uncle Otto's top soldiers be so useless?

'Move out of the way, Chirrupp!' boomed *another* voice from the doorway. 'I'll handle this!'

'Mother!' gasped Seren, this time sounding genuinely worried.

The twins' mother shoved Chirrupp to one side and stormed towards the window. 'You four may have outwitted me once with your singing, but you will *not* do it again!'

Before any of them could move, she lunged forwards and grabbed the twins by their tunics. Ella clutched the window frame to keep her balance.

'Get off, Mother!' Ade shouted, struggling against her iron grip. 'We're going on an ADVENTURE!'

'You are *banned* from adventures!' With a final grunt, she yanked the twins away from the window, and the three of them tumbled across the room and landed in a sprawling heap, taking Chirrupp with them.

Seren sat up and yelled at Ella and Freddie, 'Go! Just *go!*'

Ade shook his head, tears forming in his eyes. 'Mother, I can't believe you did that!' he spluttered. 'You are so ANNOYING!'

Freddie clambered back onto the windowsill next to Ella, but behind them, Chirrupp was reaching for anything he could find. His face was beetroot with what must have been both rage *and* embarrassment at his attempts to take control of the situation, and his ears turned a deeper shade of violet by the second. He managed to grab an enormous wooden instrument that had fallen off the wall in the kerfuffle. It must have been carved out of a tree trunk, it was so long, and it curled upwards and opened out at the far end, just like one of those Swiss horns that Ella had seen on a TV advert.

'Father, not the blarehorn!' said Seren, grappling with him on the ground. 'You have no idea how to play it! What are you doing?'

Chirrupp ignored his daughter's pleas and aimed the instrument straight at Ella and Freddie. He took a gigantic breath.

'Jump!' Ella yelled to Freddie. 'JUUUUUMP!'

They stamped their feet as hard as they could and took off out of the window, towards the Palace walls.

*DOOOOOOOOOOOOOOOT!*

The extraordinary force of the blarehorn whipped up the air behind them and launched them high over the walls. The blast was so strong that Ella's arms thrashed about as if she were conducting an invisible orchestra. Groups of Stradbow locals ran into the street to see what was going on.

Then the inevitable descent began. With the Palace roof fast approaching, Ella felt the blood drain out of her face. She couldn't possibly survive *another* plunge to the ground unscathed. Could she?

Through the din of the wind roaring past her ears, she was sure she heard Freddie yell the word *toy*. But why would he be saying 'toy' of all things?

Wait a minute…

TOY! Ella's eyes sprang open, and she plunged her hand into her pocket and pulled out the whirlsock that Mandoleena had given her earlier that day. She raised it over her head and swung it around with every ounce of energy she had, groaning through gritted teeth. The whirlsock whirred into life and slowed the last few metres of her fall like an invisible parachute. She and Freddie skidded down a sloping roof and came to an inelegant stop against a low stone wall.

They lay there, catching their breath, staring up at the oppressive sky.

'Another successful flying attempt on Drumendus,' Ella chuckled.

'We're getting better each time,' Freddie said, standing up and rubbing his wrist. 'But that's not saying much!'

'Thanks for the whirlsock reminder.'

Freddie nodded, and they rushed over the Palace rooftops to a scruffy trapdoor that led into a tower. Without Seren and Ade to guide them, they had no idea where they would end up. Ella racked her brain for clues that the twins had divulged during their vague chat earlier, but the songs Ade had sung about forbidden shortcuts and secret gaps in walls all merged into one blurry mash-up.

They climbed down a rusty ladder into a tall room with three doorways.

'All locked,' Ella said, trying each one. 'Perhaps we should—'

'Stand back,' said Freddie, positioning himself in front of the weakest-looking door.

'Er… what are you—'

'Ya!' Freddie shrieked, sending his best sonorance air kicks and punches towards the door. 'Ya, ya!' The rickety wood panels started to buckle and splinter, and after a final spectacular spinning kick, which wasn't *really* necessary, Freddie had well and truly finished off the innocent door. 'This way,' he said, a proud grin plastered across his face.

Along the next corridor, the faint sound of a choir echoed around the smooth stone walls.

Ella stopped abruptly and tilted her head to listen. 'I'm sure Seren said something about singing in the Palace.'

'Yep,' said Freddie. 'Otto orders a choir to sing whenever he's stressed. The voices calm him down, apparently. I thought Seren was joking!'

'Ha! I bet Uncle Otto doesn't tell many people about that!'

They followed the voices down a flight of stairs and through another door. It was thankfully unlocked, so there was no need for Freddie to deploy his blue-belt skills, much to his obvious annoyance. They crept through the same hall in which Uncle Otto had performed his outlandish sonorance display a couple of days ago. The sound of the choir grew, and the song itself became clearer. It was slow and repetitive but had a haunting quality to it, hypnotic almost.

'Look, there are the paintings Ade told us about,' Ella said softly. 'We must be getting near the guest rooms.'

They scurried to a wall on which dozens of dusty portraits hung. All eyes stared down at them.

'What was that riddle Ade sang to find the secret passage?' said Freddie. 'Something about jumping…'

Ella sighed. 'I wish I'd paid more attention to him…'

The click of a closing door at the other end of the hall startled them both, but when they looked around, there was no-one there.

'Otto's spies,' Freddie said, his tone nervy.

'Hurry up, brain!' Ella muttered to herself. 'What was the riddle?'

'Ah – got it! *Leap up, up, up to a B, then hush!*'

'That's the one! But… what did it mean again?'

They stepped in closer and studied the portraits of Stradbow men and women posing proudly, holding weird and wonderful musical instruments. Incredible names such as Duke Didjeriggle, Countess Croon and Lord Lyricall adorned the golden frames, and the sheer flamboyance of the outfits and hairstyles would have fitted perfectly at the most outrageous fancy-dress party.

The bang of another door closing in the distance echoed around the eerie hall.

'*Up, up, up to a B,*' Ella repeated to herself. 'Why three *ups*…? Maybe… up three portraits!'

They looked up at the third row of paintings, which stretched the entire length of the wall.

'That narrows it down – a bit,' said Freddie, but then he too seemed to have a eureka moment. '*Up to a B!* We need to find names beginning with B.'

Ella smiled. 'Okay. You start that side, I'll start this side. There can't be that many.'

Her optimism didn't take long to wear thin. Most of the portraits on the row began with B. If it wasn't Baron Babbler, it was Baron Barkeroo; if it wasn't Baroness Buzzoffee, it was Baroness Bagpipple. She even counted five Banjojos, all redorker players.

'This is hopeless,' said Freddie, rubbing the back of his neck. 'What are we missing?'

A third door thudded shut somewhere nearby, and the sound of footsteps approached.

'*Then hush,*' Ella whispered. '*Then hush, then hush…*'

Her gaze settled on a painting of a man called Brynnn wearing an old-fashioned top hat and a white tie. A sleepy animal with a fluffy tail sat on his lap. 'Of course! Look at *him.*'

Freddie ran over. 'What about him? Apart from the three Ns at the end of his name, that is.'

'He's not holding an instrument. And he's not singing. He's—'

'*Hushed!*'

'Yep – the only *B* with no sign of music in the portrait.'

Agitated voices rang around the hall.

They stared up at the man in the hat. 'So now, we…?' Freddie started.

'Leap!' said Ella, jumping up and stretching out her arm. Her hand tapped Brynnn plumb on the nose, and before she had even landed back on the ground, the portrait edged its way into the wall. Two large stones moved inwards in front of her, revealing a low entrance. 'We did it!'

Ella felt a chilly breeze on her leg from the secret passage. She crouched down and crawled into the darkness, with Freddie close behind. 'Get your melodonk ready,' she said, taking her trombolino out of her pocket. 'If we're found, we use *everything* we've got, okay? Our instruments, our voices, our clapping, our clicking, our—'

'I get the idea!'

'Whatever it takes to rescue Aunt Belinda and get her out of the Palace and to the Hammerklav and… get her to fly us home and… and…' She stumbled over her words, they poured out so rapidly. 'And…'

'Ella, you're talking faster than "Flight of the Bumblebee"!' Freddie said, then paused and added calmly, 'It's okay to be scared, you know.'

'I know… it's just…'

'I'm scared too.'

'You… you are?'

'Of course, Ella. And d'you know why? Because

I care – just like you.' He smiled kindly, and among the endless barrage of echoey door slams, snippets of choral singing and distant drums, the two of them shared a moment of quiet friendship, there in a cramped, dimly lit secret passage in the heart of Plectrumm Palace. '*And*,' Freddie added, 'I'm worried I may never eat another plate of chips in my life if I'm stuck here forever. That *would* be a disaster. Come on.'

They emerged into the light of a circular hall with many doors leading off it. A grand balcony towered over them at the far end, and a scattering of percussion instruments decorated the walls, with Ella's attention drawn to one in particular.

'The yellow gong!' she said, running over to one of the most imposing instruments she had ever seen. 'Ade said that's next to the guest wing – where Aunt Belinda lives now. Freddie…?'

Freddie stood in the centre of the room, glancing at each door in turn, melodonk at the ready.

'Freddie, what is it?'

'The choir. It's stopped.'

A door swung open, and a scruffy-looking figure wearing red tassel trousers rushed into the room and stood in front of them.

Ella gasped. 'You?'

# CHAPTER 27

# LOYALTY

'Scarp!' blurted Freddie, staring at the man known across Gurdee as one of Isolde's most loyal followers... here in the heart of enemy territory.

'What are you...?' Ella began. 'How did you...?' A hundred questions sprang up in her mind. 'Oh, never mind all that! Let's join forces. We could use your help right now.' She made for the door by the big yellow gong. 'I'll explain on the way. Follow me!' Although she and Scarp hadn't exactly got off to the best start a couple of days ago in Crumhorn Forest, she knew he could be a useful ally in Aunt Belinda's rescue attempt, and against Uncle Otto if need be.

Scarp stood in the middle of the room, his gaunt face cold and expressionless.

'Wait a second,' Ella said, slowly realising that she might have given Scarp too much credit. 'What are you *really* doing here?'

Still Scarp said nothing.

'Don't tell me… *please* don't tell me, you're on… Uncle Otto's side?'

Scarp gave a tiny nod, his face barely readable.

Ella's mind flashed back to the walkway in Gurdee, and the figures she saw running on the forest floor. 'It was *you* helping Uncle Otto's soldiers capture Gurdee!'

Another slow nod.

'I knew I recognised those red trousers! Who else would wear *them*?'

Scarp's left eyebrow flickered, but otherwise there was still no real reaction.

Ella felt the rage building inside her. Her mind again returned to Gurdee. What was it Isolde had said outside the Jumblehut?

'*Otto's soldiers know where to attack, they know our traps, they know our weapons… They are a step ahead…*'

'It all makes sense now!' she yelled. '*You* showed them the secret walkways, that *you* made.'

'I knew you were shifty from the moment I saw you,' Freddie growled, his chin jutting forwards as he spoke. 'But not… a traitor!'

'No wonder Gurdee was lost,' Ella said. 'That was all *you*, Scarp?'

'Yes, it was ALL Scarp!' a familiar voice boomed across the hall. Ella and Freddie whipped around to see Uncle Otto standing on the balcony. He strolled forwards and placed his hands on the rail, a knowing grin etched on his face. 'Scarp is one of my best spies. He tells me everything I need to know.'

'But… but… why?' Ella struggled.

'I offered him the chance to *be* somebody. To be respected. To be heard. Not hiding in the Gurdee trees like an outcast in his own home, with only Isolde giving him the time of day. No. Scarp deserves better than that. And here in Stradbow, with *me*, that's exactly what he gets.'

'Don't pretend you care about him!' Freddie raged. 'He's just part of your Gurdee power grab. And anyway… can't he speak for himself? It's pathetic!'

'Some people talk very little, Freddie. *Some* people talk too much.' They stared at each other for an unnervingly long time. 'Time to stop your silly games – whatever they are.' Ella and Freddie stood shoulder to shoulder, their glances darting between Uncle Otto and Scarp. 'And Freddie, you must control your urge to break things. Like doors, for example.'

'What? You… you know about that?'

Uncle Otto's smirk returned. 'Of course. My people have tracked your every step since you and Ella landed on the north roof.'

Freddie visibly shuddered at the thought of the Palace guards watching them this whole time, a step ahead, yet always unseen. The twins had warned them, but it didn't make it any less creepy.

Yet again, Ella realised that Uncle Otto was more powerful and cunning than she could ever imagine.

And here *she* was, a trombone-playing schoolgirl from Belton-on-Snare, trying to mount a rescue on the King's own doorstep!

'Scarp,' Uncle Otto said, 'now's your chance to show me your sonorance when it *really* matters.'

'He has sonorance too?' Freddie groaned.

'He does *now* – thanks to you two, in fact.'

'Us?'

'Yes. He had no idea where the Rain Cavern was until he followed you through Crumhorn Forest. After he saw it, how could I refuse him access? And besides, how else should I reward my most *loyal* Gurdee spy?' The way he emphasised the word *loyal* was sickening. He clearly knew that loyalty was what *Isolde* valued most about Scarp. 'Nobody in Gurdee knows of Scarp's sonorance. But he's been practising night and day... as you are about to find out.'

Scarp stepped forwards, his face finally changing to a look of steely determination, his eyes as wide as an owl's. Reaching inside his waistcoat pocket, he pulled out what looked like an organ pipe. Sharp wooden spikes dangled down from it on thin pieces of rope.

Ella felt as though her breath had been stolen from her. Scarp was now more than just a spy and a traitor: he was the enemy, on the brink of attack. What kind of sonorance would he unleash, and what would she and Freddie do to defend themselves?

They stood across the hall from each other, motionless. Ella realised she could sense the sonorance of everyone around her, as if those who possessed it were bound together by the magic itself.

'Neutralise the children, Scarp,' Uncle Otto ordered from the balcony.

In the moment Ella took to muster up the nerve to take on Scarp, Freddie had already jumped in front of her, yelling, 'Nobody *neutralises* us, thank you very much!' With a plucky smile, he looked over his shoulder and said to Ella, 'Whatever it takes, remember?'

Turning back to Scarp, he fired off a combination of air punches, and Ella joined in with a few of her own, as well as some trusty trombolino blasts.

They were no match for Scarp, though; he stood his ground and blocked them all. Twirling the pipe in his hand, he summoned the dangling spikes into action. They spun in rapid circles, like a Catherine Wheel on Bonfire Night. Dazzling purple sparks crackled out towards Ella and Freddie, who launched themselves out of the way and ended up on the floor beneath the yellow gong. The sparks ricocheted around the walls above them, and Scarp grunted in apparent irritation.

'This isn't going well...' Freddie puffed. 'We're *bound* to be captured now—'

The door by the gong burst open and thumped into the stone wall perilously close to Ella's head. Two soldiers rushed in; Ella recognised them instantly as Trebble and Cloff, the long- and short-legged duo who had spectacularly failed to stop her and Freddie escaping the dungeon. Trebble was pushing an old-fashioned keyboard on wheels.

'That *has* to be a pianarack,' Ella muttered.

'We're here, Your Musical-ness!' Trebble called. 'We heard the Earthian intruders were... intruding!'

'We're your reinforcements!' Cloff chimed in, her tone overly triumphant considering her recent history with Ella and Freddie.

Uncle Otto rolled his eyes so clearly from the balcony that Ella noticed it from the other side of the hall. 'Actually, Scarp was doing just fine without you two *drumbeciles*,' he said, his voice weary.

A hurt look flooded their faces, and Trebble began wheeling the pianarack back towards the door, his head bowed. Cloff didn't notice his change of direction, though, and their feet became tangled up.

'Careful!' Trebble yelled.

'You be careful!' said Cloff, just as the wheels of the pianarack bumped over the uneven floor.

Trebble slammed both hands down on the keyboard in a desperate attempt to keep his balance. An extraordinary clang echoed around the hall, and a sonorance wave shot upwards from the pianarack and morphed into a pulsating, kaleidoscopic ball of energy. It hovered above Trebble, as if taunting him, then plunged back down with ferocious speed. The direct sonorance hit seized control of his body, and his arms and legs jolted into a star shape. As he attempted to wrestle his limbs back under control, his hands crashed down onto the keyboard again. Dismay spread across his face as another wave of unintended sonorance shot into the air above him, formed a perfect sphere, lingered there for a tantalising moment, then attacked him exactly as it had done the first time. It was as though the sounds he made on the pianarack, in this case two horrendously clashing chords, created matching sonorance for him and him *alone*.

Ella sat there, astounded. This was a whole new level of magical weirdness.

As if to add insult to injury, the pianarack slid off its base and dropped to the floor.

'Noooooo!' Trebble cried, diving and stretching like a goalkeeper in a penalty shootout.

CRUUUUNCH!

The pianarack crumpled into the stone slabs, one corner landing flush on Cloff's toes.

'OWWWWWWEEEEE!' Cloff squealed, clutching her foot and hopping in a circle.

'What have I told you about being *careful*?' Uncle Otto barked from the balcony. 'Especially with the pianarack, the most unwieldy of all instruments.'

'M… my apologies, Your Drumendus-ness,' Trebble said, straining to lift up the sorry-looking remains of the pianarack and balance it back on its base.

'Sonorance is a big problem if you *think* you know what you're doing, but in fact you *don't*.' Uncle Otto gestured towards Ella and Freddie and added, jeeringly, 'As my niece and her friend are all too aware.'

Ella glanced at the open door and prepared herself for a sprint, nudging Freddie to join her.

Unexpectedly, Freddie shook his head and scrambled to his feet, clearly riled by Uncle Otto's mocking tone. 'I'll show them sonorance skills,' he hissed, stamping on the floor and soaring up towards the ceiling beams and down again. 'Come on then, Scarp!'

'Freddie, NO!' Ella cried as he landed on a table across the hall. 'Bad idea!' She couldn't fault his courage, just his decision to renew a battle with someone much more skilled, especially as the chance to escape the hall had recently presented itself.

Scarp reached into his pocket and pulled out a set of valves that looked like they belonged to a trumpet. He then rolled up his sleeve to reveal a rope tied around his wrist. It had the same markings as the rope he had used to tie Ella's hands back in Crumhorn Forest. 'Meet the ropechaser,' he said in a gravelly voice. In one deft movement, he swung his arm over his head and unleashed the other end of the rope at Freddie, who had no choice but to leap to the floor and land with a roll. This wasn't just any old rope; *this* rope whistled around the hall and changed its length on command. Scarp controlled it with the valves tucked in the palm of his hand, as if he were flying a remote-controlled plane. It was one of the most surreal and dangerous contraptions Ella had seen on Drumendus, which was an achievement in itself.

In his other hand, Scarp began to move the dreaded pipe in circles. The razor-sharp spikes whirred into life again and released a trail of sparks that flew after Freddie. Scarp was toying with him, hunting him around the hall until he was ready for the capture. This was a sonorance masterclass.

Ella had to help her friend. She took a running jump and soared over Trebble and Cloff, who were still floundering around with the pianarack. Hands outstretched, she went to swipe Scarp's weapons away and tackle him to the ground.

She never did reach Scarp. A burst of drumming filled her ears, and she felt herself being blasted off course. She crashed into a wall and slid to the floor beside the yellow gong, the magical energy sapped from her body. Lying on her back, winded and confused, she caught sight of Uncle Otto standing at the front of the balcony, drum in hand. 'You...?' she said.

Trebble and Cloff jumped on top of her and pinned her down. She spluttered under their weight, her eyes streaming from the crush.

Freddie collapsed next to her, panting heavily. Beads of sweat glistened on his forehead. He stared at the ropechaser, which snaked towards him, ready to pounce on Scarp's command. 'One last idea,' he whispered, a tiny glint of hope still in his eye. '*Roll*, Ella. Now!'

Trusting Freddie, Ella did as she was told. She dug her knees into Cloff to give herself space and rolled onto her side. At the same moment, Freddie reached above him and heaved the gong off the wall. It dropped onto Trebble's head with almost comedic precision.

Freddie then lunged at the ropechaser and grabbed it with both hands. The whistling rope screeched in apparent disapproval but wriggled free under Scarp's expert instruction. More spine-chilling screams pierced the air as it coiled itself around Freddie, forcing his feet together and jamming his arms against his body. He dropped to the floor like a falling tree trunk, and for the first time, Scarp let out a quiet, ugly snicker.

'There,' he murmured. 'Neutralised.'

# CHAPTER 28
# PIANARACK ATTACK

In a fit of fury at seeing her best friend tied up like an oversized Christmas parcel, Ella battled free from Cloff, not with sonorance but with good old-fashioned elbows and squirms. Indeed, Cloff herself seemed more concerned about *her* best friend, Trebble, who had just been sent to sleep by an innocent gong.

'Run, Ella!' Freddie spluttered, the rope squeezing him ever tighter on the floor. 'We're no use... to anyone... if we're both... caught...'

'I can't just leave you h—' she started.

'GO! Find Belinda!'

Scarp closed in behind Ella, spinning his pipe. In front of her, Trebble had woken up and was singing away to nobody in particular, his eyes glazed over and his head bobbing from side to side. Cloff hauled him to his feet and dragged him to the open door, to block Ella's escape path. She stood with her arms out, ready to catch Ella if she attempted a charge.

Ella looked around in a desperate attempt for inspiration.

'The pianarack!' Freddie strained from the floor. 'You've always said you... *can't* play! Now – prove it...! One... horrible... chord!'

*One horrible chord...*

Ella recalled the sonorance Trebble had caused moments earlier when he'd accidentally slammed his hands down onto the keyboard. *And*, the sonorance had gone after *him*, and nobody else. She dashed over to the worse-for-wear pianarack and lifted her arms above it.

'Sorry,' she whispered down to the keyboard. 'I *will* learn to play you properly one day!'

She dropped her arms and spread her fingers as wide as she could across the keys. The pianarack responded with the most clashy, random and painful-sounding chord imaginable. Precisely as before, a sonorance wave flew up from the keyboard and formed a flawless sphere, its angry colours reflecting around the walls as it hung there. Ella turned and sprinted at Trebble and Cloff. The sphere whooshed back down and chased her as she pelted towards the door. It struck her in the back, a short, sharp shock between her shoulder blades that catapulted her forwards at ten times the speed of her running. Her surroundings turned into a blurry mess, and she closed her eyes, preparing for impact.

Trebble and Cloff didn't stand a chance against the fearsome pianarack attack. They were little more than skittles, and Ella was the supercharged bowling ball. She zoomed through them and flew along the empty corridor, rolling to a halt underneath a tapestry covered in merry musicians. Her battered body ached all over, but the sound of Uncle Otto barking furious instructions spurred her to her feet yet again. She tried every door she passed, but they were all locked.

'Focus!' she chuntered. 'Think!'

A few metres ahead, the passage split into two dark corridors. Neither looked particularly inviting, and she didn't remember the twins mentioning it earlier. Her eyes rested on a shaft of purple light shining through a key-shaped hole in the wall. It looked like one of those narrow windows for firing weapons, like in castles back on Earth.

A streak of light scorched past her ear. Then another. Off balance, she turned to see guards rushing at her along both corridors as well as from the circular hall, their weapons raised and their faces ferocious.

'This is the end of your stupid escapade, Ella,' Uncle Otto's voice boomed around the smooth walls. 'There's nowhere left to run.'

The decision to jump through the key-shaped hole in the wall was one that seemed to happen before Ella's brain had fully agreed to it. But that's exactly what she found herself doing as the gaggle of baying soldiers bore down on her. She only just squeezed through, the cold stone grazing her arms on her way past. Rolling down the roof towards a pair of galops tucking into their hay dinner, she briefly wondered if she would land on top of one and accidentally speed off into the distance on its back.

She didn't.

The roof came to an abrupt end, and she landed on the straw-filled ground between the two nonplussed galops. She sprinted on and noticed for the first time the wisps of purple smoke trailing from her shoes as she jumped over walls and across neat flowerbeds with a series of sonorance stamps. The shouts behind her came and went, but all she could think of were Freddie's words: '*We're no use to anyone if we're both caught.*' She hid behind a gate and crouched down to catch her breath. The familiar feeling of brain scramble came over her, and her heart sank as she realised that she was alone for the first time on Drumendus, the only one free of Uncle Otto's clutches.

Through a gap in the gate, she spotted the Hammerklav down the hill, standing proudly on its platform alongside the marvelodrums. There were no crowds around it, no spontaneous songs being performed in its honour, not even any guards keeping watch. In fact, Aunt Belinda's finest invention looked rather peaceful down there, if a little tired and dirty.

'Keep searching!' bellowed a gruff voice nearby. '*Find* the Earthian!'

As the soldiers' footsteps drew closer, Ella was sure she'd be spotted. Just in time, she clambered on top of the wall by the gate and lay flat on her back, her arms squeezed into her sides. Heavy purple clouds dominated overhead, and for a few seconds, she wondered if she'd ever see another clear sky… another sunset… another star…

A shout from a soldier below snapped her out of her brief daydream. 'I need a rest, Major!' Ella heard him slump to the floor, directly underneath her hiding place. 'Don't tell the King,' he laughed, biting into something. 'He would *not* be happy if he knew we were—'

'ELLA CRINKLE!' a voice thundered across the Palace grounds.

Ella nearly fell off the wall in shock. She heard the guards scramble to their feet.

'ELLA CRINKLE!'

She caught sight of Uncle Otto striding out onto a pyramid-shaped terrace in front of the Palace.

'What's he doing?' said the guard whose mouth was stuffed with food. 'He never comes onto the Pyramidee Stage.'

'*Pyramidee*,' Ella whispered, wondering why it sounded so familiar. 'Pyramidee…'

A snippet from yet another of the twins' songs popped into her mind:

*'The Pyramidee Stage is for honoured guests alone,*
*Stone Stacks is known as the competition zone,*
*But Slane is reserved for the King and his throne!'*

'The concert stages,' she said under her breath, remembering what Ade had told her.

She craned her neck and looked over at the other two stages, Stone Stacks with its imposing pillars and Slane, Uncle Otto's personal stage, which was of course in the middle and was much bigger and more ornate than the other two. This was the stage he had used to parade Aunt Belinda in front of his Stradbow subjects earlier, and to gloat about Earthians being a superior species. Behind each stage, glass doors led inside the Palace.

Uncle Otto dragged a reluctant figure to the front of the Pyramidee Stage.

It was Freddie.

Holding him roughly by his tunic collar, Uncle Otto stared out across the grounds and gardens. 'I know you're out there, Ella! My soldiers *will* find you. They are relentless – like me.'

'Yes, that's us, *relentless*!' the same soldier chuckled beneath Ella. From his muffled voice, he had clearly shoved in *another* mouthful of food before talking.

'Will you be quiet!' barked another soldier.

Uncle Otto scanned his Palace grounds. 'Now, what about your *friend* here, Ella? I don't really need him.' Ella tried to stay still, despite her agitation growing. '*You*, Ella, you're my family. And Belinda too. But *Freddie*, what use is he to me?' He paused, his dramatic timing as predictable as ever, then added, 'That's right, NO USE whatsoever!'

Freddie wasn't going to let Uncle Otto have his big moment without a struggle. 'He's bluffing, Ella!' he yelled, trying but failing to wriggle free. 'He wouldn't dare do anything to me!'

Uncle Otto laughed. 'That's where you're wrong, Freddie Molto. *Very* wrong.' He looked back out over the grounds. 'Ella, give yourself up, or there'll be trouble ahead for your friend!' He stormed back inside, bundling Freddie in before he could say another word.

Ella was sure she caught a glimpse of Aunt Belinda looking through a window behind the Pyramidee Stage.

She closed her eyes and clenched her fists. Was this it? Was it really time to give up? She couldn't just lie there and allow terrible things to happen to Freddie. And what about Aunt Belinda? *She* was at the mercy of Uncle Otto's changing moods too.

Forcing her weary eyes to open again, she glanced down at the Hammerklav. She wished she could climb in there and take refuge for a while, instead of trying to think whilst perched precariously on a narrow wall.

Out of nowhere, a frenzied argument broke out amongst the soldiers below.

# CHAPTER 29
# FINGERTIPS

Ella peered down at the hot-tempered soldiers. One of them guzzled exotic-smelling foods and drank what must have been Drumendus beer. The other two, though, were in a heated debate about who would win this year's Stradbow music competition.

'Flonflon will prevail, *easily*!' said one of them.

'Ridiculous! This is Rimshott's year.'

The soldier with the permanent mouthful decided to join in. 'You must be *drunk* to think that!' he guffawed, sipping his beer.

'Drunk? That's rich, coming from *you*!'

A song jumped into Ella's head, as they so often did. Something about a drunken soldier. Or was it about a *sailor*? She hummed the tune:

*What shall we do with the drunken sailor?*
*What shall we do with the...*

She shook her head to try and get rid of it – there were so many more pressing things to think about than an annoying sea shanty – but it would *not* budge; the song had lodged itself in her mind. '*An earworm to end all earworms*' – that's what her music teacher at St Hildegard's would have said. More alarming still, she felt compelled to sing it out loud, and the more she tried to resist, the stronger the urge became. Although she didn't understand it, she knew sonorance was at play. Her gut told her to answer this magical command to sing; besides, if she didn't, she was sure she'd burst.

'*WHAT SHALL WE DO WITH THE DRUNKEN SAILOR,*' she blurted out, looking down at the guards. '*WHAT SHALL WE DO WITH THE DRUNKEN SAILOR—*'

The perplexed soldiers dropped their food and drink and scrambled around for their weapons.

'*WHAT SHALL WE DO WITH THE DRUNKEN SAILOR—*'

'It's *her!*' yelled the greedy guard. 'The *Earthian!*'

'*ER-LYE IN THE MORNIN'...?*' Ella ploughed on ever more forcefully, channelling her inner pirate as she sang. '*HOORAY AND UP SHE RISES...*' Something had taken hold of her, a deep sense that singing *this* song at *this* moment was the right thing to do.

It soon became clear why.

The soldiers began staggering around and tripping over each other, much like *drunken sailors* might do. Their limbs flailed as they tried to reach up and grab Ella, and they ended up in a giggling, hiccupping heap on the ground.

Ella's self-confidence soared at discovering yet another astonishing strand of sonorance: the *words* were just as powerful as the music itself! A simple folk song she'd learnt in Junior Choir had made Uncle Otto's highly trained soldiers lose their senses and act like a band of incapable imbeciles.

With renewed energy and a determined grimace, Ella sprinted down the hill and leapt over the Palace walls with a sonorance stamp. She landed with a light thud on the Hammerklav's wheeled platform, thanks to the whirlsock slowing her fall. Climbing down, she slipped through the same hatch she and Freddie had used earlier, hardly noticing the cold, dark atmosphere of Aunt Belinda's cherished Hammerklav. She rushed over to the cockpit and scanned the dials and levers on the control panel. Wild ideas flashed across her mind. Maybe she could start up the engines? Maybe she could fly over to the Pyramidee Stage and rescue Freddie and Aunt Belinda? There must be an instruction manual somewhere in the cabin. How hard could it be to turn this thing on…?

Harder than she ever could have imagined.

Not only were there no obvious buttons to fire up the rockets but every inch of the control panel was covered in Aunt Belinda's indecipherable squiggles and symbols. They meant nothing whatsoever to Ella.

Sitting in the pilot's seat, she switched *every* switch, pulled *every* lever and repeatedly tapped Mozart the mascot on the head. She *willed* the Hammerklav to come to life and even tried singing 'Fly Me to the Moon' whilst sonorance jumping against the ceiling. The stubborn spacecraft remained silent and rooted to the spot, and Ella had no choice but to crumple to the floor in an exhausted heap.

She was all out of ideas. There was no way she could outwit Uncle Otto and his soldiers, sonorance or no sonorance. She crawled over to a dark corner and pulled a thin, musty blanket over her head. Rubbing her eyes, she curled up and waited for the guards to find her and frogmarch her back to the King in disgrace.

Ella Crinkle, the most wanted person in Stradbow. The entire Palace was looking for her, but she had never felt so alone. Rubbing a tear from her grubby cheek, she wondered if she would ever return to Earth. Would she ever see Mum again? Or would she be a prisoner on Drumendus for the rest of her life?

Through a small rip in the blanket, she spotted something peculiar poking out of a container: a thin stick, which caught the light for a moment and turned a hint of purple.

It was Aunt Belinda's baton.

Ella shuffled over and eased it out. It was lighter than she had expected. She balanced it across the palm of her hand and watched as it rocked gently up and down. Closing her thumb and fingers around the delicate handle, she recalled Aunt Belinda's joy at waving it through the air as she conducted her favourite music.

What was it her aunt had said? '*The power is quite literally at your fingertips.*'

*...quite literally at your fingertips...*

Hang on a minute.

Ella had heard that phrase on Drumendus too... But when?

That was it!

Aunt Belinda *herself* had said it just a few hours ago on the Slane stage, when she was pleading for Ella and Freddie to give themselves up and join her in Plectrumm Palace. '*The power is quite literally at your fingertips.*'

How could she have missed it? Aunt Belinda was giving her a clue. She wanted Ella to find the baton before anybody else did! But why...?

'Let's see,' she said, standing in the middle of the cabin. She swooshed the baton around in front of her, pretending to lead an orchestra. Keeping her sounds as soft as she could, so as not to alert the guards outside – which proved difficult in her excitement – she stamped, tapped and clicked her fingers to the beat.

Nothing happened. Undeterred, she tried every combination of arm movements and body percussion she could think of.

It was no good. There was no baton sonorance in sight, and Ella couldn't work out what she was supposed to be *thinking*. She dropped her aching arms down and let out a frustrated grunt.

The baton woke up. A tiny trail of rainbow-coloured light zipped out towards the floor.

'Woah!' She moved the baton up and down and grunted again, this time on purpose. The same harmless trail of light beamed out for a split second. 'Finally!' she said, realising that the baton seemed to answer to her *voice* only. She waved it at the reinforced piano stool in the living quarters. 'ONE,' she said in a firm tone, counting out the beat just like her music teacher did in school orchestra rehearsals.

She didn't get to *two*.

A bright flash of rainbow light whizzed out and blew a hole right though the flowery cushion on the stool.

'Oops,' Ella said, breaking into a sheepish smile when she saw the damage. She stared down at the innocent-looking baton. 'Let's see what else you can do.' She pointed it at a folded-up map in the corner. 'Hey, you!'

The map jumped upwards, as if taken by surprise, then opened itself in the air and landed back on the floor facing Ella.

Grinning ear to ear, she rummaged around in the open container and scattered various objects across the floor. 'Hey, you!' she said to each of them, and without fail, the objects obeyed her command for attention and turned themselves towards her.

There was no stopping her now she had found out the secret to baton sonorance – her voice. Imitating the *neeeeaaaaoooo* sound of a racing car, she sent an uneaten bag of popcorn flying across the room with a swipe of her arm. She then whipped up a whirlwind of Aunt Belinda's papers with a dramatic whooshing sound and rapid circle shapes with the baton. She even levitated a few centimetres above the ground, simply by laughing and beating in time.

It was so easy! And it felt so natural. The baton channelled her voice into such powerful sonorance that her whole body trembled in delight and her mind exploded with wonder and possibility. This was it. This was the sonorance moment she'd been waiting for.

With her new-found weapon, Ella had a chance to mount a rescue, and even face Uncle Otto if she had to.

Without fully realising it, her voice became louder as she rattled off as many vocal sounds as she could think of. She forgot all about the dangers of being at the top of Stradbow's most-wanted list. Her enthusiasm had got the better of her, and during one particularly flamboyant arm-flap, the baton slipped out of her hand and zoomed around the Hammerklav like an out-of-control firework, leaving a trail of rainbow light in its wake. Ella leapt behind the cockpit chairs to avoid having her eye poked out, and the baton landed gracefully back inside the container, as if signalling that *that* was quite enough excitement for one day.

The door of the hatch burst open.

# CHAPTER 30

# UNCLE OTTO DOES NOT NAP

Scarp jumped into the Hammerklav and fired off a hefty barrage of sonorance spells. Crouched behind the pilot's seat, Ella covered her head until it died down. Had he come in a few seconds earlier, it would have been game over for her, such was the ferocity of his onslaught.

'But... where's the girl?' she heard him grunt.

Ella took her chance. She scrambled over to the container and pulled out the baton. The teardrop handle was still warm, and to Ella's amazement, the warmth spread up her arm like a protective sleeve, then across her shoulders and down through her body, energising her every fibre.

'Take *that*!' she roared, jumping to her feet and pointing the baton at Scarp with a clumsy thrust of her arm. Unfortunately, the dim trail of light that appeared barely made it halfway across the cabin before sinking to the ground and fizzling out pathetically. Realising her mistake – the baton needed a *proper* movement and a proper instruction to go with it – she went to try again. 'I mean… er…'

In that tiny moment of hesitation, Scarp lunged forwards and forced her flat to the ground. 'What are you going to do now, *Ella Crinkle*?' he croaked in her ear, snatching at the baton in her outstretched arm.

Ella fought to breathe as Scarp dug his knee into her spine. Her wheezing turned into a hissing sound, and she knew it wouldn't be long before she'd have to give up the fight. The baton swooshed up and down in the struggle.

Astonishingly, out of the same open container across the cabin, a grimy musical instrument emerged all by itself and dropped to the floor. It looked like an old French horn, its brass tubing coiled together neatly. It untwisted itself and began twitching up and down to the movement of the baton. It was answering Ella's hissing sound!

Ella breathed as much air as she could into her squashed lungs, then let out a steady hiss and beckoned the tube towards her. Scarp was too busy trying to prize the baton out of her hand to notice it slithering over, like a snake on the hunt for its next victim. Ella made sure the baton kept moving, up and down, up and down, luring the tube closer, until it was right in front of her face. She felt her cheeks burning from the effort.

'You're stronger than you look, Earthian,' Scarp said, frustration bubbling in his voice.

'You got that right, you *traitor*!' Ella rasped through gritted teeth, her head starting to spin from lack of oxygen. Her eyes remained fixed on the tube, and with one final sonorance swish of the baton, she sent the tube hurtling up towards Scarp's nose. 'NEEEEAAAAOOOO!'

A moment later, Scarp flopped to the floor in a stupor and murmured something that sounded suspiciously like 'Hot cross buns.'

Gasping for air, Ella lay beside him to recover, then clambered to the hatch without looking back. She checked all was clear outside, squinting as her eyes adjusted to the daylight. The only activity nearby was the incessant beat of the marvelodrums, obediently sending up purple lightning every few seconds.

Baton in hand and fire in her belly, Ella rushed through a deserted gate and up the hill towards Plectrumm Palace. She only hid once, as a group of soldiers marched past urgently in the opposite direction. She leapt and crept her way to the Pyramidee Stage and skirted around its edge until she reached an extravagant glass door. Pressing her nose against the windowpane, she heard a strange yelp emerge from inside, then a dull thump, but couldn't make out what was going on.

The door opened without warning, and she toppled forwards into the room.

'Ella?'

'ELLA! It *is* you!'

'Beethoven's belt!'

'That's a new one,' said Ella, muttering at Aunt Belinda and Freddie. They lifted her to her feet, and Aunt Belinda squeezed her so tightly that she accidentally hissed again. 'Wow,' she managed eventually, 'what a welcome!' She stepped back and looked at Freddie. Quite out of the blue, a streak of anger rushed through her. 'Did Uncle Otto hurt you? After he said he didn't need you anymore?'

Freddie smiled. 'No, don't worry.'

'*Really?* 'Cos I thought… when he said there was trouble ahead for you, I just—'

'It's okay, Ella. He hasn't done a thing… yet.' There was kindness in his voice. 'Anyway, do you think I'd go down without a fight? Me?' He pointed to the far side of the room at a Palace guard slumped on the floor. 'Nope.'

'So *that's* what I heard just now from outside!' Ella said. 'You were fighting the guard!'

'More of an ambush than a fight. He's been staring at me and humming a sonorance lullaby, to keep me sleepy. So irritating! Every time he'd finish, he'd swig his drink and gargle to keep his high notes working. Even *more* irritating!'

Aunt Belinda rested her arm on Freddie's shoulder. 'I *accidentally* knocked over his drink, and Freddie did the rest.'

'I did *try* to be gentle,' Freddie said, blushing, 'but the guard ended up… slightly unconscious on the floor.'

Ella made a mental note not to hum at Freddie in

case *she* ended up slightly unconscious on the floor too. 'What are you doing in here anyway?' she said. 'I was *sure* you'd be down in the dungeon.'

'Belinda insisted I stay with her, and Otto agreed. They're best mates now, you know – according to Otto, anyway!'

'Ugh!' Aunt Belinda scoffed. 'Best mates, I don't think so!' She put her spare arm around Ella and pulled her close. 'I knew you'd come for us. I just *knew* it.' She pointed at the baton resting in Ella's hand. 'And there it is. *At your fingertips.* Thank goodness you got to it before anyone else did.'

'Yeah, thanks for the clue,' Ella said. 'But how did you know the baton would work with sonorance?'

'As I said back on the Hammerklav, the baton's one of the greatest objects in all music, in the hands of the right person. Of course it should work with sonorance. And it rather suits you, Ella, now that you're a *magician!*'

'I think the word's sonorator, but thanks anyway.' A memory jumped into Ella's mind, that of Aunt Belinda standing with Uncle Otto on the terrace earlier, her arms aloft in supposed triumph as she announced that she was staying on Drumendus. 'Er... just to check for *certain*, all that stuff you said outside to the crowds... about staying here – you didn't actually *mean* any of it... did you?'

'Not a word! That was an outright fib to Otto... and to half the population of Stradbow, it seems. Whoops.' She shuffled on her toes. 'I wouldn't normally fib, you know... it's not my style.' She looked at Ella, as if seeking approval. 'But it was the only way I could get him to start treating me like a human being. Another few hours in that awful dungeon, I would have lost my mind and started singing my favourite Christmas descants at full volume on repeat. I built up Otto's trust by helping him with his practice, of all things. And of course, I agreed with everything he said, even if it was utter rubbish.' Her expression turned to a scowl. 'Can you imagine life here with my megalomaniac brother in charge, ordering us about and parading us to his subjects like a collection of rare instruments? Well, I *can* imagine it… and that's the problem!'

'Otto won't be in charge for much longer, I reckon,' Freddie said to Ella, with a hint of glee. 'Thanks to us.'

Ella felt her eyebrows shoot up. 'How come? What do you know?'

'You must have guessed? Isolde's on her way here, with her army! That's what we overheard, anyway. *And* they have sonorance now, because *we* showed them the Rain Cavern!' His delight clearly growing, he added, 'Why do you think the Palace is so empty? It should be crawling with soldiers, but they're all marching to the plain to defend the city. Didn't you see them?' Ella nodded. 'Well, it's all down to *us*!'

Shaking her head in disbelief, Aunt Belinda said, 'You two have made *quite* the impact.' There was a note of caution in her voice. 'Anyway, plenty of time to think about that on the journey home. Shall we get out of here?'

'Yep!' said Ella, striding over to the glass doors. 'Follow me!'

The Hammerklav stood waiting for them down the hill, glinting in the early-evening light, despite being covered in grimy streaks.

'LAAAA, LA-LA, LA-LA, LAAAAAAAA!'

The unexpected sound of singing filled the air. It was the same song that Ella and Freddie had heard echoing around the Palace walls earlier.

The door clattered open, and Uncle Otto barged in, followed by a line of breathless singers. 'I knew it!' he snarled. 'Ella Crinkle to the rescue. I warned you earlier – NOTHING gets past me, not in my own PALACE!' His exasperated voice sounded almost comical.

'Quick!' said Ella, ushering the others out onto the Pyramidee Stage.

'Surround them, Ottovox!' Uncle Otto yelled at his choir, who stamped as one and formed a tight circle around Ella, Freddie and Aunt Belinda.

Freddie tutted. '*Ottovox*... Of course his choir would be called that...'

The singers' voices strained as they continued their tune. 'LAAAA... LA-LA, LA-LA... LAAAAAAAA...'

'Why are you all still SINGING?' Uncle Otto bellowed. 'I'm clearly not resting ANYMORE!'

The choir stopped in an instant, and Uncle Otto elbowed his way to the front of the circle.

'I'll handle this,' Ella said to Freddie and Aunt Belinda, whose faces revealed the same uncertainty she had seen all too often. 'I *mean* it.'

She held the baton down by her leg and stood as tall as she could as Uncle Otto squared up to her.

'One thing I hate more than anything, Ella Crinkle,' he growled, 'is having my rest disturbed.'

Ella's heart pummelled her chest. 'Yeah, it's common knowledge you need a *choir* to calm you down.'

A flicker of disbelief crossed Uncle Otto's face, and he moved in closer. 'First of all, *child*, don't try anything stupid – you'll regret it if you annoy the singers, believe me. Secondly, you are officially becoming a nuisance! Do you have any idea how hard I've worked to keep the Rain Cavern a secret?' His tone had changed to a coarse whisper. 'Do you? How many times I've crushed the rumours and denied its existence? Until yesterday, only my closest advisors knew about it – and now it's common knowledge! Thanks to you and *him*.' He motioned his chin towards Freddie. 'My *enemies* have sonorance, thanks to *you* and *him*.' His voice grew again. 'And now I have to defend my kingdom, thanks to YOU and HIM!'

'You're not defending your kingdom!' said Ella, determined to give as good as she got. 'You're here, having a *nap*!'

A few Ottovox singers gasped, as if the idea of napping was a terrible insult to throw at the King.

'I do not… *nap*,' he seethed. 'I *rest*. It helps me think. I was just about to leave, if you must know.'

Ella ignored him. 'Isolde's army will beat you and chuck you out of Stradbow!' She heard another ripple of gasps from the choir, but there was far *less* outrage this time than after accusing the King of taking naps. 'Stradbow is *her* kingdom, not yours!'

Uncle Otto made a strange huffing sound, as if no-one had ever dared say that to him. They probably hadn't.

To everyone's surprise, the choir leader sprang into action and instructed the members of Ottovox to begin another song. 'From the top. One, two, three, four and—'

Uncle Otto wheeled around and glared at her, his eyes bulging. 'What are you doing? Can't you see I'm in the middle of something?'

'You seem stressed, Your Majesty,' she said, as the choir started a gentle song. 'You made… the *noise*.'

'The noise?'

'Yes, Your Majesty. The one that sounds like a galop burping.' She demonstrated the sound and wiggled her head in the same way Uncle Otto had done. 'It's a clear sign that your stress levels are high. We can calm you down.'

If anything, Uncle Otto was becoming *more* agitated. 'I don't need calming down! Now, where was I…?' He turned back towards Ella, but Aunt Belinda had stepped between them.

'This ends here, Brother,' she said, her voice calm but serious.

'I didn't see *you* stopping Ella's little escape plan,' Uncle Otto replied, then after a pause, said, 'Belinda, please don't tell me… you're in on it too?'

'It's time to let us go. You have other battles to fight.'

'But… all that talk about you staying with me on Drumendus…?' An unexpected sadness filled Uncle

Otto's eyes, and for a moment, Ella felt almost sorry for him. 'Was it all a lie?'

'Let us go, Otto,' Aunt Belinda said again.

'But... we could have built... an *empire* across Drumendus... brother and sister!' Uncle Otto's voice cracked as he spoke, and rage crept back into his face. 'I... I should never have trusted you. You'll pay for this. *All of you!*' He shoved Aunt Belinda to the ground.

'NO!' Ella yelled. 'You do NOT do that!'

She lifted her baton and aimed it point-blank at her uncle.

# CHAPTER 31
# THE PATCHWORK PARACHUTE

'ONE! TWO! THREE! FOUR!' Ella screamed, waving the baton at Uncle Otto like a furious conductor. Dazzling flashes of rainbow light careered into his chest and sent him flying backwards through the mass of singers. '*Nobody* pushes my Aunt Belinda! NOBODY!'

Thumping to the floor across the stage, Uncle Otto rolled to a halt and sat up in an astonished daze. The singers who *hadn't* been unintentionally flattened stepped back and stared at Ella's baton, dumbfounded.

Ella helped Aunt Belinda to her feet, then pulled her and Freddie close in, so the three of them were a solid, rotating mass. 'Stay away!' she spat, pointing the baton around the circle of Ottovox singers, some of whom had their hands in the air in panic. 'Let us through!'

The choir leader moved to one side, and Ella and the others edged to the corner of the stage.

'We can get down to the Hammerklav in a few seconds with sonorance jumps,' Ella said to Aunt Belinda, 'as long as you hold on tight.' She looked back at the singers, who had silently reformed into a perfect semicircle. They stretched their arms out towards the trio. 'Wait,' Ella started. 'What are you doi—'

'LAAAAAAAAAAAA!'

The choir sang the most complex, haunting chord she had ever heard. It was piercing yet beautiful, and Ella staggered forwards, unable to resist. Her body gave way and she wilted to the floor, leaving Freddie and Aunt Belinda teetering on the edge of the stage. The singing drained the energy out of her limbs. All she could do to try and protect herself, and her precious baton, was roll onto her side, close her eyes and curl up in a tight bundle. Even then, her body scraped along the stone floor in slow circles. Ottovox moved in tight again, clearly enjoying getting the better of her. The more intense their singing, the faster she spun.

Uncle Otto *had* warned her about annoying singers…

Through the dizzy haze, all she could think of was to heave as much air as she could into her lungs and blast out a whooshing noise.

'WHOOOOOSH!'

She channelled her thoughts into the baton and tried again, unsure if anything was happening.

'WHOOOOOSH!        WHOOOOOOOSH! WHOOOOOOOOOSH!'

The singing around her slowly turned to shrieking. Ella opened her eyes.

A blistering whirlwind, the height of the Palace itself, had whipped up around Ella. It whisked the Ottovox singers off their feet and scattered them effortlessly around the stage. Ella's spinning body came to an undignified stop, and she waited until the tornado she'd created disappeared before wobbling to her feet on the third attempt. She rested her hands on her knees to try and regain her balance, then veered over to Freddie and Aunt Belinda at the edge of the stage, her dizziness dictating the route she took.

'Look out!' Freddie screeched as a missile fizzed past her ear.

Ella turned to see Uncle Otto storming over, his chin thrust forward in obvious rage. 'You've really done it now, ELLA! I'll show you!'

Beater in hand, he played a ferocious rhythm on the drum that hung around his neck, and a volley of sonorance missiles flew towards Ella. There was no time to duck, but she somehow managed to deflect them with a swish of her baton and a desperate 'Neeeaaaooo!'

Uncle Otto attacked again, a man possessed with fury and dead set on revenge. He intensified the onslaught by shouting in time as he beat the drum. The ground shook in violent waves across the stage.

'I can't defend much longer,' Ella gasped, losing her balance as the stones beneath her cracked. 'It's hopeless!'

But Uncle Otto had gone too far. The stage itself started crumbling away, and Ella's corner broke off and plummeted towards the path below.

'JUMP!' Ella yelled, grabbing Aunt Belinda's hand.

'Hold tight!' said Freddie, taking her other hand.

The best friends stamped and soared into the air, just as the stones smashed to the ground in a cloud of dust. They didn't get as much height as usual, with Aunt Belinda clinging onto them for dear life, but that didn't matter – they were still in one piece and were finally heading for the Hammerklav. Yet another flurry of missiles shot by as they bounded through the Palace grounds in giant leaps. Uncle Otto roared in frustration and barked orders at anyone who happened to be nearby.

Jumping onto the wheeled platform and through the Hammerklav's emergency hatch, Ella and Freddie hauled Aunt Belinda inside, just as one of the marvelodrums blasted out a lightning bolt towards the purple clouds.

The golden gates down the road caught Ella's eye. Soldiers rushed back and forth like busy ants, and the sound of frantic activity filled the air, coupled with a sense of agitation. Further away, outside the city walls, a battle was raging.

'Isolde,' whispered Ella. 'It must be.'

Aunt Belinda beamed as she looked around her

beloved spacecraft once again. 'My old friend,' she said. 'I thought I'd *never* see you again.' She tripped over something at her feet. 'I say, what's all this?'

Scarp lay befuddled on the floor next to the coiled instrument that had attacked him earlier.

'Oh, don't worry about him,' Ella said, dragging Scarp to the door and rolling him out of the hatch. 'He wouldn't have liked Earth, anyway.'

'There's a hole in my cushion!' Aunt Belinda said, grimacing as she looked at the reinforced piano stool. 'Hmm – I won't even ask!' She rushed over to the cockpit, sat down and flicked a few switches in sequence. The dashboard lit up.

'You make it look so easy!' Ella said, remembering her own failed attempts to bring the Hammerklav to life earlier.

'Otto's coming!' Freddie called from one of the windows. '*Hurry*, Belinda... er... please...'

Aunt Belinda shook her head. 'There's no time for the launch sequence. I could try manual flight mode, but there's not much time for that either...'

The road around the Hammerklav filled up by the second with panicked Stradbow soldiers, and there were shouts of, 'The Gurdee army's coming!' and 'Retreat to the Palace!'

A hand appeared through the hatch and grabbed hold of Ella's ankle, pulling her clean out of the spaceship. 'YOU'RE NOT GOING ANYWHERE, ELLA CRINKLE!' Uncle Otto's voice bellowed.

Ella yelped as she and her uncle fell hard onto the platform below.

'You *maddening* little girl!' he spluttered, locking his arm around her neck. 'Drop the baton! NOW!'

Ella tried to wriggle free, but she was stuck fast, wheezing for air.

Her eyes lost focus, and she had the overwhelming urge to fall asleep…

She had to try something…

One last chance…

Summoning *everything* she had left in her heart, mind and body, Ella pointed the baton towards the Hammerklav's hatch and let out the most thunderous roar. It was a sound like none other she had ever made.

'ROOOOOOOOOOOOOAAAAAAAAAAAR!'

The Hammerklav jolted upwards at the sheer power of Ella's outburst and hovered in the air above the platform.

Uncle Otto's body shivered in shock, and Ella clenched her jaw and squirmed free of him. The sonorance flowed back into her veins a thousand times over.

'ROOOOOOOOOOOOOAAAAAAAAAAAR!' she yelled again, the strength of all the lions on Earth channelled into her outstretched baton.

Again, the Hammerklav answered, lurching higher into the air above Stradbow.

Freddie appeared at the hatch opening. 'Jump in!' he called, gesturing wildly. 'Quickly!'

Ella got to her feet and leapt gracefully upwards with a sonorance stamp.

But Uncle Otto leapt up too and snatched hold of Ella's trail leg as she clambered into the cabin.

'You don't give up, do you?' Ella cried, grabbing the hatch door and clinging to it by her fingertips. Uncle Otto dangled beneath her, his legs swinging around in a ludicrous mid-air dance.

'Of course not,' snarled Uncle Otto. 'I'm a CRINKLE!'

Out of the corner of her eye, Ella noticed Aunt Belinda pull what looked like a bundle of rags from a container.

Rushing over to the hatch, Aunt Belinda shouted down at Uncle Otto, 'Pick on someone your own… *AGE*! FOR ONCE!'

Ella realised that her aunt was brandishing the parachute from her mini flying machine back home.

'Meet Josephine,' Aunt Belinda said, her voice cutting. 'Another of my successful flying inventions.'

Uncle Otto's bloodshot eyes filled with dread as Aunt Belinda leaned down and threw the parachute straps over his free arm in one rapid movement.

'You are not worthy of my spaceship, OTTO CRINKLE!' She threw Josephine out of the hatch and let gravity to do the rest. 'Goodbye. And GOOD RIDDANCE!'

Josephine whooshed out of the Hammerklav and opened up in the wind. Uncle Otto didn't stand a chance against Aunt Belinda's sewn-together patchwork parachute. He shrieked as his body was yanked away from Ella's long-suffering leg. 'NOOOOoooo…'

At last, the King of Drumendus was gone.

'Who needs sonorance anyway?' Aunt Belinda

smirked, pulling Ella inside and slamming the hatch shut.

Outside, the crowd had swelled to a roaring mob, and those with sonorance started attacking the spacecraft with every spell imaginable. Ottovox had miraculously reformed, their once-immaculate uniforms torn and covered in dust, and they chanted so piercingly that Ella even heard them from inside the sealed spacecraft.

'We're losing height,' Freddie said from the window. 'We need another Ella-special!'

Ella gladly obliged, pointing her baton to the ceiling and roaring again with as much vigour as she could muster. This time, the Hammerklav juddered upwards but tipped violently to one side. 'What's happening?'

'It's the chanting,' Freddie said. 'It's pulling us back!'

The Hammerklav shook and groaned in complaint at being forced one way then the other. Staring out of the window, Ella's eyes darted between the streaks of purple light filling the air and the lines of missiles that ricocheted off the windows and dissolved. A few metres further away, another enormous lightning bolt shot up towards the clouds from one of Uncle Otto's giant drums.

One final idea forced its way into her exhausted mind. 'The *marvelodrum*! It's our only way to get into space without the rockets.'

'But... how?' Freddie said.

'Fly over it and let the lightning shoot us up!'

'You mean… use Otto's favourite invention against him?'

'Exactly! He deserves it.'

Aunt Belinda nodded. 'Strap in and connect yourselves to the air supply,' she said, guiding the shuddering Hammerklav towards the marvelodrum. 'Steady,' she muttered as it pitched to the side, her knuckles white from clutching the gear stick so tightly. 'Steady, my love.'

In the agonising seconds before the marvelodrum's next beat, Ella peered out at Stradbow for what she *hoped* was the last time. The imposing gates of the city wall had been flung open, and a small army of determined-looking soldiers had rushed through and made straight for the Palace up the hill. Even from the Hammerklav, Ella recognised the unforgettable bright-coloured clothes of the Gurdee rebels.

Isolde and her people were back in Stradbow.

BOOOOOOOOM!

The marvelodrum did what it did best and released a flash of lightning into the air above Stradbow. This time, though, the lightning took with it the unsuspecting Hammerklav and its three petrified occupants, flinging them through the dense clouds and into the clear skies above Drumendus. It moved at such speed that Ella was sure half of herself had been left behind.

The brilliant sunshine was unbearable after days of purple gloom, but Ella soon became drowsy from the force of the lightning lift-off. She drifted in and out of consciousness as the Hammerklav forged its way through Drumendus' merciless atmosphere.

Once in space, she fell into a deep sleep, the best sleep she'd ever had, in fact. It may have been a few hours; it may have been a couple of days.

It didn't matter. Ella, Freddie and Aunt Belinda were on their way home.

# CHAPTER 32
# A SHOPPING BAG

For the first time in days, Ella's dreams were not restless or terrifying or crammed full of jeopardy. Instead, the most wonderful images cascaded through her mind, of Gurdee halls filled with immaculate instruments, of Stradbow streets echoing with singing and laughter, of consorts and musings and vivid sounds at every turn. Ella emerged from her sleep sporting a wide smile, delighted by the reminder that her brief time on Drumendus had been more than just perilous sonorance battles and fierce rivalries: much more.

Even *without* sonorance, Drumendus had been a magical place... a true musical wonderland, in fact.

Ella stretched, rubbed her eyes and glanced over at her aunt.

'Just look at that,' said Aunt Belinda, pointing out of the cockpit window. Earth floated in front of them in the enormous nothingness of space, its majestic landscapes and feathery cloud formations punctuated by the deep blue of mysterious oceans. 'What a beautiful sight, eh? Far too few people see Earth like this. So… serene.'

Ella stared out at the seas and continents of her home planet. 'I'm… guessing the Drumendus mission didn't quite go as you expected?' she ventured.

Aunt Belinda scrunched up her forehead. 'You could say that. I wasn't alone, to start with. Then there was all that *magic* tomfoolery to contend with… quite unexpected, I must say…'

'I did wonder one thing. Did Uncle Otto…' The words got caught in Ella's throat for a moment. 'Did he… *force* you to show him where the Hammerklav was?'

To Ella's surprise, Aunt Belinda chuckled. 'Goodness me, no! That was all my idea.'

'Your… idea?'

'Yes! Otto's ego had grown so huge that I knew he would relish the chance to show off the Hammerklav in Stradbow. You saw how he was outside the Palace – he *loved* boasting to his subjects about "what Earthians are capable of". And the nearer the Hammerklav was to *me*, the easier it might be to escape.' She paused and tapped her Mozart mascot on the head. 'And here we are!'

'Nice work.'

'Besides,' Aunt Belinda said, 'I'm not a hundred

per cent sure I could have found my way back to our landing site – it didn't go very well the first time I tried, remember?'

'Er, yeah… we had no idea where you'd gone, and you ended up in a cage.' Ella's smile faded. 'I wonder what will happen to Uncle Otto… and Isolde, and everyone else. Especially now so many of them have sonorance?'

'It doesn't look good for Otto, does it? The power struggle won't be pretty, but he'll find a way to survive – he always does.' Sighing, Aunt Belinda fixed her gaze on a faraway galaxy out of the window. Her eyes revealed both regret and sadness. 'No-one among us is perfect. But your uncle is not the man I remember. Not the *brother*. I know there were thousands of miles of space separating us for a quarter of a century, but I thought I might at least find someone I recognised. But a power-hungry tyrant? No – I did not for one moment think I'd find that.'

'But… how did he get that way?'

'I've been asking myself the same thing. He was never easy, and he never had much self-control. And on Drumendus, he went from being alone and stranded, and surely *scared*, to being the most powerful person on the planet. That's quite a transformation! But at what cost? At *what cost*? The pursuit of power can corrupt any of us.' She stopped to think, then said, 'I find it both fascinating and alarming, that people can change over years, or they can change overnight. *You* are proof of changing overnight, Ella.'

'Me?'

'Yes!'

Ella pressed her lips together in thought. 'Wait – is that a good thing?'

'For you, a resounding *YES!* You rescued Freddie and me. You showed such courage, perhaps more than you thought you were capable of?'

'I suppose so.'

'I *know* so! I would go so far as suggesting that your legs didn't wobble as much as they might have done, even when you *were* afraid?'

'Hey, how do you know about my wobbly legs?'

'They're legendary, Ella, I'm afraid. But perhaps not anymore?' They laughed, then Aunt Belinda added, 'You and Freddie did a lot more besides the rescue. Without you, Isolde and her people wouldn't have found the Rain Cavern. Without you, she wouldn't be trying to reclaim Stradbow as we speak. *Without you*, we wouldn't have used Otto's marvelodrum to propel us back into space!'

'So I've pretty much changed the course of history on Drumendus?' said Ella, not knowing whether to laugh or cry. 'Not bad for a few days' work.'

'That sums it up perfectly.' Aunt Belinda shuffled forwards in her chair and looked at the dials above her head. 'Right, let's get this machine safely on solid ground, shall we? Prepare for re-entry and landing!'

Ella strapped herself in and shut her eyes for the journey into Earth's unforgiving atmosphere.

An hour or so later, the Hammerklav touched down in the field next to Racket Lodge and came to an ungainly stop after a couple of bounces on the grass.

Aunt Belinda ran her fingers over the dashboard. 'Well done, my dear Hammerklav.' She leaned in closer and whispered, 'You really are my *favourite* invention. Don't tell the others.'

Through the shimmering early-dawn sunshine, a herd of cows stood and stared as the weary travellers left the Hammerklav and trundled towards Racket Lodge. A severe metal fence had been put up around the garden and threatening red *No Entry* signs had been hammered into trees and fence posts all around.

'That'll be Larry Lark and those meddling BASS folks,' Aunt Belinda muttered, pulling off one of the signs and dropping it on its face. 'But they don't scare me.'

Although it was less than a week since Larry Lark's spy-drone had crashed in the garden, it felt like another lifetime. It took a moment for Ella to remember that BASS was the British Agency of Space Study, and that Larry Lark was Aunt Belinda's sworn nemesis in the world of homemade space travel.

'What happened to the garden shed?' Ella said, glancing over at the sorry-looking remains of Aunt Belinda's launch station. There was barely a wall left standing.

'Destroyed during lift-off,' said Aunt Belinda casually. 'I expected it to happen, don't worry.' She marched up to the front door. 'Could I borrow your baton, Ella?'

'You mean, *your* baton.'

'No, my dear, after everything that's happened

this week, I think we can all agree it's yours now. I just need it to get into the cottage.'

Ella beamed and handed it over.

'Now, let's see... I've never had to do this before.' Aunt Belinda leaned down to an instrument made of upturned glass bottles that sat by the door. Ella always thought it was just a quirky decoration, but it turned out to be yet another of her aunt's curious musical contraptions. With the handle of the baton, Aunt Belinda tapped out a tune on the filthy bottles, and a moment later, a wooden hatch in the wall popped open to reveal a set of keys. 'There we are! I must have lost my other keys in Dingringer Hall... or was it Twangbuzzer?'

Inside the cottage, everything was exactly as they had left it. A half-eaten packet of crisps was still perched on the arm of the sofa, Ella's trombone lay on the coffee table gathering dust and Aunt Belinda's sheet music was strewn on the floor by the fireplace – she had started a 'grand sort' but hadn't got far.

Ella looked at her watch. 'Isn't Mum picking me up this morning? It is Wednesday... I think?'

'Oh, yes,' said Aunt Belinda, 'I hadn't thought of that. Good timing, all in all, our mission. Anyone would think I'd planned it! First, though, time for a hearty astronaut's breakfast.'

Freddie hesitated at the porch door. 'I should... get going... My family might be wondering where I am.'

Ella turned to him, and they shared a look through bleary eyes that spoke a million words. 'Write soon?'

she managed eventually. 'You're my only pen pal, remember?'

'Yes!' Freddie said, then his face dropped in disappointment. 'Won't see you for ages, though.'

Ella tried to hide the knot of sadness building up inside by staring down at the patterned doormat. 'What will you tell your family when you get home?'

'The truth, of course, that I went on a last-minute mission to Drumendus. They'll laugh, tell me what a vivid imagination I have, and that'll be the end of it.'

'Really?'

'Yep!'

And with that, they high-fived, hugged, and Freddie trotted down the path and round the corner, waving as he went.

Ella wolfed down a delicious breakfast to distract herself from missing her best friend, then hastily packed her things. Mum's noisy old car turned into the drive a while later, and Ella hauled her suitcase outside.

'Welcome back, Jude!' Aunt Belinda said, bustling out and standing in front of another *No Entry* sign.

'Thanks! How was your week?' Mum said, stepping out of the car and hugging them both.

Ella looked at Aunt Belinda, and Aunt Belinda looked at Ella, each waiting for the other to speak. Eventually, Aunt Belinda piped up with, 'Oh, Ella helped me with a project I was working on. Turned out to be quite a... mission.'

'I know,' said Mum. 'I saw.'

Ella and Aunt Belinda's mouths fell open at

precisely the same moment. Aunt Belinda put her hand on her chest as if she were about to faint. 'You... you *saw*?'

'Yes! The garden shed – you've demolished it. I have to say, it's a bit of a mess from the road.'

'Phew!'

'Sorry? Didn't catch that?'

'I mean, ah yes... the shed... I'll build another one, don't you worry. Where would I house my inventions otherwise?' She let out an uneasy chuckle, then ushered Ella towards the car with a mutter. 'Bye, then.'

Ella knew Aunt Belinda was terrible at goodbyes, but she couldn't fight the urge to throw her arms around her aunt and hang on for the most monumental hug. 'Thank you,' she whispered. 'That was fun.'

'Yes, it was rather, wasn't it?'

Ella shuffled into the back seat, where there was room to spread out, and waved goodbye to her tearful aunt. As they left Racket Lodge and drove through Nether Rumpus, she barely noticed the convoy of cars with tinted windows passing by in the opposite direction.

'You're quiet, sweetie,' Mum said a few minutes later. 'Aunt Belinda must have kept you busy. Demolishing a shed can't be *that* tiring, surely. Unless there's something else?'

Ella shuffled in her chair but didn't answer. She couldn't bring herself to confirm or deny Mum's suspicions. Luckily, Mum's favourite song came on the radio, something about a spaceman and some kings, which distracted her from any further interrogation.

Ella rested her head on her hand and looked down at the baton in her lap. It didn't look like much, lying there innocently, but it was the best present Aunt Belinda could have given her.

She frowned as she realised something: she hadn't thought to check if she had sonorance *here*, on Earth…

Surely not?

There were no drums from the deep, no purple lightning flashes. Why would there be any sonorance?

There was only one way to found out.

Ella lifted the baton a centimetre above her lap and waved it along to the music as discreetly as she could.

Nothing happened.

She focused her mind on a shopping bag at her feet and counted under her breath as she beat again, up and down, up and down. 'One, two, one, two…'

A tiny streak of rainbow light zipped out of the baton and sizzled into the bag, singeing the canvas into a dark circle.

Ella tucked the baton down the side of the seat as Mum's song finished.

'Everything okay?' Mum said, glancing over.

Ella nodded and tried to hide her grin.

Yes. Everything *was* okay.

Ella Crinkle had sonorance on Earth.